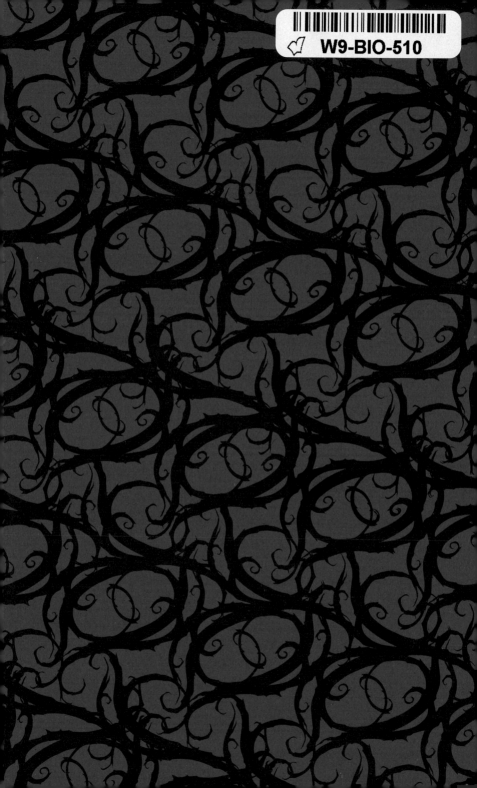

the Isle of the Lost

of the

Lost

A DESCENDANTS NOVEL

MELISSA DE LA CRUZ

DISNEP • HYPERION
LOS ANGELES   NEW YORK

First Edition, May 2015
10 9 8 7 6 5 4 3 2 1
G475-5664-5-15046

Printed in the United States of America

Library of Congress Cataloging-in-Publication Data
De la Cruz, Melissa, 1971–
The Isle of the Lost/Melissa de la Cruz.—First edition.
pages cm
Summary: Imprisoned on the Isle of the Lost, the teenaged
children of Disney's most evil villains search for a dragon's eye—
the key to true darkness and the villains' only hope of escape.
ISBN 978-1-4847-2097-4 (hardback)
[1. Villains—Fiction. 2. Magic—Fiction. 3. Prisoners—Fiction.] I. Title.
PZ7.D36967Is 2015
[Fic]—dc23   2014049881

Reinforced binding

Visit www.DisneyBooks.com
and www.DisneyDescendants.com

SUSTAINABLE FORESTRY INITIATIVE   Certified Sourcing
www.sfiprogram.org
SFI-00993

THIS LABEL APPLIES TO TEXT STOCK

For Mattie,
without whom this book would not be possible

And for the two baddest ladies in the biz,

*Emily Meehan and
Jeanne Mosure,*

who offered me a chance to work on an island full of
villains and believed in me—thank you, ladies,
for everything

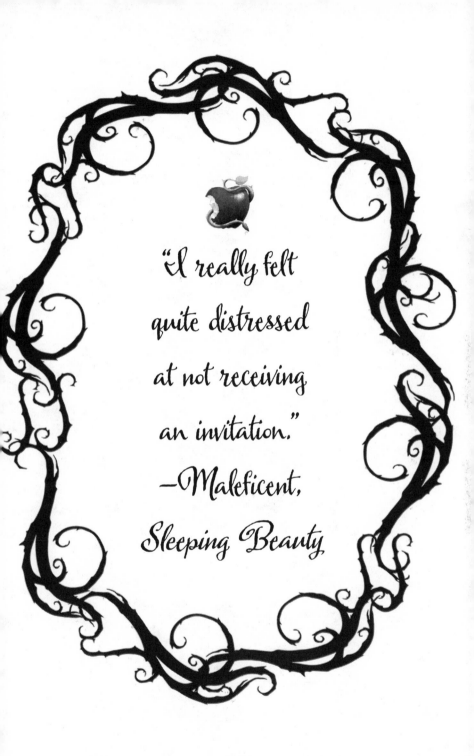

"I really felt
quite distressed
at not receiving
an invitation."
—Maleficent,
Sleeping Beauty

prologue

Once upon a time, during a time after all the happily-ever-afters, and perhaps even after the ever-afters after that, all the evil villains of the world were banished from the United Kingdom of Auradon and imprisoned on the Isle of the Lost. There, underneath a protective dome that kept all manner of enchantment out of their clutches, the terrible, the treacherous, the truly awful, and the severely sinister were cursed to live without the power of magic.

King Beast declared the villains exiled forever.

Forever, as it turns out, is quite a long time. Longer than an enchanted princess can sleep. Longer, even, than an imprisoned maiden's tower of golden hair. Longer than a week of being turned into a frog, and certainly much longer than waiting for a prince to finally get around to placing that glass slipper on your foot already.

Yes, forever is a long, long, long time.

Ten years, to be specific. Ten years that these legendary villains have been trapped on a floating prison of rock and rubble.

Okay, so you might say ten years isn't *such* a long time, considering; but for these conjurers and witches, viziers and sorcerers, evil queens and dark fairies, to live without magic was a sentence worse than death.

(And some of them were *brought back* from death, only to be placed on this island—so, um, they should know.)

Without their awesome powers to dominate and hypnotize, terrorize and threaten, create thunderclouds and lightning storms, transform and disguise their features or lie and manipulate their way into getting exactly what they wanted, they were reduced to hardscrabble lives, eking a living selling and eating slop, scaring no one but their own minions, and stealing from each other. It was hard even for them to imagine they once had been great and powerful, these poisoners of forest apples and thieves of undersea voices, these usurpers of royal powers and owners of petulant mirrors.

Now their lives were anything but powerful. Now they were ordinary. Everyday.

Dare it be said? Dull.

So it was with great excitement and no small fanfare that the island gathered for a one-of-a-kind event: a six-year-old princess's wickedly wonderful birthday party. *Wicked* being something of a relative term under a dome that houses a bunch of powerless former villains.

In any event, a party it was.

It was the most magnificent celebration the isolated island and its banished citizens had ever seen, and tales of its gothic grandeur and obnoxious opulence would be told for years to come. The party to end all parties, this lavish occasion transformed the ramshackle bazaar and its rotting storefronts in the middle of the island into a spookily spectacular playground, full of ghostly lanterns and flickering candles.

Weeks before, a flock of vultures had circled the land, dropping invitations on every shabby doorstep and hovel so that every grubby little urchin from every corner of the island would be able to partake in this enchanting and extraordinary event.

Every little urchin on the island, that is, *except for one malicious little fairy.*

Whether her invitation was lost to the winds and torn to tatters or devoured by the hungry buzzards themselves— or—gasp!—*never even addressed* in that looping royal scrawl, as was suspected, we will never know.

But the result was the same.

Above the tumultuous bazaar, up high on her castle balcony, six-year-old Mal pulled on the locks of her thick, purple hair and pursed her lips as she observed the dark and delicious festivities below. What she could make of them, at least.

There she saw the tiny princess, the fairest of the (is) land, sitting on her rickety throne, her hair as blue as the ocean, eyes as dark as night, and lips as pink as roses. Her hair was pulled back from her face in a pretty V-braid, and she laughed in delight at the array of marvels before her. The princess possessed a darling giggle that was so entrancing, it brought a smile to haughty Lady Tremaine's face, she of the thwarted plans to marry her daughters to Prince Charming; the ferocious tiger Shere Khan was practically purring like a contented kitty; and for old times' sake, Captain Hook bravely stuck his head between Tick-Tock's open jaws, if only so he could make her laugh and hear that lovely peal again.

The princess, it would seem, could make even the most horrible villains smile.

But Mal wasn't smiling. She could practically smell the two-story cake made of sour apples, sinfully red and lusciously wormy; and try as she might, she couldn't help but overhear the screeches of the parrot Iago as he repeated, over and over again, the story of talking caves that held riches beyond measure, until the assembled villagers wanted to wring his feathered neck.

Mal sighed with green-eyed jealousy as the children gleefully tore into their baddie bags. The crumpled containers held a variety of evil sidekicks to choose from—pet baby moray eels akin to the slinky Flotsam and Jetsam swimming in tiny bowls; little spotted, cackling hyenas who were no quieter than the infamous Shenzi, Banzai, and Ed; pouncing and adorable black kittens from Lucifer's latest litter. Their badly behaved recipients screamed with excitement.

As the party escalated in feverish merriment, Mal's heart grew as black as her mood, and she swore that one day, she would show them all what it meant to be truly evil. She would grow up to be greedier than Mother Gothel, more selfish even than Cinderella's stepsisters, more cunning than Jafar, more deceptive than Ursula.

She would show them all that she was just like her—

"Mother!" she yelped, as the shadow of two looming and ominous horns made their way toward the balcony, and her mother appeared, her purple cape fluttering softly in the wind.

Her mother's voice was rich, melodious, and tinged with menace. "What is going on here?" she demanded as the children below tittered at the sight of a highly inappropriate shadow-puppet show mounted by the frightening Dr. Facilier.

"It's a birthday party," sniffed Mal. "And I wasn't invited."

"Is that right?" her mother asked. She peered at the celebration over Mal's shoulder, and they both took in the sight of the blue-haired princess giggling on a moth-eaten velvet pillow as Gaston's hairy and handsome young twin sons, Gaston Jr. and Gaston the Third, performed feats of strength—largely balancing their enormous booted feet on each other's squashed faces—to impress her. From the sound of things, it was working.

"Celebrations are for the rabble," her mother scoffed. Mal knew her mother despised parties of any kind. She despised them almost as much as she did kings and queens who doted on their precious babies, chubby little fairies with a knack for dress design, and obnoxious princes on even more obnoxious valiant steeds.

"Nevertheless, Evil Queen and her horrid progeny will learn soon enough from their spiteful little mistake!" her mother declared.

For her mother was the great Maleficent, Mistress of Darkness, the most powerful and wicked fairy in the world and the most fearsome villain in all the land.

Or at least, she had been.

Once upon a time, her mother's wrath had cursed a princess.

Once upon a time, her mother's wrath had brought a prince to his knees.

Once upon a time, her mother's wrath had put an entire kingdom to sleep.

Once upon a time, her mother had had all the forces of hell at her command.

And there was nothing Mal desired more in her heart than to grow up to be just like her.

Maleficent stepped to the balcony's edge, where she could see out to the whole island all the way to the sparkling lights of Auradon. She raised herself to her full height as thunder and lightning cracked and boomed and rain began to pour from the heavens. Since there was no magic on the island, this was just wickedly good coincidence.

The party came to a halt, and the gathered citizens were paralyzed at the sight of their leader glaring down at them with the full force of her wrath.

"This celebration is over!" Mal's mother declared. "Now, shoo, flee, and scatter, like the little fleas you are! And you! Evil Queen and your daughter! From now on, you are dead to the entire island! You do not exist! You are nothing! Never show your faces anywhere ever again! Or else!"

Just as quickly as it had gathered, the group dispersed, under the wary eye of Maleficent's frightening henchmen, the boar-like guards wearing aviator caps pulled down low over their hooded eyes. Mal caught a last glimpse of the blue-haired princess looking fearfully up at the balcony before being whisked away by her equally terrified mother.

Mal's eyes glittered with triumph, her dark heart glad that her misery had caused such wondrous maleficence.

Ten Terrible Years Later

"Magic Mirror
on the Wall,
who is the fairest
of them all?"
—Evil Queen,
Snow White

chapter

This Is the Story of
a Wicked Fairy. . . .

t has to be a dream, Mal told herself. *This couldn't be real.* She was sitting by the edge of a beautiful lake, on the stone floor of an ancient temple ruin, eating the most luscious strawberry. The forest all around her was lush and green, and the sound of the water rushing at her feet was soothing and peaceful. Even the very air all around her was sweet and fresh.

"Where am I?" she asked aloud, reaching for a plump grape from the gorgeous picnic set before her.

"Why, you've been in Auradon for days now, and this is the Enchanted Lake," answered the boy seated next to her.

She hadn't noticed him until he spoke, but now that she had noticed, she wished she hadn't. The boy was the worst part of all this—whatever *this* was—tall, with tousled honey-brown hair, and painfully handsome with the kind of smile that melted hearts and made all the girls swoon.

But Mal wasn't like all the girls, and she was starting to feel panicked, like she was trapped here somehow. In *Auradon*, of all places. And that it might not be a dream—

"Who are you?" she demanded. "Are you some kind of prince or something?" She looked askance at his fine blue shirt embroidered with a small golden crest.

"You know who I am," the boy said. "I'm your friend."

Mal was instantly relieved. "Then this *is* a dream," she said with a crafty smile. "Because I have no friends."

His face fell, but before he could answer, a voice boomed through the peaceful vista, darkening the skies and sending the water raging over the rocks.

"FOOLS! IDIOTS! MORONS!" it thundered.

Mal awoke with a start.

Her mother was yelling at her subjects from the balcony again. Maleficent ran the Isle of the Lost the way she did everything—with fear and loathing, not to mention a healthy supply of minions. Mal was used to the shouting, but it made for a seriously rude awakening. Her heart was still pounding from her nightmare as she kicked off the purple satin covers.

What on earth was she doing dreaming of Auradon?

What kind of dark magic had sent a handsome prince to speak to her in her sleep?

Mal shook her head and shuddered, trying to blink away the horrid vision of his dimpled smile, and was comforted by the familiar sound of fearful villagers begging Maleficent to take pity on them. She looked around her room, relieved to find she was right where she should be, in her huge, squeaky, wrought-iron bed with its gargoyles on each bedpost and velvet canopy that sagged so low, it threatened to fall on top of her. It was always gloomy in Mal's room, just as it was always gray and overcast on the island.

Her mother's voice boomed from the balcony, and the floor of her bedroom rattled, causing her violet-lacquered chest of drawers to suddenly spring open, disgorging its purple contents on the floor.

When Mal decided on a color scheme, she stuck to it, and she had been drawn to the layers of gothic richness in the purple continuum. It was the color of mystery and magic, moody and dark, while not being as commonplace in popular villainswear as black. Purple was the new black, as far as Mal was concerned.

She crossed the room past her grand, uneven armoire that prominently displayed all of her freshly shoplifted baubles— trinkets of cut glass and paste, shiny metallic scarves with trailing strands, mismatched gloves and a variety of empty perfume bottles. Pushing the heavy curtains aside, from her window she could see the whole island in all its dreariness.

Home, freak home.

The Isle of the Lost was not a very large island; some would say it was but a speck or a blight on the landscape, certainly more brown than green, with a collection of tin-roofed and haphazardly constructed shanties and tenements built on top of one another and more or less threatening to collapse at any moment.

Mal looked down at this eyesore of a slum from the tall-est building in town, a formerly grand palace with soaring tower spires that was now the shabby, run-down, paint-chipped location of the one and only Bargain Castle, where *slightly* used enchanter's robes were stocked in every color and *slightly* lopsided witch's hats were always 50 percent off.

It was also the home of some *not-so-slightly* bad fairies.

Mal changed out of her pajamas, pulling on an artfully constructed purple biker jacket with a dash of pink on one arm and green on the other, and a pair of torn jeans the color of dried plums. She carefully put on her fingerless gloves and laced up her battered combat boots. She avoided glancing at the mirror, but if she had, she would have seen a small, pretty girl with an evil glint in her piercing green eyes and a pale, almost translucent complexion. People always remarked how much she looked like her mother, usually just before they ran screaming the other way. Mal relished their fear, even sought it. She combed her lilac locks with the back of her hand and picked up her sketchbook, stuffing it into her backpack along with the spray-paint cans she always carried with her. This town wasn't going to graffiti itself, was it? In a perfectly magical world it would, but that wasn't what she was dealing with.

Since the kitchen cupboards were bare as usual, with nothing in the fridge but glass jars full of eyeballs and all sorts of moldy liquids of dubious provenance—all part of Maleficent's ongoing efforts to whip up potions and conjure spells like she used to—Mal headed to the Slop Shop across the street for her daily breakfast.

She studied the choices on the menu—black-like-your-soul coffee; sour-milk latte; crusty barley oatmeal with a choice of mealy apple or mushy banana; and stale, mixed cereal, dry or wet. There were never many options. The food, or scraps, more like it, came from Auradon—whatever wasn't good enough for those snobs got sent over to the island. Isle of the Lost? More like Isle of the Leftovers. Nobody minded too much, though. Cream and sugar, fresh bread, and perfect pieces of fruit made people soft. Mal and the other banished villains preferred to be brittle and hard, inside and out.

"What do you want?" a surly goblin asked, demanding her order. In the past, the disgusting things had been foot soldiers in her mother's dark army, ruthlessly dispatched across the land to find a hidden princess; but now their tasks were reduced to serving up coffee as bitter as their hearts, in tall, grande, and venti sizes. The only amusement they had left was to ruthlessly misspell each customer's name, written with marker on the side of each cup. (The joke was on the goblins since hardly anyone could read Goblin; but that never seemed to make any difference.) They kept blaming their imprisonment on the island on their allegiance to Maleficent, and it was common knowledge that they kept petitioning King Beast for amnesty, using their flimsy familial ties to the dwarfs as proof they didn't belong here.

"The usual, and make it snappy," said Mal, drumming her fingers on the counter.

"Room for month-old milk?"

"Do I look like I want curds? Give me the strongest, blackest coffee you've got! What is this, Auradon?"

It was like he'd seen her dreams, and the thought made her ill.

The runty creature grunted, wiggling the boil on his nose, and pushed a dark, murky cup toward her. She grabbed it and ran out the door without paying.

"YOU LITTLE BRAT! I'LL BOIL *YOU* IN THE COFFEEPOT NEXT TIME!" the goblin shrieked.

She cackled. "Not if you can't catch me first!"

The goblins never learned. They had never found Princess Aurora either, but then again, the dimwits had been looking for a baby for eighteen years. No wonder Maleficent was always frustrated. It was so hard to find good help these days.

Mal continued on her way, stopping to smirk at the poster of King Beast admonishing the citizens of the island to BE GOOD! BECAUSE IT'S GOOD FOR YOU! with that silly yellow crown on his head and that big grin on his face. It was positively nauseating and more than a little haunting, at least to Mal. Maybe the Auradon propaganda was getting to her head, maybe that's why she had dreamt she was frolicking in some sort of enchanted lake last night with some pretentious prince. The thought made her shudder again. She took a gulp of her scalding, strong coffee. It tasted like mud. Perfect.

In any event, she had to do something about this blister on the wall. Mal took out her paint cans and sprayed a mustache and goatee on the king's face and crossed out his ridiculous message. King Beast was the one who had locked them all up on the island, after all. That hypocrite. She had a few messages of her own for him, and they all involved revenge.

This was the Isle of the Lost. Evil lived, breathed, and ruled the island, and King Beast and his sickly sweet billboards cajoling the former villains of the world to do *good* had no place in it. Who wanted to make lemonade from lemons, when you could make perfectly good lemon grenades?

Next to the poster she sprayed a thin, black outline of a horned head and a spread cape. Above Maleficent's outline, she scrawled *EVIL LIVES!* in bright green paint the color of goblin slime.

Not bad. Bad*der*. And that was *much* better.

chapter

2

A Wily Thief . . .

f Mal lived above a shop, Jay, son of Jafar, actually lived *inside* one, sleeping on a worn carpet beneath a shelf straining under ancient television sets with manual dials, radios that never worked, and telephones that had actual cords attached to them. His father had been the former grand vizier of Agrabah, feared and respected by all, but that was a long time ago, and the evil enchanter was now the proprietor of Jafar's Junk Shop, and Jay, his only son and heir, was also his sole supplier. If Jay's destiny had once been to become a great prince, only his father remembered it these days.

"You should be on top of an elephant, leading a parade,

waving to your subjects," Jafar mourned that morning as Jay prepared for school, pulling a red beanie over his long, straight dark hair and choosing his usual attire of purple-and-yellow leather vest and dark jeans. He flexed his considerable muscles as he pulled on his black studded gloves.

"Whatever you say, Dad!" Jay winked with a mischievous smile. "I'll try to steal an elephant if I come across any."

Because Jay was a prince, all right. A prince of thieves, a con man, and a schemer, whose lies were as beautiful as his dark eyes. As he made his way through the narrow cobblestone streets, dodging rickshaws manned by Professor Ratigan's daredevil crew, he took advantage of their frightened passengers ducking under clotheslines weighed down by tattered robes and dripping capes to filch a billfold or two. Ursula chased him away from her fish and chips shop, but not before he had managed to grab a handful of greasy fries, and he took a moment to admire a collection of plastic jugs of every size and shape offered by another storefront, wondering if he could fit one in his pocket.

Every manner of Auradon trash was recycled and repurposed on the island, from bathtubs to door handles, as well as from the villains' own formerly magical accoutrements. A shop advertised USED BROOMS THAT DON'T FLY ANYMORE BUT SWEEP OKAY, and crystal balls that were only good as goldfish bowls these days.

As vendors laid out rotten fruit and spoiled vegetables

under tattered tents, Jay swiped a bruised apple and took a bite, his pockets bulging with pilfered treasures. He waved a cheerful hello to a chorus of hook-nosed witches gathered at a slanted balcony—Madam Mim's granddaughters, who, while relieved to be out of his sticky fingers' reach, swooned at his greeting nonetheless.

Maleficent's henchmen, large boar-like men in leather rags with the familiar aviator-style caps pulled down over their eyes, snuffled an almost unintelligible hello as they passed him on their way to work. Jay deftly took their caps without their noticing and shoved them down the rear of his trousers, planning to sell them back to the guys the next day like he did every week. But he resisted the urge to trip them up as well. There just wasn't time to do everything in one day.

Looking for something to wash down the sour taste of the apple, Jay caught sight of a familiar face taking a sip from a paper cup bearing the Slop Shop logo and grinned.

Perfect.

"What in Lucifer's name?" Mal cried as the cup disappeared from her fingers. She hesitated for a second before realization hit. "Give it back, Jay," she said, hands on her hips, addressing the empty space on the sidewalk.

He snickered. It was so much fun when Mal was mad. "Make me."

"Jay!" she snarled. "Make you what? Bruise? Bleed? Beg? Thief's choice, today."

"Fine. Jeez," he said as he slunk out from the shadows.

"Mmm, pressed hot mud, my favorite." He handed her back her cup, feeling wistful.

Mal took a sip and grimaced. "Actually, it's disgusting, you can have it. You look hungry."

"Really?" He perked up. "Thanks, Mal. I was starving."

"Don't thank me, it's particularly awful today. I think they threw some raw toads into the brew this morning," she said.

"Bonus! Extra protein." Amphibians or not, Jay drained it in one shot. He wiped his lips and smiled. "Thanks, you're a pal," he said in all honesty, even though he and Mal weren't friends, exactly, although they were partners in crime.

Like his, Mal's jeans and jacket pockets were stuffed with all manner of junk, shoplifted from every storefront in town. A knitting needle was sticking out of one pocket, while the other contained what looked like a sword handle.

"Can I trade you a teapot for that old sword?" he asked hopefully. Everything his father sold was stuff Jay had stolen from somewhere else.

"Sure," she said, taking a rusty kettle in exchange. "Look what else I got," she said. "Ursula's necklace." She rattled it in the air. "I nabbed it this morning when the old sea witch waved hello."

"Sweet." He nodded. "All I got was a handful of fries. Too bad it can't capture anything anymore, let alone a mermaid's voice."

Mal huffed. "It's still valuable."

"If you say so." He shrugged.

Jay and Mal were in a constant competition for who was the more accomplished thief. A clear winner would be hard to call. You could say they had bonded on their love of swiping things, but they would tell you that bonds of any kind were for the weak.

Even so, they fell into step on the walk to school. "Heard the news?" he asked.

"What news? There's no new news," she scoffed, meaning nothing new ever happened on the island. The island's old-fashioned fuzzy-screened televisions only broadcast two channels—Auradon News Network, which was full of do-gooder propaganda, and the DSC, the Dungeon Shopping Channel, which specialized in hidden-lair décor. "And slow down, or we'll get there on time," she added.

They turned off the main road, toward the uneven, broken-down graveyard that was the front lawn of Dragon Hall. The venerable school for the advancement of evil education was located in a former mausoleum, a hulking gray structure with a domed ceiling and a broken-down colonnade, its pediment inscribed with the school's motto: IN EVIL WE TRUST. Scattered around its haunted grounds, instead of the usual tombstones, were doomstones with horrible sayings carved into them. As far as the leaders on this island were concerned, there was never a wrong time to remind its citizens that evil ruled.

"No way, I heard news. Real news," he insisted, his heavy

combat boots stomping through the root-ripped graveyard terrain. "Check it out—there's a new girl in class."

"Yeah, right."

"I'm totally serious," he said, narrowly avoiding stumbling over a doomstone inscribed with the phrase IT IS BETTER TO HAVE NEVER LOVED AT ALL THAN TO BE LOVED.

"New girl? From where, exactly?" Mal asked, pointing to the magical dome that covered the island and shrouded the sky, obscuring the clouds. Nothing and no one came in or out, so there wasn't ever a whole lot of *new*.

"New to us. She's been castle-schooled until now, so it's her first time in the dungeon," said Jay as they approached the wrought-iron gates, and the crowd gathered around the entrance parted to let them through, many of their fellow students clutching their backpacks a little more tightly at the sight of the thieving duo.

"Really." Mal stopped in her tracks. "What do you mean, 'castle-schooled'?" she asked, her eyes narrowing suspiciously.

"A real princess too, is what I've heard. Like, your basic true-love's-kiss-prick-your-finger-spin-your-gold-skip-the-haircut-marry-the-prince-level princess." He felt dizzy just thinking about it. "Think I could lift a crown off her somewhere? Even a half-crown . . . ?" His father was always talking about The Big Score, the one fat treasure that would free them from the island somehow. Maybe the princess would lead them to it.

"A princess?" Mal said sternly. "I don't believe you."

Jay wasn't listening anymore. "I mean, think of the loot she'd have on her! She's got to have a ton of loot, right? Hope she's easy on the eyes! Better yet, on the pockets. I could use an easy mark."

Mal's voice was suddenly acid. "You're wrong. There aren't any princesses on the island, and certainly not any who would dare to show their faces around here. . . ."

Jay stared at her, and in the back of his mind he heard alarm bells and had a faint memory of an awesome birthday party concerning a princess . . . and some sort of scandal that involved Mal and her mother. He felt bad, remembering now that Mal hadn't received an invitation, but he quickly suppressed the icky emotion, unsure of where it came from. Villains were supposed to revel in other people's sadness, not empathize!

Besides, when it came down to it, Mal was like a sister, an annoying, ever-present pest, and a pain in the . . .

Bells. Ringing and echoing through the island from the top of the tower, where Claudine Frollo was tugging the rope and being pulled up along with it as she rang in the official start of the Dragon Hall school day.

Jay and Mal shared a smirk. They were officially tardy. The first thing that had gone right all morning.

They passed through the crumbling and moss-covered archway and into the main tomb, which was buzzing with activity—members of the Truant Council putting up signs for a Week-Old Bake Sale; the earsplitting sounds of the junior orchestra practicing for the Fall Concert, the sea witches leaning over their violins.

Frightened students scrambled to get out of their way as Mal and Jay walked past the dead ivy–covered great hall toward the rusting double doors that led to the underground class-tombs. A tiny first-year pirate who ran with Harriet Hook's crew got lost in the shuffle, blocking their path.

Mal came to a halt.

The boy slowly lifted his head, his eye patch trembling.

"S-s-so s-s-sorry, M-m-m-mal," he said.

"M-m-m-MOVE IT," Mal said, her voice high and mocking. She rolled her eyes and kicked the torn textbooks out of her way. The boy scampered toward the first open door he saw, dropping his fake hooked hand in his haste and sending it tumbling away.

Jay kept his silence, knowing to tread lightly as he picked up the hook and stuffed it inside his jacket. But he couldn't help asking, "Why not just throw a party of your own instead of sulking about it?"

"What are you talking about?" said Mal. "As if I care."

Jay didn't reply; he was too busy hugging himself tightly and wishing he'd thought to bring a warmer jacket instead of a sleeveless vest as the temperature dropped the usual twenty degrees as they ventured down the cold marble stairs to the damp basement gloom of campus.

Mal had gone silent for a moment, and Jay assumed she

was still brooding on what happened ten years ago, when she suddenly snapped her fingers and said, with a wicked gleam in her eyes, "You're absolutely right, Jay. You're a genius!"

"I am? I mean, yes, I am," replied Jay. "Wait—what am I right about?"

"Having a party of my own. There's a lot to celebrate, after all. You just said there was a new princess in our midst. So I'm going to throw a party."

Jay goggled at her. "You are? I mean, I was just kidding. Everyone knows you hate . . ."

"Parties." Mal nodded. "But not this one. You'll see. It's going to be a real howler." She grinned. "Especially for the new kid."

Jay smiled back weakly, wishing he had never mentioned it. When Mal got like this, it usually had terrible consequences. He shivered. There was a definite chill in the air—a new wild wind was blowing, and he was smart enough to worry about where it would lead.

chapter
3

A Beautiful Princess . . .

In the Castle-Across-the-Way lived a lived a mother-and-daughter duo very different from Maleficent and Mal. Unlike the shabby Victorian confines of the Bargain Castle, this one was full soot and dust, with broken chandeliers and spiderwebs in the corners. It wasn't so much a castle as a cave—yet another prison within the prison of the island. And for ten years, this mother and daughter had only each other for company. Banishment to the far side of the island had made Evil Queen a little odd, and Evie couldn't help but notice how her mother insisted on making declarations just like some legendary "magic mirror."

"Magic Mirror in my hand, who is the fairest on this

island?" Evil Queen asked as Evie was getting ready that morning.

"Mom, you're not holding *anything* in your hand. And anyway, is that really the *first* thing on your mind? Not breakfast?" asked Evie, who was starving. She perused the day's offerings—hard croissants and watery coffee from the basket the vultures left on their doorstep every day.

"Your daughter has grace but should take better care of her face to be the fairest," her mother declared in somber tones that she called her "Magic Mirror" voice.

Fairest, prettiest, most beautiful. The thickest hair, the fullest lips, the smallest nose. It was all her mother cared about. Evil Queen blamed all her troubles on not being more beautiful than Snow White, and it seemed no matter how well Evie did her hair or put on her makeup, she would never be beautiful enough for her mother. It made Evie sick to her beautiful stomach sometimes. Like mother, like daughter—or so she'd always been told. The poison apple never fell far from the tree.

And even if Evie suspected there *might* be more to life than being beautiful, that wasn't something she could ever say to her mother. The woman had a one-track mind.

"You didn't put on enough blush. How will you ever win a handsome prince, looking like that?" her mother scolded, pinching her cheeks.

"If only there was one around here," said Evie, who dutifully took out her compact and reapplied. There were no princes to be found on the island, as all the princes lived in Auradon now. That's where *all* the world's royalty lived— and that's where *she* should live too. But it was not to be. Like her mother, she would be trapped on the Isle of the Lost forever.

Evie checked the hallway mirror one last time and adjusted her blue cape around her shoulders, the back of it embroidered with a crown in the middle. Her poison-heart necklace winked red in between the soft blue folds. Her raggedy black skirt with the splashes of red, white, and blue paint went well with her forest-print-like black-and-white leggings.

"Your hair!" Evil Queen said with despair, tucking a loose strand back into her daughter's neat V-braid, which swept her hair off her forehead. "Okay, *now* you're ready."

"Thanks, Mom," said Evie, whose only goal was to survive the day. "Are you sure it's safe to go to school?"

"No one can keep a grudge for ten years! Also, we're all out of wrinkle cream! Pick up some from the bazaar—I don't trust the vultures to send the right one."

Evie nodded and hoped her mother was right.

But when she stepped out of their castle gates, she froze. Maleficent's curse echoed in her ears. But nothing happened, and she kept going. Maybe, for once, the wicked old fairy had forgotten about it.

When Evie arrived at school that morning, everyone stared at her as she walked through the halls. She felt a bit self-conscious, and wondered if she'd ever fit in. She was supposed to check in with Dr. F, the headmaster, when she arrived. But where were the administrative chambers? Evie wondered, whirling around in a full circle.

"May I help you?" a handsome if somewhat hairy and very large boy asked when he saw her.

"Oh—I'm looking for the headmaster—?"

"Follow me," he said with a broad grin. "Gaston, at your service . . . and this is my brother, Gaston." He pointed to his identical twin, who gave her the same beaming, arrogant smile.

"Thank you, uh, Gastons." Evie replied. The boys led her down the hall to the administrative-tombs.

"Dr. F, you got a visitor," Gaston said reaching for the door handle.

"I want to open it," his brother said, elbowing him away. But the first Gaston punched him without even a backward look. "After you, princess," he offered grandly, as his brother slithered to the floor, holding his jaw.

"Um, thanks, I think," said Evie.

Dr. Facilier looked up and gave the three students a jack-o'-lantern smile. "Yes? Oh, Evie, welcome to Dragon Hall. It's a delight to see you again, child. It's been too long. Ten years, is it? How is your lovely mother?"

"She's well, thanks." Evie nodded politely but hurried to get to the point. "Dr. Facilier, I just wanted to see if I could swap my Wickedness class for Advanced Vanities that meets at the same time?" she asked.

The shadowy man frowned. Evie batted her eyelashes. "It would mean so much to me. By the way—" She pointed to his bolo tie, with its unfortunate silver chain. "That is so cool!" she said, thinking exactly the opposite.

"Oh, this? I picked it up in the Bayou d'Orleans right before I was brought here." He sighed, and his frown softened into a real smile. "I suppose Vanities is a better fit for your overall schedule. Consider it done."

"Good, I'm in that class," the Gastons chorused. "On Tuesdays it's right after lunch."

"Lunch!" Evie slapped her forehead.

"What's wrong?"

"I forgot to bring mine!" In all the excitement and anxiety about finally leaving the castle, she'd left her basket at home.

"Don't worry," the twins replied. "You can share ours!" they added, holding up two huge baskets of food. A giant block of some particularly smelly cheese poked out, along with two loaves of brown bread speckled with mold and several thick slices of liverwurst.

Evie was touched they had offered to share, even though they looked like they could eat a horse and a half between them, with or without the mold.

They led her down the winding hallway. The stone walls were covered in the same pea-green moss as outside, and seemed to be leaking some sort of brown liquid all over the dusty cement floor. Evie felt something furry circling her ankles and found a fat black cat with a smug grin looking up at her.

"Hi, kitty," she cooed, leaning down to pet it.

"That's Lucifer," said one of the Gastons. "Our mascot."

Several yelps from first-year students could be heard from inside the rusty lockers that haphazardly lined the corridor. With only a few lightbulbs flickering overhead, Evie nearly walked into a giant cobweb woven over a heavy steel door. A spider the size of a witch's cauldron sat in its center. *Cool.*

"Where does that lead to?" she asked.

"Oh that? That's the door to the Athenaeum of Evil," the other Gaston said.

"Come again?"

"The Library of Forbidden Secrets," he explained. "Nobody is allowed down there, and only Dr. F has the key."

"What kind of secrets?" asked Evie, intrigued.

"Forbidden ones, I guess?" Gaston shrugged. "Who cares? It's a library. Sounds pretty boring to me."

Finally, they arrived at the classroom's arched wooden door. Evie stepped inside and made her way to the nearest open desk, smiling at those who came to gather curiously around her. Everyone was looking at her with such awe and admiration, she seemed to be making waves.

The desk she'd chosen had a remarkably large cauldron and a great view of the professor's lectern. She took a seat, and there was a gasp in the crowd. Wow, these kids sure were easy to please.

Evie was feeling pretty good about her first day until she heard the sound of a throat clearing.

When she looked up, there was a pretty, purple-haired girl standing in front of her cauldron, staring at her with unmistakable venom. Her mother's "mirror" would have had a few choice words about this one, that's for sure. Evie felt a cold dread as the memory of a certain infamous party came flooding back. Maybe if she played dumb and flattered her, the girl wouldn't remember what had happened ten years ago. It was worth a shot.

"I'm Evie. What's your name?" Evie asked innocently, although she knew exactly who was standing in front of her. "And by the way, that jacket is amazing. It looks great on you—I love all the patchwork leathers on it."

"Girl, that's her cauldron. You should bounce," a student Evie would find out later was named Yzla whispered loudly.

"Oh, this is yours . . . ?" Evie asked the purple-haired girl.

The purple-haired girl nodded.

"I had no idea this was your desk, I'm so sorry! But it has such a great view of the lectern," Evie said with her trademarked bright smile, so blinding, it should have come with sunglasses. Evie finally realized why the students had been staring at her. They had been watching a train wreck about to happen.

"Yes, it does," the purple-haired girl replied, her voice soft and menacing. "And if you don't move your blue-haired caboose out of it, you'll get some kind of view, all right." She snarled, brusquely brushing past Evie and noisily plonking her backpack down into the middle of the cauldron.

Evie got the message, grabbed her things, and found an empty cauldron in the back of the classroom, behind a column where she couldn't see the blackboard.

"Is that who I think it is?" she asked the small boy seated next to her, whose hair was black at the roots but white at the tips. Actually, everything he wore was black and white with a splash of red: a fur-collared jacket with one black and one white side and red leather sleeves, a black button-down shirt with streaks of white, and long shorts with one white and one black-and-white leg. It was a pretty cool look. For a bloody skunk.

"If you mean Mal, you're right, and I would stay out of her way if I were you," he said.

"Mal . . ." Evie breathed, her voice trembling nervously.

"Yeah. Her mom's the Big Bad around here. You know—" He made horn signs with his hands on either side of his head. You didn't need to have lived on the Isle for long to know exactly whom he was talking about. Nobody dared speak her name, not unless absolutely necessary.

Evie gulped. Her first day, and she'd already made the worst enemy in school. It was Maleficent who had banished Evie and her mother ten years ago and caused Evie to grow up alone in a faraway castle. Her own mother might be called Evil Queen, but everyone on the Isle of the Lost knew that Maleficent wore the crown in these parts. From the looks of it, her daughter did the same in the dungeons of Dragon Hall.

Magic Mirror on the wall, who's the stupidest of them all?

chapter
4

A Smart Little Boy . . .

Carlos De Vil looked up from the contraption he was assembling and shot the new girl a shy smile. "It'll be okay. Mal just likes to be left alone," he said. "She's not as tough as she seems. She only talks a big game."

"She does? What about you?" the blue-haired princess asked.

"I don't have a game. Unless you consider getting beat up and pushed around a game, which in a way I guess it is. But really it's not that entertaining, unless you happen to be the one doing the beating and the pushing."

Carlos turned his attention back to the mess of wires in front of him. He was smaller and younger than the rest of the class, but smarter than most of them. He was an AP student: Advanced Penchant (for Evil). It was only right, since the infamous Cruella was his mother. His mother was so notorious, she had her own song. He hummed it under his breath sometimes. (What—it was catchy!) Sometimes he would do it just to send her into hysterics. Then again, that wasn't so difficult. Cruella's witch doctors believed she was sustained by pure metabolic fury. Privately, Carlos thought of it as her Rage Diet: no carbs, just barbs—no hunger, just anger—no ice cream, just high screams.

His thoughts were interrupted by his friendly new seat-mate. "I'm Evie. What's your name?" she asked.

"Hi, Evie, I'm Carlos De Vil," he said. "We met once before, at your birthday party." He'd recognized her the minute she walked in. She looked exactly the same, just taller.

"Oh. Sorry. I don't remember much about the party. Except how it ended."

Carlos nodded. "Yeah. Anyway, I'm also your neighbor. I live just down the street in Hell Hall."

"You do?" Evie's eyes went wide. "But I thought no one lived there but that crazy old lady and her—"

"Don't say it!" he blurted.

"Dog?" she said at the same time.

Carlos shuddered. "We—we don't have dogs," he said weakly, feeling his forehead begin to perspire at the very thought. His mother had told him dogs were vicious pack animals, the most dangerous and terrifying animals on earth.

"But she's always calling someone her pet. I thought you were a d—"

"I told you, don't say it!" warned Carlos. "That word is a trigger for me."

Evie put up her hands. "Okay, okay." Then she winked. "But how do you fit in the crate at night?"

Carlos only glared.

Their first class was Selfishness 101, or "Selfies" for short, taught by Mother Gothel, who took way too many self-portraits with an old Polaroid camera.

The photos were littered around the classroom: Mother Gothel making a duck face, sleepy-eyed Mother Gothel in an "I woke up like this" pic, Mother Gothel in "cobra" pose. But Mother Gothel herself was nowhere to be found. She was always at least a half hour late, and when she finally arrived, she was irritated to find the students there before her. "Have I taught you nothing about being fashionably, annoyingly late to every engagement?" she asked, letting out an exasperated sigh and collapsing dramatically into her chair, one hand fanned over her eyes.

For the next half hour or so they studied Portraits of Evil, comparing the likenesses of the most famous villains in history, many of whom lived on the island and some of whom were their parents. Today's class just happened to feature Cruella De Vil.

Of course.

Carlos knew the portrait by heart, whether or not he was looking at it.

His mother. There she was in all her finery, with her tall hair and her long red car, her eyes wild and her furs flying in the wind.

He shuddered again and went back to tinkering with his machine.

Class ended, and students began to file out of the classroom. Evie asked Carlos what his next subject was, and looked happy to discover they both had Lady Tremaine for Evil Schemes. "That's another advanced class—you must have a really high EQ," he told her. Only those who boasted off-the-charts evil quotients were allowed to take it. "It's this way," he said, motioning up the stairs.

But before they could get too far, a cold voice cut through the chatter. "Why, if it isn't Carlos De Vil," it said behind them.

Carlos would know that voice anywhere. It was the second-most terrifying on the island. When he turned, Mal was standing right behind him, next to Jay. Carlos automatically checked his pockets to make sure nothing had disappeared.

"Hey, Mal," he said, trying to appear nonchalant. Mal never spoke to anyone except to scare them or to complain that they were in her way. "What's up?"

"Your mom's away at the Spa this weekend, isn't she?" Mal asked, elbowing Jay, who snickered.

Carlos nodded. The Spa—really just a bit of warmish steam escaping from the crags of rock in the ruined basement of what had once been a proper building—was Cruella's one bit of comfort, her one reminder of her luxurious past.

How far the De Vils had fallen, just like the rest of the Isle.

"Y-yes," he said uncertainly, unsure if that was the correct answer even though it was the truthful one.

"Right answer," Mal said and patted him on the head. "I can't exactly give a party at my place without my mother yelling at everyone, not to mention the whole flying crockery issue."

Carlos sighed. Like the rest of the Isle, he knew parties brought out Maleficent's worst behavior. There was nothing she hated more than people openly having fun.

"And we can't have it at Jay's because his dad will just try to hypnotize everyone into being his servants again," Mal continued.

"Totally," agreed Jay.

Carlos nodded again, although he wasn't sure where this was leading.

"Great. Perfect. Party at your house. Tonight."

Party? At his house? Did he hear that right?

"Wait, what? Tonight?" He blanched. "I can't have a party! I mean, you should understand, my mom doesn't really like it when people come over—and, um, I've got a lot of work to do—I have to fluff her furs, iron her undergarments, I mean—" He gulped, embarrassed.

Mal ignored him. "Spread the news. Hell Hall's having a hell-raiser." She seemed to warm to the thought. "Get the word out. Activate the twilight bark, or whatever it is you puppies do."

"Bowwow," barked Jay with a laugh.

Carlos glared at the two of them, in spite of himself.

"There's a party?" Evie asked shyly. Carlos had forgotten she was standing right next to him, and he jumped at the sound of her voice.

"Eavesdrop, much?" Mal said, snarling at her although it was obvious Evie couldn't help it, as she was standing right there.

Before Evie could protest, Mal sighed. "Of course there is. The party of the year. A real rager, didn't you hear?" Mal looked her up and down and shook her head sadly. "Oh, I guess you didn't hear." She mock-winced, looking at Carlos conspiratorially. "Everyone's going to be there."

"They are?" Carlos looked confused. "But you only just told me to have it—" He quickly got the message. "Everyone," he agreed.

Evie smiled. "Sounds awesome. I haven't been to a party in a long, long time."

Mal raised an eyebrow. "Oh, I'm sorry. This is a very exclusive party, and I'm afraid you didn't get an invitation."

With those parting words, Mal went ahead of them into the classroom—she was in their next class too, of course (her EQ was legendary)—and left them to each other.

"Sorry," Carlos mumbled. "I guess I was wrong, Mal doesn't just *talk* a big game."

"Yeah, me too. The party sounds like fun," Evie said sadly.

"You want to see what I'm making?" he asked, trying to change the subject as they settled into their seats. He took out of his bag a black box, with wires and an antenna poking out from one side—the same contraption he'd been fiddling with earlier. "I made it from some old magician's stuff."

"Sure." Evie smiled. "Hey, is that a power core? It looks like you're making a battery, right?"

Carlos nodded, impressed. "Yeah."

"What does it do?"

"Can you keep a secret?" he asked, whispering.

Evie nodded. "I keep them from my mom all the time."

"I'm trying to poke a hole in the dome."

"Really? Can you do that? I thought it was invincible."

"Well, I thought I could maybe try to get a signal with this antenna here. It's actually an old wand, and I think if I hit the right frequency, we might be able to bring some of the outside world into the dome, and we can watch something other than that hairy old beast king telling us to be good, or that channel that only sells shackles."

"I sort of like the Auradon channel," Evie said dreamily.

"Especially when they feature the Prince of the Week. They're so dreamy."

Carlos snorted.

She looked from the boy to the battery. "Frequency? But how?"

"I'm not sure, but I think if I can break through the dome, we'd be able to pick up Auradon's radio waves—you know, Internet and wi-fi signals. I'm not exactly sure what the frequency is, but I think that's how they get all those channels and stuff."

Evie sighed again. "What I'd give to go to Auradon. I've heard that everything is so beautiful there."

"Um, I guess. If you're into that kind of thing," Carlos said. He didn't care about princes or enchanted lakes or chirping animals or cheerful dwarfs. What he did care about was discovering more of the online world, a safe virtual refuge, where he'd heard you could even find people with whom you could play videogames—that sounded like fun, as he never had anyone to play with.

There *had* to be something more to life than kowtowing to the cool kids, organizing his mother's fur coats, and hiding from her tantrums.

There *had* to be. Although right now it wasn't just his mother he had to answer to. If Mal was serious, which it looked like she was, in the next few hours he somehow had to figure out how to throw the party of the year.

chapter
5

And a Handsome Prince
Who Lived Far, Far Away

eanwhile, across the Sea of Serenity, which separated the Isle of the Lost from the rest of the world, lay the USA—the United States of Auradon, a land of peace and enchantment, prosperity and delight, which encompassed all the good kingdoms. To the east lay the colorful domes of the Sultan's seat, where Aladdin and Jasmine lived, not far from where Mulan and Li Shang guarded the imperial palace. To the north was Charming Castle, owned by Cinderella and her king, next door to "Honeymoon Cottage," the forty-bedroom palace that Aurora and Phillip called home. And to the south, one could spy the lanterns of Rapunzel and Eugene Fitzherbert's divine domicile, near the spot on the coast where Ariel and Eric had made their under-and-over-the-sea royal residence at Seaside.

But right in the center was the grandest castle in all of Auradon, with lavish turrets and balconies, its highest towers flying the proud blue-and-gold banner of the good old USA. Inside the magnificent building were many ballrooms, great rooms and state rooms, a formal dining room that could seat hundreds, where everyone was made to feel like a pampered guest, and a wondrous library that held all the books that were ever written.

This was all fitting, of course, because this was Castle Beast, home of King Beast and Queen Belle, the seat of Auradon. Twenty years ago, King Beast united all the fairy-tale lands into one under his crown; and for the past two decades he had ruled over its good citizens with strong and fair judgment, and only occasionally a tiny bit of his beastly temper.

Belle had a calming influence on the hotheaded Beast: she was not just the love of his life but the pacifier of his moods, the voice of reason in a gathering storm, and the mother of his only child.

The jewel in the crown was their handsome son, fifteen-year-old Prince Ben. There had been no fairies at his christening to bestow gifts, perhaps because he did not need any. Ben was as handsome as his father, with his strong brow and chisel-cut cheekbones, but he had his mother's gentle eyes and keen intellect. He was a golden boy in every way, with a good heart and a winning spirit—captain of the tourney team, friend to all, destined to rule Auradon one day.

In short, he was the very sort of person that the people of the Isle of Lost despised. And, as on the Isle of the Lost, magic was no longer a factor in daily life in Auradon either. King Beast and Queen Belle stressed scholarship above enchantment, exhorting the young people to work hard instead of relying on fairy spells or dragon friends for help. Because Beast was the most powerful figure in all the kingdoms, when he proposed the new work ethic, nobody argued against him. It was indeed a new (once upon a) time for the people of the fabled fairy-tale lands.

But even without magic, life in Auradon was close to perfect. The sun always shone, the birds always chirped, there was never more than a five-minute wait at the DFMV (the Department of Formerly Magical Vehicles); and if everyone wasn't happy *all* the time (it's not as if this were *heaven*—get a grip, people), everyone was content.

Except, of course, when they weren't.

Isn't that always the way?

The kingdom's various short or fluffy or furry or minuscule—and sometimes animal—sidekicks were causing problems again. Sidekicks United, they called themselves, and they were far from happy. They were, in a word, disgruntled.

"Well, then, how can we help you today? Let's see. . . ." Ben wasn't talking to anyone but a piece of paper—or a thousand pieces. He stared down at the documents in front of him, tapping them with his pen. His father had asked him to lead the Council meeting that morning, part of the training for becoming king in a few months.

As was tradition, the firstborn child of the royal household would take the throne of Auradon at sixteen years of age. Beast and Belle were ready to retire. They were looking forward to long vacation cruises, early-bird dinners, and playing golf (Beast), bingo (Belle), and generally taking it easy. Besides, Belle had a stack of unread bedside reading so high, it threatened to topple over on a huffy Mrs. Potts when she came to take away the breakfast tray every morning.

The complaint wasn't the only thing on his mind. Ben had woken up that morning from a bit of a nightmare. Or it felt like a nightmare—and it certainly looked like one. In the dream, he was walking around a strange village full of shabbily dressed, miserable people who ate rotten fruit and drank black coffee. No cream. No sugar. No coffee cake to dip in it. The horror! And he had fallen into some kind of ditch, but someone had helped him out.

A beautiful, purple-haired girl who looked nothing like anyone in Auradon . . .

"Thank you," he said gratefully. "And who are you?"

But she'd disappeared before he could catch her name.

He went back to the papers in his hand and tried to forget about her.

Ben studied the Sidekicks United complaint—the first of its kind—and his heart beat a little faster at the thought of having to talk to all these people and convince them that there was no need for this level of discontent.

He sighed, until a familiar voice interrupted his reverie.

"Be careful about the sidekicks, son. Sooner or later they steal the spotlight."

Ben looked up, surprised to see his father standing in the doorway. King Beast looked like he always did, as smiling and happy and fulfilled as on his billboards. All over Auradon, they read *Good job being good! Keep it up! King Beast roars his approval!*

His father motioned to the stack of papers on Ben's desk. "Looks like you're working hard."

Ben wiped his eyes. "Yeah."

King Beast clapped his paw of a hand on his son's shoulder. "That's my boy. So what is it that they want, exactly?"

Ben scratched behind his ear with his pen. "It seems they're a bit upset, as they do all the work around here and are hardly compensated for their efforts. If you think about it from their perspective, they have a point."

"Mmm." King Beast nodded. "Everyone gets a voice in

Auradon. Although you can't let too many voices drown out reason, of course. That's what it means to be kingly," he said, perhaps a little more forcefully than was necessary.

"If you keep raising *your* voice, my darling, you're going to crack all the china, and Mrs. Potts will never allow you either a cup of warm milk or a warm bath again." Ben's mother, the goodly Queen Belle, arrived in the room and slipped her hand under her husband's muscled arm (yet another Beastly quality the king still seemed to possess—the strength of a wild creature in the form of a mere man). She was as beautiful as the day she had come upon Beast's castle, and resplendent in a pretty yellow dress. If there were laugh lines around her eyes now, no one seemed to notice; and if anything, they only served to make her look more appealing.

The second he saw his mother, Ben found himself more at ease. He shy and quiet, his mother gentle and under-standing, Ben and Belle had always been two like peas in a castle-garden pod—always preferring to have their noses in books rather than affairs of the state.

"But half the castle staff has signed this petition—see, there's Lumiere's scrawl, and Cogsworth's," Ben said, his forehead wrinkling. Injustice of any kind was upsetting to think about, and it bothered him that the very people on whom his family depended to keep their lives in running order believed that they had cause for complaint.

"Lumiere and Cogsworth will sign anything anyone asks them to sign. Last week they signed a petition to declare every day a holiday," his father said, amused.

Ben had to laugh. King Beast had a point. The fussy Frenchman and the jolly Brit would agree to anything so they could get back to their work. Chip Potts, who was known to make a little mischief around the castle, had probably put them up to it.

"That's the ticket. Listen to your people, but assert your right to rule. Lead with a gentle heart and a firm hand. That's the way to be a king!"

King Beast extended his own fist, and Ben just stared at it. He gazed down at his own hand, which looked like a small child's in comparison to his father's.

Beast pulled Ben up by the arm, closing his hand around his son's. "There. Strong. Powerful. Kingly."

King Beast's hand was so enormous Ben found he could no longer see his own.

"Strong. Powerful. Kingly," Ben repeated.

Beast growled, then slapped his son on the back, almost sending him flying into the nearest decorative lamp. The floor shook as he strode out of the room, still chuckling.

Queen Belle looked relieved; Beast was not above making a joke at his own expense—though he was much less forgiving when anyone else attempted the same line of humor. She put her arms around her son, drawing him close.

"Ben. You don't have to be another King Beast. Just be yourself—it's more than enough."

"That's not what Father says."

Belle smiled. They both knew there was no use trying to explain away his father's logic, and she didn't try. "No matter what, your father and I believe in you. That's why we wanted you to start meeting with the Council. It's time for you to learn how to rule. You will make a wonderful king, all on your own. I promise."

"I hope so," Ben said, uncertainly.

"I know so," Belle said, kissing his cheek.

As the feather-light steps of his mother faded away, Ben took up his pen and turned back to his pages. This time, though, all he could see was his fist, with the same golden beast-head ring that his father wore.

Strong. Powerful. Kingly.

He clenched his fingers harder.

Ben swore he would make his father proud.

chapter

6

Mean Girl

"Well, you look very pleased with yourself," said Jay as Mal settled into her front-row seat and propped her feet up on the desk next to her.

"I am," she said. "I just taught that little blueberry what it means to feel left out."

"Carlos looked like he was going to have a cow when you told him he was hosting your party."

"You mean a dog?" Mal laughed, even though the joke was getting old.

Jay elbowed her with a wink before melting away to his desk in the back of the room.

Mal was in a good mood. This class was her favorite:

Advanced Evil Schemes and Nasty Tricks, taught by Lady Tremaine, otherwise known as the Wicked Stepmother. Mal was particularly fond of Mean-Spirited Pranks.

"Hello, you dreadful children," Lady Tremaine said, entering the room with a swish of her petticoats and casting a bored look at the class in front of her. "Today we will embark on our annual class project: Crafting the Ultimate Evil Scheme."

She turned toward the chalkboard and wrote in earsplitting cursive: *The Cinderella Story: Once Upon a Broken Glass Slipper.* "As you well know," she said, as she turned back to the students, "my manipulation of Cinderella was my greatest evil deed. For years I kept her in the attic and treated her as a virtual servant. If not for some horrid meddling mice, one of my daughters would be the queen of Charming Castle right now, instead of that ungrateful girl. And so, the goal of every teacher at Dragon Hall is to train the new generation of villains not to make the same mistakes we did. You must learn to adapt, to be faster, more cunning, and wickeder than ever before. You will spend this year working on an evil scheme of your choosing. The student with the best nasty trick will win Dragon Hall's Evilest of the Year award."

The class nodded their heads in unison, each filling with a variety of ideas for awful tricks. Mal scratched her nose with the end of her purple-plumed fountain pen, wondering what her year-long scheming project would be. She looked around the room at her fellow students scribbling away on notepads, brows furrowed, some cackling softly under their breaths. Her mind was racing with horrid ideas, each more horrid than the last. *Lock all the first-years in the dungeon?* Been there, done that. *Fill the hallways with cockroaches?* Child's play. *Let a stampede of goblins loose in the slop hall?* That would be just a regular Tuesday. . . .

Across the room, Mal heard a soft giggle. She looked over her shoulder to find that annoying new girl Evie chatting cheerfully with Carlos De Vil as they played with some sort of black box on his desk. Ugh. That girl had nothing to be happy about. Why, hadn't she, Mal, just told her she couldn't come to the howler of the year? Mal was slightly disconcerted for a moment, until she realized: the evil scheme of the year was right in front of her.

A twisted smile formed on her lips, and she chewed her fountain pen for a moment before scribbling a page's worth of notes.

She would show that blue-haired princess a thing or two.

Of course, she'd already told Evie that she couldn't come to the party, but that wasn't *enough*. It was too simple, too blunt. Mal had to be sneaky, like Lady Tremaine had been, pretending to be working in Cinderella's best interests when she had been doing exactly the opposite.

Mal realized that she'd been waiting years for this chance, whether or not she'd consciously known it. The memory of the "lost" invitation—if indeed it had ever existed in the

first place (it was still unclear what had truly happened)—
grated on her feelings as sharply today as it had when she
was six years old.

A day like that can only happen once in sixteen years.

A day like that changes a person.

A day like that was never going to happen again.

Not if Mal could help it.

And to be honest, Mal wanted to do more than ruin
Evie's day, she wanted to ruin her *year*. On second thought,
maybe keeping Evie out of the party was the wrong move. If
Evie wasn't there, then Mal wouldn't have the opportunity
to torture her to her heart's delight.

Mal finished writing down her plans just as the bell rang
and caught up to Jay, who was all cheer and charm—and
by the time they reached the door, his pockets were full of
much more than that.

"Hold up," Mal said as she spotted Carlos and Evie
coming toward them.

Evie looked genuinely fearful and Carlos wary as they
approached Mal, who blocked the doorway.

"Hey, Evie, you know that party I'm having?" Mal
asked.

Evie nodded. "Um, yeah?"

"I was only kidding earlier," Mal said with the sweetest
smile she could manage. "*Of course* you're invited."

"I am?" Evie squealed. "Are you sure you want me
there?"

"I don't want anything more in the world," said Mal grandly, and truthfully. "Don't miss it."

"I won't," promised Evie with a nervous smile.

Mal watched her and Carlos skitter away with satisfaction. Jay raised an eyebrow. "What was that all about? I thought you didn't want her there," he said, as he deftly stole a rotten banana from a first-year's lunch pail.

"Plans change."

"An evil scheme, huh?" Jay waggled *both* eyebrows.

"Maybe," Mal said mysteriously, not wanting to give anything away. It wasn't like Jay could be trusted. "Thieves' honor" meant neither of them had any.

"Come on. It's me. The only one you can stand on this island."

"Don't flatter yourself," she said, only half smiling.

"Don't you hate parties? You didn't go to Anthony Tremaine's kickback the other week, and you missed my cousin Jade's 'Scary Sixteenth.' They were off-the-hook, as the pirate posse would say." He smirked.

"Those were different. Anyway, you need to hop to it. Carlos can't throw my party alone." She grabbed his arm. "We need jugs of spicy cider, bags of stale potato chips, sparkling slop, the works."

Jay peeled the banana and took a bite. "Done."

"And make sure it's the good stuff from the wharf, from the first boats. I've got a reputation to uphold."

He saluted and tossed the banana peel on the floor, and they both watched gleefully as a fellow student slipped and fell. Things like that never got old.

Mal smiled, her green eyes glittering a little more like her mother's than usual. "Let's go. I have a party to throw." *And someone to throw it at.*

chapter

7

Hell Raiser

Carlos never shied from a mission, and if Mal wanted a howler, there was no alternative but to provide one. There was nothing he could do about it, AP Evil Penchant or not. He knew his place on the totem pole.

First things first: a party couldn't be a party without guests. Which meant people. Lots of people. Bodies. Dancing. Talking. Drinking. Eating. Playing games. He had to get the word out.

Thankfully it didn't take too long for everyone he crossed paths with at school, and the minions of everyone *they* crossed paths with, to spread the word. Because Carlos didn't so much issue an invitation as deliver a threat.

Literally.

He didn't mince words, and the threats only grew more exaggerated as the school day wore on. The rumors spread like the gusty, salty wind that blew up from the alligator-infested waters surrounding the island.

"Be there, or Mal will find you," he said to his squat little lab partner, Le Fou Deux, as they both dissected a frog that would never turn into a prince in Unnatural Biology class.

"Be there, or Mal will find you and ban you from the city streets," he whispered to the Gastons as they took turns stuffing each other in doomball nets in PE.

"Be there, or Mal will find you and ban you and make everyone forget you, and from this day onward you will be known only by the name of Slop!" he said almost hysterically to a group of frightened first-years gathered for a meeting of the Anti-Social Club, which was planning the school's annual Foul Ball. They turned pale at his words and desperately promised their attendance, even as they trembled at the thought.

By the end of the day, Carlos had secured dozens of RSVPs. Now, *that* wasn't too hard, he thought, putting away his books in his locker and releasing the first-year who'd been trapped inside.

"Hey, man." Carlos nodded.

"Thanks, I really have to pee," squeaked the unfortunate student.

"Sure," Carlos said, scrunching his nose. "Oh, and there's a party. My house. Midnight."

"I heard, I'll be there! Wouldn't miss it!" the first-year said, raising his fist to the air in excitement.

Carlos nodded, feeling mollified and more than a little impressed that even someone who'd been trapped inside a locker all day had heard the news about the party. He was a natural! Maybe party planning was in his blood. His mother certainly knew how to enjoy herself, didn't she? Cruella was always telling him how boring he was because all he liked to do was fiddle with electronics all day. His mother declared he was wasting his time, that he was useless at everything except chores, and so maybe if he threw a good party, he could prove her wrong. Not that she would be around to witness it, though. She'd probably be enraged to discover her Hell Hall crawling with teenagers. Still, he wished that one day Cruella could see him as more than just a live-in servant who happened to be related to her.

He made his way home, his mind awhirl. With the guests secured, all he had to do was get the house ready for the blessed event—and that couldn't be too hard, could it?

A few hours later, Carlos took it all back. "Why did I ever agree to have this party?" he agonized aloud. "I never wanted to have a party." He raked his fingers through his curly, speckled hair, which made it stick up in a frazzle, a lot like Cruella's own do.

"You mean tonight?" A voice echoed from the other end of the crumbling ballroom, from behind the giant, tarnished statue of a great knight.

"I mean *ever*," sighed Carlos. It was true. He was a man of science, not society. Not even *evil* society.

But here he was, decorating Hell Hall, which had seen better days long before he'd been born. Still, the decrepit Victorian mansion was one of the grandest on the island, covered in vines more twisted than Cruella's own mind, and gated with iron more wrought than Cruella's own daily hysterias.

The main ballroom was now draped in the sagging black-and-white crepe paper and partly deflated black-and-white balloons that Carlos had pilfered from a sad stack of dusty boxes stashed in his building's basement. Those few boxes, stamped *De Vil Industries*, were all that remained of the former De Vil fashion empire—the merest scraps of a better life that had long since faded away.

His mother, of course, would be furious when she saw that Carlos had gotten into her boxes again—"*My stolen treasures*," she'd scream, "*my lost babies!*"—but Carlos was a pragmatist, and a scavenger.

Why his mother had ever been obsessed with black-and-white Dalmatian puppies, he had no idea. He was terrified of those things; but she had been prepared to own one hundred and one of them, so there was a lot of stuff to scavenge.

Over the years, he'd repurposed more than a few empty

crates—*scientists requiring bookshelves as they did*—abandoned leashes—*nylon withstanding the elements as it did*—and unsqueaked squeaky toys—*rubber repelling electricity as it did*—that had fallen by the wayside when his mother's plans were foiled.

An AP Evil scientist and inventor like Carlos couldn't afford to be choosy. He needed materials for his research.

"Why did you agree to this party? Easy. Because Mal asked you to," Carlos's second-best friend Harry said, shaking his head as he wiggled his fingers, tape dangling from each one. "Maybe you should try, for your next invention, to build something that would free us all from her mind control."

His third-best friend, Jace, tried to take a piece of tape but only succeeded in taping himself to Harry. "Yeah, right. No one can stand up to Mal," said Jace. "As if."

Harry (Harold) and Jace (Jason) were the sons of Horace and Jasper, Cruella's loyal minions, the two blundering thieves who had attempted to kidnap the one hundred and one Dalmatian puppies for her and failed miserably. Just like their fathers, Harry and Jace tried to look like they were more capable and less nervous than they actually were.

But Carlos knew otherwise.

Harry, as short and fat as his father, could barely reach to fasten his side of the ebony streamer. Jace, taller even than his own tall, scrawny father, didn't have that same problem but, as previously mentioned, couldn't manage to figure out the tape dispenser. Between them, they didn't exactly constitute a brain trust. More like a brain *mis*-trust.

Carlos wouldn't have chosen them as his friends—his mother chose them for him, just like she did everything else.

"They're all we've got," Cruella would say. "Even when we have nothing else, we'll always have . . ."

"Friends?" Carlos had guessed.

"Friends?!" Cruella had laughed. "Who needs friends when you have minions to do your bidding!"

Cruella certainly ruled Jasper and Horace with an iron leash, but one could hardly say that Harry and Jace did Carlos's bidding. They only seemed to hang around because their fathers made them, and only because they were all scared of Carlos's mother.

Which was why he considered them only his *second*- and *third*-best friends. He didn't have a *first* best friend, but he knew enough about the concept of friendship, even without having any proper ones of his own, to know that an actual best friend would have to be able to do something more than follow him around, tripping over his feet and repeating his not-worth-saying-the-first-time jokes.

All the same, it was good to have some help for the party, and it was Harry who nodded sadly at him now. "If Mal doesn't like this party, we're doomed."

"Doomed," echoed Jace.

Carlos surveyed the rest of the room. Every piece of broken-down old furniture was covered in a dusty white linen cloth. Every few feet of plaster wallboard was punctured by a crumbling hole that revealed the plywood and plaster underneath.

The overachiever in him bristled. He could do better than this! He had to. He rushed upstairs and dug out his mother's antique brass candelabras and rigged them up around the room. With the lights off, the candles glimmered and flickered as if they were floating in midair.

Next, was the chandelier swing—a staple at any Isle party, or so he'd heard. He had Jace climb up a makeshift ladder and tie a rope swing to the light fixture. Harry jumped off from one of the sheet-covered couches to test it out, which caused a cloud of dust to settle over the whole room. Carlos approved—it kind of looked like a fresh snowfall had been sprinkled over the hall.

He picked up the rotary phone and called his cousin Diego De Vil, who was the lead singer in a local band called the Bad Apples.

"You guys want a gig tonight?"

"Do we ever! Heard Mal's having a full-moon howler!"

The band arrived not too long after, setting up the drum set by the window and practicing their songs. Their music was loud and fast, and Diego, a tall, skinny guy who sported a black-and-white Mohawk, sang out of tune. It was marvelous. The perfect soundtrack for the evening.

Next up, Carlos dug out an old-fashioned instant Polaroid

camera he'd found in the attic. He fashioned a private booth by removing the sheet from a couch and rigging it on a rod in a secluded corner. "Photo booth! You take their photo," he said to Jace. "And you hand it to them," he told Harry.

Carlos admired his handiwork. "Not too shabby," he said. "Now we're talking."

"And it's about to get a whole lot better," said an unfamiliar voice.

Carlos turned to see Jay entering the room holding four huge grocery bags filled with all manner of party snacks: stinky cheese and withered grapes, deviled eggs (so appropriate) and wings (sinfully spicy), and more. Jay pulled a bottle of the island's best spicy cider out of his jacket and dumped it into the cracked punch bowl on the coffee table.

"Wait! Stop! I don't want things to get out of hand," Carlos said, trying to grab the bottle and cap it. "How did you get your hands on all of that sugar!"

"Oh, but that's where you're wrong," Jay said, grinning. "Better your party gets out of hand than Mal gets out of sorts."

Jay sank to the couch, putting his combat boots up by the punch bowl. The minions shrugged, and Carlos sighed.

The guy had a point.

As the clock struck midnight, Mal's guests began to arrive in force. There were no gourd-like carriages or rodent-like servants to be seen, not anywhere. Nothing had been transformed into anything, especially not what anyone would consider a cool ride.

There were only feet, in varying degrees of shoddy footwear. Perhaps because their feet were the largest, the Gastons arrived first, as usual. They never risked a late entrance, so as not to miss a buffet table full of food they might swallow whole before anyone else got a taste.

During the awkward silence that followed the Gastons head-butting their hellos and competitively slamming pitchers of smuggled root beer, a whole ship's worth of Harriet Hook's pirate crew came marauding through the door.

As Carlos stood against the faded wallpaper nursing his spicy punch, the Gastons and the pirate posse busied themselves with chasing the next group of guests through the house. This happened to be an entire cackling slew of evil step-granddaughters, festooned with raggedy ribbons and droopy curls, elbowing their way around the corners at top speed. "Don't chase us!" they begged, just waiting to be chased. "You're horrible!" they screamed, horribly. "Sto-o-o-o-o-o-p," they said, refusing to stop.

Their cousin, Anthony Tremaine followed them into the room, rolling his eyes.

The band struck up a rollicking tune. Dark-haired Ginny Gothel arrived with a bushel of wormy apples, and a game of bob-for-the-wormiest-apple broke out in the tub. Everybody wanted a turn on the chandelier swing, and the rest of the guests were engaged in a serious dance-off over by the band. All in all, it was shaping up to be a wicked good time.

More than an hour after the party had officially started, there was a sharp knock on the door. It wasn't clear what made this knock different from all the others, but different it was. Carlos leapt to his feet like a soldier suddenly called to attention. Jay stopped dancing with a posse of evil step-granddaughters. The Gastons looked up from the buffet table. Little Sammy Smee held an apple between his teeth questioningly.

Carlos steadied his nerves and opened the door. "Go away!" he yelled, using the island's traditional greeting.

Mal stood in the doorway. Backlit by the dim hall light, in shiny purple leather from head to toe, she appeared to have not so much a halo as a shimmer, like the lead vocalist of a band during a particularly well-lit rock concert—the kind with smoke and neon and bits of sparkly nonsense in the air.

Carlos half-expected her to start belting a tune with the band. Perhaps he should have felt excited that such an infamous personality had decided to come to his party.

Er, *her* party.

There would be no unplugging this party like one of his rebuilt stereos, not once it had begun, especially not the sort of party Mal seemed to have in mind.

"Hey, Carlos," she drawled. "Am I late?"

"Not at all," said Carlos. "Come in."

"Excited to see me?" Mal asked with a smile.

He nodded yes. Except that Carlos wasn't excited.

He was *terrified*.

Somewhere, deep down, he even wanted his mommy.

chapter

Only Human

"*T*oad's-blood shots!" declared Mal, leaping into the room as if she were just another guest. "For everyone!"

And just like that, the party began again, as quickly as it had stopped. It was like the entire room exhaled in one relieved breath. *Mal isn't mad. Mal isn't banning us from the streets. Mal isn't renaming us Slop.*

Not yet.

Mal could see their relief on their faces, and she didn't blame them. They were right. The way she'd been feeling lately, it was certainly something to celebrate.

So the crowd cheered, and toad's-blood shots splashed

across the room by the cupful, and Mal, in a show of generous sportsmanship, chugged a slimy cup right along with the rest.

She circled the party, pilfering a wallet from one of the Gastons, stopping to share a mean giggle with Ginny Gothel about the dress Harriet Hook was wearing, ducking under an overenthusiastic pirate swinging from the chandelier, taking a bite out of someone else's devil dog and grabbing a mouthful of dry popcorn. She walked into the hallway and bumped into Jay, who was out of breath after winning the latest dance-off.

"Having fun?" he asked.

She shrugged. "Where'd Carlos go?"

Jay laughed and pointed toward a pair of black shoes poking out from behind a sheet covering the biggest of the bookcases. "Hiding from his own party. Typical."

Mal knew how Carlos felt, though she'd never admit it. Truly, she'd rather be almost anywhere on the whole Isle than at this party. Like her mother, she hated the sights and sounds of revelry. Fun made her uncomfortable. Laughter? Gave her hives. But a vendetta was a vendetta, and she had more planned for this evening than just Deep, Dark, Secret or Death-Defying Dare.

"Come on," said Jay. "They're playing pin the tail on the minion over there, and Jace has like, ten tails. Let's see if we can make it a dozen."

"Maybe in a minute. Where's Princess Blueberry?" Mal

asked. "I did a whole loop of this party, and I didn't see her anywhere."

"You mean Evie? She's not here yet. Nobody seems to know if she's coming or not." Jay shrugged. "Castle kids."

"She has to come. She's the whole point. She's the only reason I'm even having this stupid party." Mal hated when her evil schemes didn't go exactly as planned. This was the first step in *Operation Take Down Evie, Or Else*, and it *had* to work. She sighed, staring at the door. Pretending to be having fun at a party when you hated parties was the most tiresome thing in the world.

Mal had to agree with her mother on that one.

"What are you two doing?" asked Anthony Tremaine, Lady Tremaine's sixteen-year-old grandson, a tall, elegant boy with dark hair swept off a haughty forehead. His clothes were as worn and ragged as everyone else's on the Isle, but somehow he always looked as if he was wearing custom tailoring. His dark leather coat was cut perfectly, his jeans the right dark wash. Maybe it was because Anthony had noble blood, and would probably have lived in Auradon except for his grandmother's being, you know, evil and banished. At one point he'd tried to get everyone on the Isle to call him Lord Tremaine, but the villain kids had all just laughed in his face.

"Just talking," said Mal.

"Evil plotting," said Jay.

They looked at each other.

Something about Anthony's handsome face brought to Mal's mind another handsome boy—the prince from her dream. He'd said he was her friend. His smile was kind and his voice gentle. Mal shuddered.

"Do you want something?" Mal asked Anthony coolly.

"Yes. To dance." Anthony looked at her expectantly.

She looked at him, confused. "Wait—with *me*?" Nobody had ever asked her before. But she'd never really been to a party before either.

"Well, I didn't mean *him*," Anthony said, looking awkwardly at Jay. "No offense, man."

"None taken." Jay grinned broadly, knowing how uncomfortable this made Mal. He found it hilarious. "You two kids go have fun out there. Anthony, make sure you pick a slow song," he said, as he slid away. "I have a step-granddaughter waiting for me."

Mal could feel her cheeks turning pink, which was embarrassing, because she wasn't afraid of anything, least of all dancing with snotty Anthony Tremaine.

So why are you blushing? she thought.

"I'm not really a dancer," she said lamely.

"I can show you," he said with a smooth smile.

Mal bristled. "I mean, I don't dance with anyone. Ever."

"Why not?"

Why not, indeed?

Mal thought about it. Her mind flashed back to earlier that evening. She'd been getting ready for the party, trying to choose between violet-hued holey or mauve patchwork jeans, when her mother had made a rare appearance at her door.

"Where on this dreadful island could you possibly be going?" Maleficent asked.

"To a party," Mal said.

Maleficent let out an exasperated sigh. "Mal, what have I told you about parties?"

"I'm not going to have *fun*, Mother. I'm going so I can make someone *miserable*." She almost wanted to share *Operation Evie Scheme* right then, but thought better of it. She would tell her mother once she had completed it successfully, lest she disappoint her once more. Maleficent never failed to remind Mal that sometimes it just didn't seem like Mal was evil enough to be her daughter. *At your age I was cursing entire kingdoms* was a familiar phrase Mal had grown up hearing.

"So you're off to make someone miserable?" her mother cooed.

"Wretched, really!" enthused Mal.

A slow smile formed on Maleficent's thin red lips. She crossed the room and stood in front of Mal, reaching out to trace a long nail along Mal's cheek. "That's a nasty little girl," she said. Mal swore she saw a glimmer of pride flicker in her mother's cold, emerald-green eyes.

Mal snapped back to reality as the band finished a punk rock number with clashing cymbals and a drum roll. Anthony Tremaine was still staring at her.

"So why don't you dance, again?"

Because I don't have time to dance when I have evil schemes to hatch, Mal wanted to say. *One that will make my mother proud of me, finally.*

She turned up her nose. "I don't have to have a reason."

"You don't. But that doesn't mean you don't have one."

He caught her by surprise, because he was right.

Because she did have a reason, a very good reason to stay clear of any kind of activity that might hint at or lead to romance. Her missing father. Otherwise known as He-Who-Must-Not-Be-Named-in-Maleficent's-Presence.

So Anthony had her there. Mal had to give him that. But instead, she glared at him. Then she glared at him again, for good measure. "Maybe I just like to be alone."

Because maybe I'm so tired of my mother looking at me like I'm weak, just because I came from her own moment of weakness.

Because maybe I need to show her that I'm strong enough and evil enough to prove to her that I'm not like my weak, human father.

That I can be just like her.

Maybe I don't want to dance because I don't want to have anything human about me.

"That can't be it." Anthony said, picking lint off his jacket. His voice was uncommonly low and pleasant, which once again brought back to Mal's mind the handsome prince by the enchanted lake. Except that Anthony wasn't quite as handsome as the boy in her dream had been, not that she thought that boy handsome, *mind you*. Not that she thought about him *at all*. "Nobody likes to be alone."

"Well, I do," she insisted. It was true.

"And besides, everybody wants to dance with a lord," he said smugly.

"Nope, not me!"

"Fine, have it your way," Anthony said, finally backing away, his head held high. In a hot second, he had already asked Harriet Hook to dance, and she'd accepted with a delighted shriek.

Mal exhaled. *Phew*. Boys. Dreams. Princes. It was all too much for one day.

"Mal. Mal. Earth to Mal?" Jay waved a hand in front of her face. "You okay?"

Mal nodded but didn't answer. For a moment she had been lost in the memory of that awful dream again. Except that this time it didn't seem so much a dream as a premonition? That one day she might just find herself in Auradon? But how could that be?

Jay frowned, holding out a cup of cider. "Here. It's like you've powered down, or something."

Mal realized that she hadn't moved from the front hall. She'd been standing there, stupidly frozen, ever since Anthony had left her side. That was three songs ago, and the Bad Apples were playing their current hit, "Call Me Never."

She perked up, not because of the cider or the catchy song but because, out of the corner of her eye, she spotted Evie through the floor-to-ceiling window in the foyer. She was coming down the road in a brand-new rickshaw, her pretty V-braid gleaming in the moonlight. *She thinks she is so special. Well, I'll show her,* Mal thought. Her eyes wandered over the room and rested upon a familiar-looking door.

It was the door that led to Cruella De Vil's storage closet. Mal only knew it was there because she and Carlos had once accidentally come across it when they were working on a skit about evil family trees in sixth grade, and Mal had been bored and had decided to go poking around Hell Hall. Cruella's closet was not for the faint of heart.

Mal would never forget that day. It was the kind of closet that would get the best of anyone. Especially a princess who was making her way up the steps to the front door and would appear at any moment now.

"Jay," she said, motioning to the front door. "Let me know when Evie arrives."

"Huh? What? Why?"

"You'll see," she told him.

"All part of the evil scheme, huh?" he said, happy to do her bidding. Jay was always up for a good prank.

But Carlos went white-faced when he saw where Mal

was heading. "Don't—" he shouted. He shook off his sheet, almost tripping over the fabric in an attempt to get to the door before Mal could open it all the way.

It slammed shut. Just in time.

But Mal crossed her arms. She wasn't backing down from this one. It was just too perfect. She glanced out the window again. Princess-Oh-So-Fashionably-Late was at the front door now.

Mal raised her voice. "New game! Seven Minutes in Heaven! And you've never played Seven Minutes if you haven't played it in a De Vil closet."

The words were barely out of Mal's mouth before most of the evil step-granddaughters practically trampled her to get to the door. They loved playing Seven Minutes and were enthusiastically wondering with whom they would end up inside. A few of them puckered their lips and powdered their noses while fluttering their eyelashes at Jay, who was stationed by the front door like a sentry.

"Who wants to go first?" Mal asked.

"Me! Me! Me!" yelped the step-granddaughters.

"She does," Jay called, holding a very recognizable blue cape.

"I do? What do I want to do?" asked the cape's owner.

Mal smiled.

Evie had arrived.

"Evie, sweetie! So glad you could make it!" Mal said,

throwing her arms theatrically around the girl and giving her a giant and fake embrace. "We're playing Seven Minutes in Heaven! Want to play?"

"Uh, I don't know," said Evie, looking around the party nervously.

"It'll be a scream," said Mal. "Come on, you want to be my friend, don't you?"

Evie stared at Mal. "You want *me* to be your friend?"

"Sure—why not?" Mal led her to the closet door and opened it.

"But doesn't a boy go in here with me?" Evie asked as Mal shoved her inside the storage room. For someone castle-schooled, Evie sure knew her kissing games.

"Did I say Seven Minutes in Heaven? No, you're playing *Seven Minutes in Hell*!" Mal cackled; she couldn't help it. This was going to be so much fun.

The crowd around the hallway had scattered in fear after it was clear Mal had no interest in having other people join the game—or Evie—inside the locked room.

But Carlos remained standing, his face as white as the tips of his hair. "Mal, what are you doing?"

"Playing a dirty trick—what does it *look* like I'm doing?"

"You can't leave her in there! Remember what happened to us?" he asked, motioning angrily to his leg, which had two distinct white scars on the calf.

"I do!" Mal said gleefully. She wondered why Carlos was

so concerned about Evie. It wasn't as if they'd been taught to care about other people.

But Carlos soon made clear that he wasn't being altruistic. "If she's not able to get out on her own, I'm going to have to clean up the mess! And my mother will freak out! You can't leave her in there!" he whispered fiercely, anxiety about Cruella's punishment written all over his face.

"Fine, go get her," said Mal with a sly smile on *her* face, knowing full well that he wouldn't.

Carlos quaked in his scuffed loafers. Mal knew there was nothing he wanted to do less than go back in there again. He remembered all too well what had happened to him and Mal in sixth grade.

There was a scream from behind the door.

Mal wiped her hands. "You want her out? You get her out." Her job was done.

Her evil scheme had worked. This was going to be a real howler.

chapter

9

Let the Fur Fly

*T*he first thing Evie thought when the door unceremoniously closed with a bang behind her was that she had worn her prettiest dress for nothing. She had been looking forward to the party all day, had run home to go through every outfit in her closet, holding up dress after dress to see which shade of blue looked best. Azure? Periwinkle? Turquoise? She had settled on a dark midnight-blue lace mini-dress and matching high-heeled boots. She'd been extremely late to the party, as her mother had insisted on giving her a three-hour makeover.

Not that it mattered, because she was now locked in a closet alone. She wasn't just imagining it—Mal really *was* out to get her, most likely for not having been invited to Evie's birthday party when they were six years old. But it wasn't as if it was her fault! Evie'd been just a kid. It had been her mother who hadn't wanted Mal at the party for some reason. Mal couldn't hold it against *her*, could she? Evie sighed. Of course she could. Evie still remembered the hurt and anger on six-year-old Mal's face, looking down from the balcony. Evie supposed that she'd probably feel the same way—not that she could see it from Mal's point of view, or anything. *There's no* me *in empathy,* as Mother Gothel liked to say.

In the end, Evil Queen probably should have dropped her grudge against Maleficent and invited her daughter to the celebration. It certainly hadn't been fun being cooped up in their castle for ten years. Evie wasn't even sure why her mother had decided that now was a safe time to leave; but so far, other than Evie being locked in this closet at the moment, nothing too bad had happened. Yet.

Besides, the darkness of the closet didn't bother her. Evie was her mother's daughter, after all, and used to the horrors of the night—to dark, hidden things with yellow eyes glittering in the shadows, to candles dripping over skull candleholders, to the flash of lightning and the fury of thunder as they rolled across the sky. She wasn't scared. She wasn't scared in the least bit.

Except . . .

Except . . . her foot just struck something hard and

cold . . . and the quiet of the closet was broken by the loud, echoing snap of steel meeting steel.

She screamed. *What was that?!* When her eyes adjusted to the dim light, she saw fur traps littered all over the floor, lying in wait for the next animal to wander through. There were so many of them that one wrong step would mean a trap would snap her leg in two. She turned back to the door and tried to open it, but it was no use. She was locked in there.

"Help! Help! Let me out!" she yelled.

But there was no answer, and the band was playing so loudly, Evie knew no one would hear her, nor care.

It was hard to see, so Evie felt her way tentatively in the darkness, sliding her left foot on the floor first. How many were there? Ten? Twenty? A hundred? And how big was this room, anyway?

Her foot came in contact with something cold and heavy, so she retreated. How was she going to get out of this place without losing a limb? Was there another door on the other side, maybe? She squinted. Yes, that was another door. There was a way out.

She headed slowly to the far end, the floorboards creaking ominously under her feet.

Evie shifted to her right, hoping to avoid the trap, to move around it, but her foot struck another, and she jumped back as it too snapped shut with a bang, springing into the air and barely grazing her knee. Her heart thundered in her chest as she slid around the next trap, careful not to strike the metal for fear that it might close around her ankle. As long as she missed the trap's center, she would be good.

She could do this. All she had to do was move slowly, carefully. She edged around another one. She was getting better at this; she could find her way to the back of the room and possibly another door. She cleared one and then another, moving more quickly, sliding one foot in front of the other, searching for and avoiding the traps. Faster. A little faster. The door must be close, then—

She struck a trap and it suddenly popped up with a snap. She jumped away, and as the trap fell on the floor, it hit another trap, which sprang up and hit the one next to it, all in succession—and this time, Evie saw that she couldn't move slowly but that she had to *run*.

The chorus of snapping metal jaws rang through the darkness, steel blades against steel blades, as she ran screaming toward the back door. The traps slammed shut, *BAM BAM BAM*, one after another, one a hairbreadth away from her stocking while another almost caught her heel as she turned the door handle, left the room, and shut the door behind her.

But just as she thought she was safe, she realized she had plunged right into a dark, furry presence.

Was it a bear? A horrible shaggy monster? Had she

gotten out of the frying pan only to fall into the fire? Evie twisted and turned, but only succeeded in wrapping herself deeper in fur—dense, thick, woolly fur—*with two armholes?*

This was no bear . . . no monster. She was trapped in a fur coat! Evie tried to shake it off, tried to shrug it off her shoulders, but she was smack-dab in the middle of dozens of coats, all of them black or white or black *and* white, made of the thickest, lushest hides—there was spotted ocelot and dip-dyed mink, silky sable and shiny skunk, all of them packed in like sardines, so full, so fluffy, so thick. This was Cruella De Vil's fur closet, her wondrous collection, her obsession, her greatest weakness.

And those fur traps back there were her security system, just in case anyone got too close to the stuff.

Evie finally managed to untangle herself and push aside the wall of fur, just as a hand grasped her wrist and pulled her through to the other side.

"You okay?" It was Carlos.

Evie took a deep breath. "Yes. I think so. Do I win the game?" she asked drily.

Carlos laughed. "Mal's going to be annoyed you survived."

"Where are we?" Evie looked around. There was a lumpy mattress on the floor next to an ironing board and a washbasin, along with a vanity table that held dozens of white-and-black wigs.

When Carlos looked embarrassed, she realized it was

his bedroom. Cruella's fur closet opened onto a dressing room, where her son slept.

"Oh."

Carlos shrugged. "It's home."

Even if her mother annoyed her sometimes, at least Evil Queen was obsessed with Evie's good looks; and even when she wasn't worried that perhaps Evie might not be the fairest of them all, she treated her daughter like the princess she was. Evie's room might be dark and musty, but she had a real bed, not a makeshift one, with a thick blanket and relatively soft pillows.

"It's not so bad in here, really!" Evie said. "I'm sure it's cozy and, hey . . . you'll never catch a cold. You can just use one of her fur coats for a blanket, right?" It was awfully drafty in the room: like her own home, Hell Hall wasn't insulated for winter.

Carlos shook his head. "I'm not allowed to touch them," he said, trying to put the furs back in order. They were so heavy, and there were so many of them. "I'll fix them later. She doesn't come back till Sunday."

Evie nodded. "This is all my mother's fault. If she hadn't tried to challenge Maleficent's leadership when they first came to the Isle, none of this would have happened."

"Your mother actually *challenged* Maleficent?" Carlos goggled. It was unheard of.

"Well, she is a queen, after all," Evie pointed out. "Yeah, she was angry that everyone on the island decided to follow

Maleficent instead of her." She walked over to the vanity and began to fix her makeup, delicately powdering her nose and applying pink gloss to her full rosebud lips. "And now here we are."

"Mal will get over it," he said hopefully.

"Are you kidding? A grudge is a grudge is a grudge. She'll never forgive me. Didn't you listen in Selfie class? I thought you were so smart." Evie smiled wryly. "Oh well, I should just face it. Go back to our castle and never come out."

"But you're not, right?"

"No, I guess not." Evie put away her compact. "Hey," she said softly. "I have an old comforter I never use . . . I mean, if you get cold and you can't . . . Oh, never mind." She'd never had any siblings, so she had no idea what having a little brother would be like. But if Evil Queen had ever stopped looking at herself in the mirror long enough to have another kid, Evie thought it would be tolerable to have a little brother like Carlos.

Carlos looked as if he didn't know what to say.

"Forget I said anything," said Evie in a rush.

"No, no, bring it. I mean, no one's ever cared whether I'm warm or not," he said, blushing red as his voice trailed off. "Not that *you* care, of course."

"I certainly don't!" agreed Evie. Caring was *definitely* against the rules at Dragon Hall and could turn anyone into a laughingstock. "We were going to throw it out."

"Excellent, just consider my home your Dumpster."

"Er, okay."

"Do you think you might have a pillow you were going to toss out too? I've never had a pillow." Carlos turned red again. "I mean, I've had *tons* of pillows, of course. So many! We have to keep throwing them away. I get so many pillows. I mean, who's never had a pillow in their life? That's preposterous."

"Yeah, I think we were going to throw away a pillow," Evie said, turning just as red as Carlos, even as a warm, sunny sensation had taken over her chest. She changed the subject. "Still working on that machine of yours?"

"Yeah, wanna see?" he asked.

"Yeah, sure," Evie replied, following Carlos out of the room toward the back of the house, away from the party. Carlos slipped outside, holding the door open for Evie.

"Where are we going?"

"To my lab," Carlos replied, pulling out a matchbook and lighting a candle to lead the way into the weedy backyard.

"Your what?"

"My science lab. Don't worry, I don't, like, sacrifice toads or something."

Evie let out a hesitant laugh.

They approached a huge, gnarled tree with a rope ladder. Carlos started climbing up it. "I have to keep it all in my tree house. I'm afraid my mom is going to get some big ideas and turn my chemicals into makeup and hair products."

Evie scrambled up the ladder behind him. The tree

house was more elaborate than any she'd ever seen, with miniature turrets and a tiny balcony that looked out onto the dark forest below. Inside, Evie spun around, gaping. The walls were lined with shelves of glass beakers, vials, and jars containing various neon-colored liquids. In the corner sat a small, old television with about fifteen different antennas strapped to it.

"What is all this?" Evie asked, picking up a jar of something white and snowy.

"Oh, that's from Chem Lab. It's sodium polyacrylate—I was trying to see if I could use it as a sponge when mixed with water," Carlos said. "But here, this is what I wanted to show you." He pulled out the wire-box contraption he'd been working on in class. "I think I got the battery to work."

Carlos fiddled with a few buttons and flicked a few switches. It sputtered to life, then died. His face fell. He tried again. This time, it emitted a high-pitched squeal before dying.

He looked up at Evie sheepishly. "Sorry, I thought I had it."

Evie looked at the black box. "Maybe try connecting this wire to that one?" she suggested.

Carlos peered at the wires. "You're right, they're in the wrong place." He switched the wires and hit the switch.

A powerful electric burst shot out of the box, sending Carlos and Evie flying back against the wall and falling to the floor. The beam of light burst up toward the plywood ceiling, blasting a hole in the tree-house roof and up to the sky.

"Maleficent!" Carlos cursed.

"Oh my goblins!" Evie screamed. "What just happened?"

They both scrambled out onto the tree-house balcony and stared up at the sky, where the light was streaking all the way up, through the clouds, up, up, up, all to the way to the dome!

The light seared through the barrier as easily as it had burned a hole in the tree-house roof.

Lightning flashed, and the very earth shook with a supersonic rumble. For a second they could see through the dome and directly into the night sky. The black box began to emit a strange beeping noise.

Carlos and Evie scrambled back inside, and Carlos picked up the box. It was making a sound neither of them had ever heard before.

And for a brief moment, there was something on the television in the room, which had burst to life all of a sudden.

"Look!" Evie cried.

The screen was flashing with so many different scenes it was dizzying. For a moment they saw a talking dog (Carlos screamed at the sight); then it switched to a pair of twins who were nothing alike (one was boyish and athletic and the other was sort of a diva, and they both sort of looked like Mal, except with yellow hair); then it switched again to two teenage boys who seemed to be running a hospital for superheroes.

"Look at all these different television shows!" Carlos said. "I knew it! I knew it! I knew there had to be other kinds!"

Evie laughed. Then the screen flickered and went dark again, and the box in Carlos's hands went dead. "What happened?"

"I don't know. I think maybe it worked? It penetrated the dome for a second, didn't it?" he asked, approaching the box fearfully and touching it with the end of one finger. It was hot to the touch, and he pulled his hand away quickly.

"It must have," Evie said. "That's the only explanation."

"Promise you won't tell anyone about what happened, especially about the dome. We could get in real trouble, you know."

"I promise," said Evie, making an X with her fingers behind her back.

"Good."

"You want to go back to the party?"

"Do we have to?" she asked, unwilling to find herself trapped in another closet.

"You have a point. And that show you like on Auradon News Network, the one that features the Prince of the Week, is going to be on in five minutes."

"Excellent!"

Unbeknown to the two villain children, far off in the distance, deep in the heart of the forbidden fortress, hidden behind a gray misty fog on the other side of the island, a long black scepter with a jewel on its end came back to life, glowing green with power again. The most powerful weapon of darkness had been awakened for a moment.

Next to the hidden staff, a stone statue of a raven began to vibrate, and when the bird began to shake its wings, the stone crumbled into dust, and in its place was that black-eyed fiend, that wicked fairy's familiar, the one and only Diablo, Maleficent's best and first friend.

Diablo shook his feathers and gave a throaty, triumphant cry. Evil would fly again.

Evil lives. . . .

chapter

10

Council of Sidekicks

*B*en nervously fiddled with the beast-head ring on his finger as he waited for the Council members to come in and take their seats around the king's conference table later that morning. His father's advice rang in his ear. *Keep a strong hand. Show 'em who's king.*

He flexed his own fingers, thinking of his father's fist. His father didn't mean it literally, but Ben was worried nonetheless. He supposed he would just have to improvise.

"Ready, sire?" Lumiere asked.

Ben took a breath and tried to sound as serious as possible. "Yes, let them in, thank you."

Lumiere bowed. Even though it had been a long time

since he had been enchanted and turned into a candela-brum, there was something about him that still resembled one, and for a moment, Ben could easily imagine two small flames flickering on his outstretched palms.

Lumiere knows who he is—and he's happy being Lumiere. Is it really so much more complicated to be a king than a candelabrum?

The thought was, for a moment, comforting to Ben. But then the Council entered the room—and he found there was nothing comforting about the sudden sight of the royal advisors.

In fact, they're pretty terrifying, Ben thought.

He didn't know why. They were chatting amiably enough, discussing last night's Tourney scores and whose Fantasy Tourney League was winning. Seats were taken, gossip exchanged, goblets of spiced cider passed around, as well as a plate or two of the castle kitchen's sugar cookies.

Representing the sidekicks were the usual seven dwarfs, still wearing their mining clothes and stocking hats. Seated next to the dwarfs (or rather, sitting along the edge of a book of *Auradon's Civic Rules & Regulations* that lay on the table nearest them, because they were much too small to take any seat at all) were the very same mice who had helped Cinderella win her prince—wily Jaq, chubby Gus, and sweet Mary. The rodent portion of the advisory board tended to speak in small, squeaky tones that could be hard for Ben to understand without the communicator in his ear, which translated everything that the animals said in the meeting.

Everyone at the table was wearing one of the clever hearing devices, one of the few magical inventions allowed in the kingdom. The mice's squeaks, the Dalmatian's barks, and Flounder's burbling were all translated so that they could be understood.

Beyond the mice, a few of Ariel's sisters (Ben could never remember which was which, especially as their names all started with *A*) and Flounder splashed along in their own copper bathtub, wheeled in by a very unhappy Cogsworth, who grimaced every time the slightest bit of water sloshed over the edge.

"Mind the splashing, please! I only just had this floor mopped. You do know this isn't a beach resort, do you not? Precisely. It's a *council* meeting. A *rrrrroyal* council," the former clock trumpeted, rolling his *r*'s with great fanfare. Andrina—or was it Adella?—only laughed and flicked him with her great, wet fins.

Rounding out the other side of the table were the three "good" fairies, Flora, Fauna, and Merryweather, looking apple-cheeked and cheery in their green, red, and blue hats and capes, seated next to the famed blue Genie of Agrabah. They were comparing vacation notes. The fairies were partial to the forest meadows while the genie preferred the vast deserts.

"I guess we should get started?" Ben ventured, clearing his throat.

No one seemed to hear him. The mice roared with

laughter, falling onto their backs and rolling across the Auradonian law book. Even Pongo and Perdita of the freed De Vil Dalmatian contingent joined in the laughter with a little lively barking. All told, it was a friendly group, or so it seemed. Ben began to relax.

And why shouldn't he? Unlike the infamous villains trapped on the Isle of the Lost, the good citizens of Auradon looked as if the last twenty years hadn't aged them one bit. Ben had to admit it: every one of the royal councilors looked just like they had in the photographs he had studied of the founding of Auradon. The mice were still small and cute, the Dalmatians sleek and handsome. The mermaids—whatever their names—remained as fresh as water lilies, and the good fairies burst with good health. Even the infamous Genie of Agrabah had toned down his usual hyper-manic performance. Dopey was still his mute, charming self, and while Doc may have had a few more white hairs than before in his beard, Grumpy looked almost cheerful.

Except for one thing—

"What—no cream cakes?" Grumpy grabbed a sugar cookie, glaring at the plate.

"It's a meeting, not a party," Doc said, harrumphing.

"Well, it's certainly not a party now," Grumpy said, examining a cookie. "There isn't even a currant or a chocolate chip? What, are we discussing budget problems today?"

"As I was saying," Ben interrupted, moving the plate of cookies away from Grumpy, "welcome, welcome, everyone.

I hereby declare this meeting of the King's Council officially open. Shall we begin?" asked Ben.

Heads nodded around the table.

Ben glanced down at the notecards he had hidden beneath his right hand. Hopefully, he was doing this correctly.

He coughed. "Excellent. Well, then."

"Don't we need to wait for your dad, kid?" Genie asked, putting his feet up on the table. Now that magic was discouraged in Auradon, the genie had taken physical form and was no longer a floating cloud.

"Yeah. Where's King Beast?" Flounder piped up.

"Isn't your father joining us today, Ben?" Perdita asked, gently.

Color crept into Ben's face. "No, sorry. My dad—I mean, King Beast—has uh, asked me to run the meeting this morning."

Everyone stared. The mice sat up. Grumpy let the cookie drop.

"Anyway." Ben cleared his throat and tried to affect a confidence he did not feel. "On to business." He was stalling.

He looked at the stack of papers in front of him. Petitions and letters and applications and motions, from sidekicks from every corner of the kingdom . . .

Show them who is king. That's what my father said.

He tried again. "In my role as future king of Auradon,

I've studied your petitions, and while I appreciate your suggestions, I'm afraid that . . ."

"Our petitions? Are you talking about the Sidekicks Act?" Grumpy sounded annoyed.

"Er, yes, I'm afraid that we cannot recommend granting these petitions as . . ."

"Who's we?" asked Mary.

Dopey looked confused.

"I guess, I mean *me*? What I mean to say is, I've taken your suggestions for change but it doesn't look like they can be approved as . . ."

One of the mermaids tilted her head. "Not approved? Why not?"

Ben became flustered. "Well, because I . . ."

Doc shook his head. "I'm sorry, son, but have you ever even set foot outside this castle? What do you know about the whole kingdom? For instance, our goblin cousins on the Isle of the Lost would like forgiveness—they've been exiled for a long time."

All around the table, the councilors began to murmur in low tones. Ben knew the meeting had taken a turn for the worse, and he desperately began to review his options. There was nothing on his notecards about what to do in the case of council revolt.

One. What would my dad do?

Two. What would my mom do?

Three. Could I run for it? What would that do?

Ben was still evaluating option number three when Grumpy spoke up. "If I may interrupt," Grumpy said, looking the exact opposite of, well, Merry, who sat next to him. "As you know, for twenty years we dwarfs have worked the mines, gathering jewels and diamonds for the kingdom's crowns and scepters, for many a prince and princess in need of wedding gifts or coronation attire." Ben turned even redder, looking at the polished gold buttons on his own shirt. Grumpy glared at him pointedly, then continued. "And for twenty years we have been paid zilch for our efforts."

"Now, now, Mr. Grumpy," said Ben. "Sir."

"It's just Grumpy," huffed Grumpy.

Ben looked at the mice. "May I?"

"Be my guest," said Gus, hopping down.

Ben pulled the Auradon law book free from beneath the mice, sending a few rodents rolling. He turned to a chart in the appendices at the back of the thick book. "Okay, then, Grumpy, as a citizen of Auradon, it looks like you and the rest of the dwarfs have been granted two-month vacations . . . twenty holidays . . . and unlimited sick days." He looked up. "Does that sound right?"

"More or less," Doc said. Grumpy folded his arms with another glare.

Ben looked relieved, closing the book. "So you can't say you've been *working* for exactly twenty years, can you?"

"The math is beside the point, young man—or should I

call you, young *beast*?" Grumpy shouted from behind Doc, who was doing his best to shove his own stocking cap into Grumpy's mouth.

"Prince Ben will do," Ben said, with a thin smile. No wonder the dwarf was called Grumpy; Ben had never met such a cantankerous person!

"If I can interject, and I don't mean to offend, but we're a bit tired of being without a voice and without a contract." Bashful spoke up. At least, Ben thought that was his name, if only from how red he turned as he spoke.

"You're here now, aren't you? I don't believe you can call that being 'without a voice,' can you?" Ben smiled again. *Two for two. Boom. Maybe I'm better at this king stuff than I thought.*

"But what will happen to our families when we retire?" Bashful asked, not looking convinced.

"I'm sure my father has a plan to take care of everyone," Ben said, hoping it was true.

A voice squeaked up from the table. Ben leaned forward to listen. "And has anyone noticed that we sidekicks do all the work in this kingdom? Since the Fairy Godmother frowns on magic, we mice make all the dresses!" Mary said indignantly. The little mouse had climbed back up on the law book to make herself heard. "By paw!"

"That's very—" Ben began, but he was cut off. He was no longer in charge of the room. That much was clear.

"Not to mention the woodland creatures who do all the

housekeeping for Snow White," added Jaq. "They aren't too happy about it, either."

Mary nodded. "Plus, Snow White needs a whole new wardrobe as she's reporting on the Coronation soon! *Your* coronation, I might add!"

Ben searched desperately through the papers in front of him. "Every citizen has the right to file—to file a—"

"I still collect everything for Ariel," burbled Flounder. "Her treasures have grown, but what do I have to show for any of it?"

Ben tried again. "You have the knowledge that what you do is a very much appreciated—"

Flounder kept going. "And the mermaids give undersea tours all year round without taking a penny. Even in the busy season!"

Ariel's sisters nodded indignantly, their shimmering tails splashing water all over the table from the bathtub. Cogsworth slapped a hand over his eyes, while Lumiere squeezed his arm in support.

Ben nodded. "Well, that is certainly something worth further consid—"

"And if I might add, living without magic has taken a toll on our nerves," sighed Merryweather. "Flora can't sew, Fauna can't bake, and I can't clean without our wands. You'll find our petition at the end there, dear boy." Flora shoved it into Prince Ben's face, and he sat back in his chair, surprised.

Fauna chimed in. "While we appreciate all that the Fairy Godmother has done, we can't see why just a little magic might not be useful?"

"But is there really any such thing as a little—" Ben began.

Pongo sat up. "And not to sound weary, but Perdy and I are a bit fatigued after caring for one hundred and one Dalmatians," said Pongo in that rich, elegant voice of his.

"If only there were one hundred and one hours in the day." Perdy yawned. "I could at least sleep for five of them. Imagine that."

Mary the mouse nodded sympathetically, patting Perdy's paw with her own.

A blur of blue appeared in Ben's face. "To put it bluntly, Prince Ben, this blows," said Genie, who blew him a mocking kiss.

The dwarfs applauded wildly.

Ariel's sisters tittered, and now the water in the tub was roiling like a small tsunami. Cogsworth left the chamber in a huff, and even Lumiere motioned for Prince Ben to cut the meeting short.

If only Ben knew how.

The room began to dissolve into absolute chaos, as the sidekicks and dwarfs began to shout at one another, while the good fairies kept on complaining about the back-breaking work even ordinary chores now entailed, and all the rest of the company advocated for relief from their own grievances.

It was hard to pick out one from the next, Ben thought, as he slunk down in his chair, trying not to panic.

Breathe, he told himself. *Breathe, and think.*

But it was impossible to think amid the ruckus in the room. The mermaids complained that the tourists left their trash everywhere; the dwarfs whined that no one liked to whistle while they worked anymore; Pongo and Perdita barked about the stress of having to pay for one hundred and one college educations; and even Genie looked bluer than usual.

Ben covered his ears. This wasn't a meeting anymore. It was an all-out brawl. He had to shut it down, before people started throwing things—or mice.

What would my father do? What does he expect me to do? How could he put me in this situation and expect me to know what to do?

The more he thought about it, the angrier he got. Finally, Ben stood up. No one cared.

He climbed on top of his chair—and still nobody noticed him.

That's it!

His father told him to be kingly, and kings were heard!

"ENOUGH!" he yelled from the top of the table. "THIS MEETING IS ADJOURNED!"

A shocked silence filled the room.

Ben just stood there.

"Why! I never . . ." growled Perdy. "How rude! To speak to us in such a way!"

"Impertinent and ungrateful, that's for certain," sniffed Flora.

"Why, that does it!" said Grumpy. "Where's King Beast? We're not deaf! Don't you know your manners, son?"

"My word, we've never been treated so poorly!" Merryweather fluttered.

The dwarfs and sidekicks left the room, shooting Ben wary glances as they filed out. The mermaids huffed and made a point of sloshing water on the floor, as Lumiere was left to drag them away, shaking his head. The mice turned their noses up as they walked past without so much as a squeak; the Dalmatians held their tails high; and even Dopey gave the prince a silent, hurt look.

Ben hung his head, embarrassed by his actions. He had tried to lead like his father, and he had failed. He hadn't been able to table the petition, and he hadn't been able to inspire confidence in the King's Council. If anything, he had made the situation worse.

Which is why I would make a terrible king, Ben thought, as he climbed down from his father's council room table.

He hadn't proven himself.

He'd only proven one thing—

That Prince Ben wasn't fit to the wear the royal beast-head ring that was currently on his finger.

chapter

11

Evil Lives?

Mal was standing alone in the corner, nursing her spicy cider, when she noticed two figures trying to sneak their way toward the buffet table to grab a couple of cans of expired sodas. It was Carlos, of course, and Princess Blueberry. Evie didn't look any worse for wear after spending time in Cruella's closet. She wasn't even bleeding! There wasn't a scratch on her or even a run in her stocking. Ugh. Carlos must have helped her somehow, the ungrateful little twerp.

Mal sighed.

Foiled again.

Just like her mother, whose own curse had failed.

Were they destined for failure forever?

This party was a bust. It was definitely time to go. Even the evil step-granddaughters looked tired of pretending to hate being chased by the rowdy pirates.

Mal tossed her empty cider cup on the floor and left without a backward glance. She spent the night rearranging her neighbors' overgrown lawns, swapping lawn gnomes, mailboxes, and outdoor furniture. She amused herself doing some light redecorating by toilet-papering a couple of houses and egging a few rickshaws. Nothing like a little property damage to make her feel better. She left her mark on each house with the message *Evil lives!* spray-painted on the lawn, to remind the island people exactly what they stood for and what they had to be proud of.

Feeling as if she had salvaged the evening, it was with some surprise and not a little shock that when she rolled home to the Bargain Castle, she found her mother awake and awaiting her.

"Mother!" Mal yelped, startled to see Maleficent sitting on her huge high-backed green chair in front of the stained-glass window. It was her throne, as it were—her seat of darkness.

"Hello, dear," Maleficent's cold voice said. "Do you know what time it is, young lady?"

Mal was confused. Since when had Maleficent imposed a curfew? It wasn't as if her mother cared where she went or when she came home, now—did she? After all, the woman wasn't called Maleficent for nothing. "Two in the morning?" Mal finally guessed.

"I thought so," Maleficent said, pushing up a purple sleeve and correcting the time on her wristwatch. She pulled the sleeve down and looked at her daughter.

Mal waited, wondering where this was going. She hadn't seen her mother in a while, and when they did come in contact, Mal was often taken aback by how small her mother looked, these days.

The Mistress of Darkness had literally shrunk with the reduction in her circumstances. Whereas once she had been towering, she was now almost a miniature version of her former self—petite, even. If she stood up, one could see that Mal was taller than she was by a few inches.

Yet the distinctive menace had not abated, it just came in a tinier package. "Where was I? Oh yes, *Evil lives!*" Maleficent hissed.

"*Evil lives*—exactly, Mother." Mal nodded. "Is that what you want to talk to me about? The tags around town? Pretty good, right?"

"No, you misunderstand me, dear," her mother said, and it was then that Mal noticed that her mother was not alone. She was petting a black raven that was perched on the arm of her chair.

The raven croaked, flew to Mal's shoulder, and nipped her ear.

"Ouch!" she said. "Stop that!"

"That's just Diablo. Don't be jealous my little friend; that's just Mal," Maleficent said dismissively. And even if Mal knew that her mother couldn't care less about her (Mal tried not to take it personally, as her mother couldn't care less about *anyone*), it still stung to hear it said aloud so bluntly.

"Diablo? That's Diablo?" said Mal. She knew all about Diablo, Maleficent's first and only friend. Her mother had told her the story many times: how, twenty years ago, now, Maleficent had battled Prince Phillip as a great black fiery dragon but had been struck down, betrayed, by a weapon of justice and peace that some irritatingly good fairies had helped aim right into her heart. Maleficent had believed herself dead and passed from this world, but instead she had woken up the next day, alone and broken, on this terrible island.

The only remnant of the battle was the scar on her chest where the sword had struck, and every so often she would feel the phantom pain of that wound. She had told Mal many times how, when she woke up, she had realized that those awful good fairies had taken everything away from her—her castle, her home, even her favorite pet raven.

"The one and only Diablo," purred Maleficent, actually looking happy for once.

"But *how*? He was frozen! They turned him into stone!" said Mal.

"Yes, they did, those horrid little beasts. But he's back!

He's back! And *Evil lives!*" Maleficent declared, with a witch's cackle for good measure.

Okay. Her mother was getting just a *wee* bit repetitive.

Mal gave her mother her best eye-roll. To the rest of the fools, minions, and morons on the island, Maleficent was the scariest thing with two horns around; but to Mal, who had seen her mother put goblin jelly on toast and drop crumbs all over the couch, polish her horns with shoe polish, and sew the raggedy hemline of her purple cape, she was just her mother, and Mal wasn't *that* scared of her. Okay, so she was still scared of her mother, but she wasn't like *Carlos*-scared.

Maleficent stood from her chair, her green eyes blazing into Mal's identical ones. "My Dragon's Eye—my scepter of darkness—Diablo says it has been awakened! *Evil lives!*— and best of all, it is on this island!"

"Your scepter? Are you sure?" Mal asked skeptically. "Hard to believe King Beast of Auradon would leave such an impressive weapon on the Isle."

"Diablo swears he saw it, didn't you, my sweet?" Maleficent purred. The raven cawed.

"So where is it?" asked Mal.

"Well, I don't speak Raven, do I? It's on this blasted piece of rock somewhere!" Maleficent fumed, tossing her cape back.

"Okay, then. But so what?"

"So what?! The Dragon's Eye is back! *Evil lives!* It means I can have my powers back!"

"Not with the dome still up," Mal pointed out.

"It doesn't matter. I thought those three despicably good fairies had destroyed it, but they had only frozen it, like they had Diablo. It is alive, it is out there somewhere, and best of all—you—my dear—will get it for me!" Maleficent announced with a flourish.

"Me?"

"Yes. Don't you want to prove yourself to me? Prove that you are worthy of being my daughter?" her mother asked quietly.

Mal didn't answer.

"You know how much you are a disappointment to me, how when I was your age, I had armies of goblins under my control, but you . . . what do you do—put your little drawings all over town? You need to do MORE!" she seethed, standing up from her chair. Diablo flapped his wings and cawed in agreement.

Mal tried not to show her feelings. She'd thought those tags were pretty cool. "Fine! Fine! I'll go get your scepter!" she agreed, if only to stop her mother from raging.

"Wonderful." Maleficent touched her heart, or the hole in her chest where it should have been. "When that sword pierced my dragon hide, and I fell off that cliff twenty years ago, I was sure I had died. But they brought me back to suffer a fate worse than death, much worse. But one day, I will have my revenge!"

Mal nodded. She'd heard the spiel so many times, she

could chant it in her sleep. Maleficent took her hand, and they chorused, *"Revenge on the fools who imprisoned us on this cursed island!"*

Maleficent urged Mal closer so that she could whisper a warning in her ear.

"Yes, Mother," said Mal, to show she understood.

Maleficent grinned. "Now, get out of here and bring it back, so we can be free of this floating prison once and for all!"

Mal trudged up to her room. She'd forgotten to tell her mother about the mean trick she'd pulled on Evie at the party, not that it would have been evil enough for the great Maleficent, either. Nothing was. Why did she even bother?

She climbed out her window and onto the balcony where could see across the entire island and the shining spires of Auradon glimmered in the distance.

A few minutes later, she heard the sound of jiggling trinkets, which meant Jay had dropped by to annoy her or to steal a late-night snack.

"I'm out here," she called.

"You left before the fun really began," he said, meaning the party. "We turned the ballroom into a mosh pit and crowd-surfed." He joined her on the balcony, a bag of smelly cheese curls in his hand.

She shrugged.

"What's with the rude raven?" he asked, chomping

noisily on the snack, his fingers turning a fluorescent shade of orange.

"That's Diablo. You know, my mom's old familiar. He's back."

Jay stopped chewing. "He's *what*?"

"He's *back*. He got unfrozen. So now Mom thinks the spell over the island might be unraveling, somehow."

Jay's eyes grew wide.

Mal looked away and continued, "That's not all. Diablo swears the Dragon's Eye is back too. That he saw it glow back to life. You know, her scepter, her greatest weapon, the one that controls all the forces of evil and darkness, blah blah blah. She wants me to find it, and use it to break the curse over the island."

Jay let out a loud laugh. "Well, she's really gone off the cliff into the deep end to take a swim with the killer alligators, then, hasn't she? That thing is hidden forever and ever, and ever and ever and—"

"Ever?" Mal smirked.

"Exactly."

Mal turned away, wanting to change the subject. "Do you ever think about what it's like over there?" she asked, nodding toward Auradon.

Jay scoffed. "Yeah, horrible. Sunny, and happy, and . . . horrible. I thank my unlucky stars every day that I'm not there."

"Yeah, I know. But, I mean—you never get sick of this

place, like you want a change?" she asked, brooding.

Jay looked at her quizzically.

"Never mind." Mal didn't think he would understand. She continued staring into the night. Jay continued munching on his cheese curls and fiddling with some newly stolen costume jewelry.

A memory came flooding back to Mal. She was five years old and was in the marketplace with her mother when a goblin tripped and fell, spilling his basket of fruit everywhere. Without thinking, she had started picking up the fruit, helping the goblin gather it all. One by one, she picked up the apples, dusted them off on her dress, and placed them back in the basket. Suddenly Mal looked up from where she was crouched. The market had gone silent, and everyone, including her mother, who was rotten-apple red and fuming, was staring at her.

"Get up this instant," her mother had hissed. Maleficent kicked the basket, and the apples all fell out again.

Mal obeyed. When they got back home, her mother locked her in her room to think about what she had done. "If you're not careful, my girl, you'll end up just like *him*—just like your father—weak and powerless. AND PATHETIC!" Maleficent had bellowed through the locked door.

Little Mal had stared into the dingy mirror leaning precariously on her vanity. Fighting back tears, she vowed never to disappoint her mother again.

● ● ●

"We have to find it," Mal said to Jay as an icy wind whipped up from the sea below and pulled her from her memory. "The Dragon's Eye. It's here."

"Mal, it's not poss—"

"We have to," Mal said.

"Eh," Jay replied shrugging his shoulders and turning toward the window to go back inside. "We'll see."

Mal took one last look out at the horizon to the bright, sparkling speck in the distance. She felt a pang in her gut, like longing. But what for, she couldn't say.

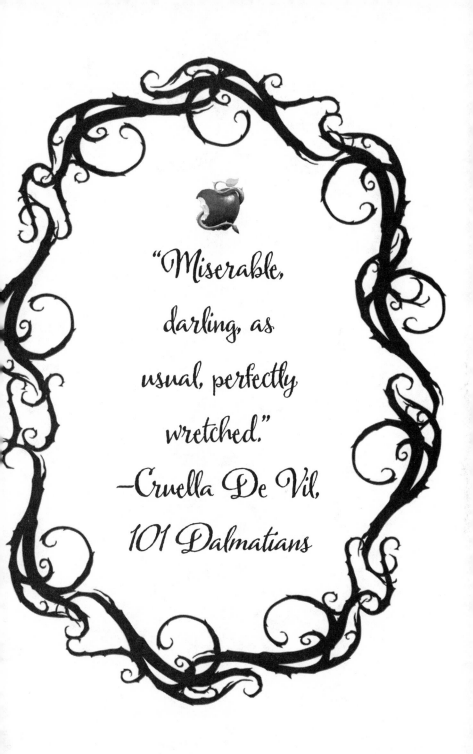

"Miserable, darling, as usual, perfectly wretched."

—Cruella De Vil, 101 Dalmatians

chapter

Score One for the Team

Jay left the Bargain Castle behind him. It was the very end of night, the time when it was just turning toward morning—when it was still dark, but you could already hear the mournful call of the vultures scavenging their way across the island. He shivered, retracing his steps through the grim backstreets and alleyways of the town, past the eerily bare trees and broken-shuttered buildings that looked as abandoned and hopeless as everyone who lived there.

Jay quickened his pace. He wasn't scared of the dark; he depended on it. Jay did some of his best work at night. He'd never get used to the way the island felt in the darkness, though. Jay picked up on it most when everyone else was asleep, and he could see the world around him clearly, for what it was. He could see that this town and this island and these bare trees and these broken shutters were his life, no matter what other life his father and his peers had known. There was no glory here. No magic and no power, either. This was it—all they would ever have or be or know.

No matter what Mal thinks.

Jay kicked a rock across the crumbling cobblestones, and an irritated cat howled back at him from the shadows.

She's so full of it.

Mal wouldn't admit it—their defeat—especially not when she was in a mood like tonight. Mal was so stubborn sometimes. Practically delusional. In moments like these, Jay had clearly seen the effects of a raised-by-a-maniacal-villain upbringing. He couldn't blame Mal for not wanting to tell her mother no—nobody would—but really, there was no way that Maleficent's scepter was somewhere on the Isle of the Lost, and even if it was, Jay and Mal would never find it.

Jay shook his head.

Eye of the Dragon? More like, Eye of Desperation.

That raven is bonkers, probably from being frozen for twenty years.

He shrugged and rounded the corner to his own street. He tried to forget about it, half-expecting (and half-hoping) Mal would probably do the same. She had her whims, but they never seemed to last. That was the good thing about

Mal; she would get all worked up about something, but totally drop it the next day. They got along because Jay had learned to just ride out the storm.

When he finally made his way through the last of the puzzle of stolen locks, chains, and deadbolts that guarded his own house (thieves being the most paranoid about burglary), he pushed the rotting wooden door open with a creak and crept inside.

One foot at a time. Shift your body weight as you step. Stick close to the wall. . . .

"Jay? Is that you?"

Crap.

His father was still awake, cooking eggs, his faithful parrot, Iago, on his shoulder. Was Jafar worried about his only son being out so late? Was he worried about where he'd been, or who he'd been with, or why he hadn't come home until now?

Nah. His father had only one thing on his mind, and Jay knew exactly what it was.

"What's tonight's haul?" Jafar asked greedily, as he set his plate of food down on the kitchen table, next to a pile of rusty coins that passed for currency on the island. The table was where Jafar practiced his favorite hobby: counting his money. There was a good-sized pyramid of coins on the table, but Jay knew it wouldn't satisfy Jafar's greed.

Nothing did.

"Nice pajamas." Jay smirked. The trick with his father

was to keep moving, to stay on your toes, and above all else, to avoid answering the question, because none of the answers were ever right. When you couldn't win, you shouldn't give in and play. That was just setting yourself up for disaster.

I mean, my dad's best friend is a parrot.

Enough said.

"Nice pajamas!" Iago squawked. "Nice pajamas!"

Jafar was wearing a faded bathrobe over saggy pajamas with little lamps printed all over them. If twenty years of being frozen could turn a raven cuckoo, twenty years of life among the lost had done just as much to diminish the former Grand Vizier of Agrabah's infamy, along with his grandeur and panache (at least, that was how his father thought of it). Gone were the sumptuous silks and plush velvet jackets, replaced by a uniform of ratty velour sweat suits and sweat-stained undershirts that smelled a little too strongly of their shop's marketplace stand, which was located, rather unfortunately and quite directly across from the horse stalls.

The sleek black beard was now raggedy and gray, and there was the aforementioned gut. Iago had taken to calling him "the sultan," since Jafar now resembled his old adversary in size; although, in all fairness, Iago himself looked like he was on a daily cracker binge.

In return, Jafar called his feathered pal things that were unrepeatable by any standard, even a parrot's.

Jay hated his father's pajamas: they were a sign of how far their once royalty-adjacent family had fallen. The flannel was worn so thin in places you could see Jafar's belly roll beneath it. Jay tried not to look too closely, even now, in the shadows of the early morning light.

His father ignored the pajama insults. He'd heard them all before. He wolfed down his midnight snack with relish without offering Jay a bite. "Come on, come on, get on with it. What'd we get? Let's have a look."

Jay eyed his carpet roll at the end of the room, beyond the table—but he also knew there was no way of getting past his father now. He reluctantly unpacked his pockets. "Broken glass slipper, got it from one of the step-granddaughters. With some glue, we could get a good price for it." The cracked, heel-less slipper shattered into a pile of glass shards the moment it hit the table. Jafar raised an eyebrow.

"Um, superglue?" Jay kept going. "One of Lucifer's collars, Rick Ratcliffe's pistol keychain—and look, a real glass eye!" It was covered in lint. "It's only a little used. I got it from one of the pirates." He held it up to his own eye and peered through the glass—then jerked it away, wrinkling his nose and fanning his face with his hand. "Why don't pirates ever bathe? Hello, it's called a *shower.* It's not like they're even out at sea anymore." With that, he rolled the eyeball across the table to his father.

Iago squawked curiously while Jay waited for the inevitable.

Jafar waved a dismissive hand over the items and sighed. "Garbage."

"Garbage!" Iago shrieked. "Garbage!"

"But that's all there is on this island," Jay argued, leaning against the kitchen sink. "This is the Isle of the Lost, the Isle of the Leftovers, remember?"

His father frowned. "You went to the De Vil place, and you didn't score a fur coat? What were you doing in there all night? Slobbering over Maleficent's girl?"

Jay rolled his eyes. "For the ten-thousandth time, *no*. And it's not like *I* was the one locked in the coat closet." As he said it, he wondered why he hadn't thought of that.

"You need to try harder! What about that princess? The one who's just come out of the castle?"

"Oh yeah, her. I forgot." Jay dug into his jeans pocket and brought out a silver necklace with a red poisoned-apple charm on it. "That's all she had on her. I'm telling you, even the castles around this place are dumps."

Jafar put on a pair of spectacles and examined the jewelry, squinting first with one eye, then with the other. His eyesight was going, and his back ached from the extra work of carrying around his own sweatsuited belly; even villains were not spared the perils of aging. "Paste and glass. In my day, a *servant* wouldn't have worn that, let alone a princess. Not quite the big score we're looking for." He tossed the bauble aside, sighing as he stopped to feed Iago another cracker.

"Score," said Iago, gleefully spitting cracker crumbs. "Big Score!"

Jay's shoulders slumped.

The big score.

It was his father's dream: that one day his only son would find a cachet of loot so big, so rich, so laden with gold, that Jafar would no longer have to preside over a junk shop, ever again. No matter that the Isle of the Lost was a floating rubbish heap; somehow Jafar believed the big score was always right around the corner—a bounty that could transport him back to his rightful place as a sorcerer, with all its power and trappings.

Talk about delusional.

Even if it did exist, could such a treasure take any of them back in time to a better day, or free them from a lifetime of imprisonment? As if an object or a jewel or any amount of gold coins could fix the mess that people like Jafar had gotten them all into, in the first place?

The big score. His father was as crazy as Mal had been tonight. Jay shook his head.

And then he just shook. Because he'd thought of something.

Hang on.

What had Mal told him tonight? That the raven believed Maleficent's scepter, the Dragon's Eye, was hidden somewhere on this island? If Diablo was telling the truth, and Jay was able to find it, it would be the biggest score of the year. Of the century! He thought it through. Was it possible? Could it be *that* easy? Could his father have been right to hold on to the faintest hope for something better, even after all these years?

Nah.

Jay rubbed his eyes. It had been a long night. There was no way that thing was on the Isle of the Lost. There was nothing of power here—not when it came to people, and not when it came to their stuff.

And even if it *was* here—however unlikely that might be—the dome over the island kept out all magic out. The Dragon's Eye was just a fancy name for a walking stick now. Like he'd told Mal, it was a useless enterprise. They were better off trying to hijack a boat out of the Goblin Wharf back to Auradon. Not that any of them would want to live there.

Maybe we belong on the Isle of the Lost, Leftover, and Forgotten. Maybe that's how this story is supposed to go.

Only, who's going to break the news to my dad?

Jay watched as his father returned to stacking the coins in neat piles. Counting coins gave him peace in some way his son would never understand. Jafar was whistling, and looked up when he saw Jay staring at him.

"Remember the Golden Rule?" his father purred as he caressed the money with his hands.

"Totally. 'Night, Dad," Jay said, heading to the worn carpet underneath the shelves in the back, where he slept. *Whoever has the most gold makes the rules.* It's what his father believed, and while Jay had never seen any gold in his life, he'd been taught to believe it too.

He just wasn't sure that he believed there was any gold to find. Not on the Isle of the Lost. Still, as he curled up on the hard bit of carpeted floor that was his bed, he tried to imagine what it would feel like to find it.

The Big Score.

He fell asleep dreaming of his father bursting with pride in a pair of pajamas made of gold.

chapter

13

After Shocks

Cruella was going to kill him if she ever found out he'd thrown a party while she was away. People on the island kept telling him Cruella had mellowed with age, that she was rounder and less shouty, but they didn't have to live with her.

Cruella De Vil's son knew his mother better than anyone.

If his mother had any idea that he'd let a bunch of people come over . . . and even worse, let anyone even come *near* her fur closet—let alone *inside* it—let alone be tackled in a pile of full-length grade-A–pelt coats—well, let's just say it wouldn't be a puppy she would be trying to skin.

But thankfully his mother was still at the Spa and hadn't

returned unexpectedly as she was wont to do sometimes, if only to keep her son and Jasper and Horace on their minion-y toes.

Carlos stumbled out of bed and found a few bleary-eyed guests wandering around Hell Hall, smelling like last night's spicy cider. "You're probably looking for the bathroom. This way. No problem!" He shoved them out the front door before they could realize what was happening. As he did, Harry and Jace, the two young, second-generation De Vil minions who had helped him decorate for the party, stumbled out of the ballroom with crepe paper in their hair.

"'Morning," said Carlos, his voice still froggy with sleep. "Why are you wearing the party?"

"I told him not to get me tangled up in his stupid streamers," Harry said, still surly.

"*You* told me? You were the one playing tag all night, dragging half the decorations around after you."

"I was entertaining guests."

"Then why was no one playing *with* you?"

As usual, there was no hope of real conversation with either of them. Carlos gave up.

His cousin Diego De Vil gave him a thumbs-up from the couch. "Great party. Total howler!" The rest of the band was packing up their gear.

"Thanks, I think." Carlos wrinkled his nose. The gloomy morning light made everything look sadder and more sordid. Even the chandelier's candles had burnt down to stubs, and someone had broken the rope swing so that it swayed gently, brushing the floor.

"We'd better get out of here so you can clean up." Diego grinned. "Or did your mom say to leave it for her to do when she got home?" He burst out laughing.

"Very funny." Carlos ignored his cousin, pushing his way through the swinging door that led to the kitchen. He was hungry, his head hurt, and he hadn't slept well—dreaming anxiously of keeping the party a secret from his mother, but also of the dazzling light that had emanated from his machine and hit the dome.

Did that really happen?

For a moment there, Carlos thought he had felt something in the air. Something wild and electric and thrumming with energy. *Magic? Could it be?*

He wondered if he could make the machine do it again.

After breakfast.

He poked his head into the kitchen, which looked like a party bomb had exploded. Every counter and surface was sticky and littered with cups, bowls, bits of popcorn and chips, rotten deviled eggs, uneaten devil dogs, and empty bottles of cider. His feet stuck and unstuck with every step on the floor, ripping up and down with a noise that was part Velcro, part pseudopod. He took a broom and began to sweep and clean, just enough so that he could get to the fridge and the shelves.

"Hey, uh, can I just . . ." Carlos said, pushing a snoring

Clay Clayton away from the kitchen counter to grab his breakfast. Clay was the son of the Great Hunter who'd almost captured Tarzan's gorilla troop (*almost* being the operative word: like every villain on the Isle, each one's evil schemes had ultimately ended in failure).

Carlos filled a bowl with some congealed, lumpy oatmeal and grabbed a spoon just as the Gastons stuck their heads inside.

"Hey, man! What've you got there? Breakfast? Don't mind if we do." The burly brothers high-fived him as they stole his cold porridge from under his nose on their way out the door. Being the Gastons, they were the last to leave and the first to steal all the food, as usual.

"I guess I wasn't hungry anyway," Carlos said out loud, although only he was listening. "We should get busy and clean this place up before my mom gets home."

He sighed and picked up the broom.

There was way too much to clean. But he was Carlos De Vil, boy genius, wasn't he? Surely he could figure out a way to make this task easier? Yes, he would. He just had to put his mind to it. He would take care of the cleanup later. First, he had to go to school.

Back at her own castle, Evie hadn't been able to sleep any better than Carlos had. Perhaps her dreams weren't plagued by Cruella De Vil or the cracking dome, but they were tormented by endless mazes of dark rooms and snapping traps—and she had woken up in a full sweat just as one was about to clamp down on her leg with its steel jaws again.

I can't go back to school, she thought. *Not after last night.*

The thought of having to face Mal again made her stomach queasy.

Besides, what was wrong with staying home? Home was, well, home. Wasn't it? So maybe it wasn't nice here, but it was safe. *Relatively.* Cozy. *In a not-exactly-traditionally-cozy way.*

Or not.

Okay, so it was cold and musty and basically a cave. Or a prison, as she had come to think of it during her years of castle-schooling. And today, like most days of her life, Evie could hear her mother talking to herself in her imaginary Magic Mirror voice again.

But at least at home there were no traps and no purple-haired wicked fairies angling for revenge. There were no confusing frenemies, if she and Mal were even that.

I don't know what we are, but I know I don't like it.

And here I thought once I got to a real school my life was going to be so much better.

Evie got up and went to her desk, which had a few of her old textbooks from her years of castle-schooling. She picked up her favorite, a worn leather grimoire, the Evil Queen's personal spell book.

Of course, it was useless on the Isle, but Evie still liked reading all the spells. It was like a catalog of her mother's finer days, of a time before she spent hour after useless hour rattling around the empty rooms of the castle doing the Voice. It made Evie feel better, sometimes. To remember that things hadn't always been like this.

She paged through the spell book's worn yellow pages like she had when she was a little girl. She had pored over them the way she imagined the princesses in Auradon pored over their stupid fairy tales. She studied them the way other princesses studied, well, other princesses.

There were truth spells involving candles and water, love spells that called for flower petals and blood, health spells and wealth spells, spells for luck and spells for doom. Trickster spells were her favorite, especially the Peddler's Disguise, which her mother had used to fool that silly Snow White. That was a good one.

A classic, even.

"Hi, sweetie," Evil Queen said, entering her bedroom. "You're looking pale again! Let me blush!" She removed a big round brush and began to work on Evie's cheeks. "Pink as an appleblossom. There. Much better." She looked down at the book in her daughter's hand. "Oh, that old thing? I never understand. Why would you want to get that out again?"

"I don't know. Maybe because I just can't picture it. I mean, did you really do this spell? You?" Evie somehow couldn't imagine her mother as a frightening old hag. Sure, she was plump and middle-aged and no longer resembled the formidable portrait of her that hung in the main gallery, but she was far from ugly.

"Oh, yes! It was a scream! Snow Why-So-Stupid? was completely fooled! What a dope." Evil Queen giggled. "I mean, hello? Door-to-door *apple* sales hag? In the middle of the forest?" She sighed. "Ah. Good times."

Evie shook her head. "Still."

Her mother fussed with her hair. "Wait. Why are you here? Shouldn't you be in school?"

"I don't feel like going," Evie confessed. "I'm not sure it's right, after all. Going to a big school. Maybe I should just stay in the castle."

Evil Queen shrugged. "Who needs an education anyway? *Pretty is as pretty is*—remember that, darling."

"Don't worry. You don't let me forget."

"It's attention to the little things. You have to work for it, and you have to want it. Your eyelashes aren't going to curl themselves, you know."

"Nope. You're going to curl them for me, even if I don't want you to."

"That's right. And why? So that one day you can have what's rightfully yours, even if you are stuck on this miserable island. It is your birthright, to be the Fairest. Of. Them. All. Those aren't simply words."

"I'm pretty sure they are, actually."

"It's a responsibility. Ours. Yours, and mine. With great beauty comes great power."

Evie just stared. When her mother got like this, it was hard to talk her down.

"I can't want this more than you do, Evie." Her mother sighed, shaking her head.

"I know," Evie said, because it was true. "But what am I supposed to do? What if I don't know what I want? Or how to get it?"

"So you try harder. You reapply. You add that extra layer of gloss over your matte lip stain. You use your blush and your bronzer, and make sure you don't confuse the two."

"*Bronzer on the bone, blush on the cheek,*" Evie said, automatically.

"You know which mascara makes your eyes pop."

"*Blue for brown. Gold for green. Purple for blue,*" Evie recited, as if these were her family's version of math facts.

"Exactly." Evil Queen clasped her fingers around her daughter's in a touching, if rare, maternal gesture. "And please, my darling girl. Never forget who you really are."

"Who am I?" Evie said, squeezing her mother's hand. She felt so lost—more than anything, it was all she wanted to know.

"Someone who needs to use elixir on her hair, or it looks too frizzy." With those parting words, Evil Queen left the room, gathering up her dark skirts behind her. "Mirror! Magic Mirror!"

Yeah, Evie thought, she could stay here, reading her old books and watching Auradon News Network, just like before. Later, if she was really lucky, her mother would come into her room to give her yet another interesting hairstyle, even though Evie had told her millions of times she preferred the V-braid.

This is my life, when I'm in the castle.

Braiding and blushing and bronzing.

That was the thing about leaving home, she guessed. Once you'd made your way out into the world, once you'd left the darkness of the cave, it was hard to go back.

Even to make your hair smooth and your eyes pop.

The more Evie thought about it, the more she knew she couldn't stay in the castle one more second. She'd read all the books and watched all the shows and there was no one to talk to other than her mother, who was only obsessed with the latest cosmetics that arrived on the Dumpster barges, the used tubes of lipstick and opened jars of cream that the Auradon princesses tossed when they didn't want them anymore.

Even school has to be better than this.

Besides, she could deal with Mal, couldn't she? She wasn't scared of her.

Not *that* scared of her.

Okay, so maybe she was. But Evie was more terrified of rotting in a cave forever. And she was far too young to start working on her own Magic Mirror voice. She shook her head at the thought.

Pretty is as pretty is?

Was that what my mother said?

But what was the point of being pretty if there was no one there to see how pretty you were?

Even the crack on her ceiling was starting to look like the Dragon's Eye.

Mal stared up at it from her bed, transfixed. She had woken up extra early—even earlier than Carlos and Evie—as she couldn't sleep, thinking of the quest her mother had all but immediately dispatched her on. Maleficent was like that: once she had an idea in her head, there was no stopping her. It didn't matter if it was her daughter or one of her minions—she expected everyone to stop and drop and risk everything to do her bidding.

That was the Maleficent way.

Mal knew there was no exception made for daughters, not when you were one of the all-time most villainous villains of the Isle of the Lost. You didn't get to be number one by being merciful, or even reasonable.

Not when you were one of the evil elite.

Maleficent wanted the Dragon's Eye back, which was great, and all, and Mal totally got it; but actually trying to find out *where* it was on the island—now that was something else entirely.

So, yeah.

It wasn't as if Diablo were any help. All the raven did was caw when Mal poked it. "Where is it, huh, D? If you're back to life, then it can't be far, right? But where?" He'd poke her eyes out if she got close enough to let him. That stupid bird had always wanted her mother all to himself; and to him, Mal wasn't even a threat as much as a nuisance.

Still, it was more than just a bird that was haunting her now.

Maleficent's threats were hard to shake. As always, her mother knew exactly where to strike. She could find her daughter's soft spots as easily now as when she had been a baby wearing one on the top of her own head.

Don't you want to prove yourself to me?

Prove that you are worthy of the name I bestowed on you, Maleficent!

Mal turned over in her hard, squeaky bed, restless.

Yes, Mal was named for her mother, but her mother liked to say that since Mal had shown so far that she was only a tiny bit evil, Mal could only have a tiny bit of her real name until she proved herself truly worthy of her dark fairy heritage. Which was ridiculous, really, if you thought about it. Mal didn't exactly have an army of evil resources at her command. She made do with what she had to work with—stolen paint cans, hapless high school kids, a closet full of old mink coats and fur traps. Sure, maybe she wasn't encasing whole castles in hedges of thorns, but then every villain had to start somewhere, didn't she?

And if she had let Evie off the hook at the end of the night, that wasn't her fault either, was it? It wasn't like you could put a time line on this kind of thing. Good scheming took a little planning, didn't it?

Mal turned over again.

It was still quiet in the Bargain Castle, which meant Maleficent hadn't gone out on the balcony yet to harangue and humiliate her subjects. When Mal finally slid out of bed, slithered into today's purple everything, and tiptoed out of her bedroom, she noticed that the door to her mother's room was locked, which meant Maleficent was not to be disturbed under any circumstance. She was adamant about getting eight hours of "evil sleep" and recommended a healthy diet of nightmares to keep the claws sharp.

It had worked for her so far, hadn't it?

Mal brooded on her mother's warning as she hurried down the crumbling staircase.

The Dragon's Eye was cursed, as Maleficent had told her, which meant that anyone who touched it would immediately fall sleep for a thousand years. That had always been her mother's specialty—putting people to sleep against their will. Of course, that hadn't exactly worked out during the Sleeping Beauty debacle, but that didn't mean that the Dragon's Eye staff would be any less powerful now. When Mal found the scepter she would have to take care not to touch it, and then to figure out a way to somehow bring it back without awakening the curse.

If it still works.

If I find it.

If it exists at all.

As Mal picked up her backpack, she only felt worse. Even dumping an extra spray can into her bag didn't lift her spirits.

Maybe Jay was right.

Maybe this whole quest was too silly to even embark on. She didn't know where to begin to find her mother's lost weapon, no matter how powerful it once had been.

Who was she to think she could find something that had been lost for so long? Maybe she should just forget about it and go back to her usual routine of tagging and shoplifting.

Besides, it wasn't as if anything Mal could do would change how her mother saw her. Even if she did succeed in finding the Dragon's Eye, Mal knew she couldn't help who her father had been, and in the end that was what Maleficent could never forgive nor forget.

The one thing Mal herself could never fix.

So why bother?

Why try?

Maybe she should just accept it and move on. That's what her mother expected from her, anyway.

To fail. To disappoint. To give up. To give in.

Just like everyone else in this place.

Mal pulled open the castle door and set out for school, trying not to think about it.

chapter

Evil Enrichments

*L*ike many nerds before him, Carlos liked school. He wasn't ashamed to admit it—he would have told as much to anyone who bothered to ask. Since no one did, however, he reviewed the argument himself.

He liked the structure and the rules of school. He liked the work, too—answering the kinds of questions that had answers, and exploring the ones that didn't. While there were parts of school that were torture, like when he was forced to run the length of the tombs in gym (why practice *fleeing on foot* when they lived *on an island*?) or when he had to work with assigned partners (usually the kind who teased him for not being able to run the length of the tombs in gym), the other parts more than made up for it.

Those were the good parts—the parts where you actually used your brain—for which Carlos liked to think he was better equipped than the average villain.

And he was right.

Because Carlos De Vil's brain, by way of comparison, was almost as big as Cruella De Vil's fur-coat closet.

That's what Carlos tried to tell himself, anyway, especially when people were making him run the tombs.

His first class today was Weird Science, one he always looked forward to. It was where he'd originally gotten the idea to put his machine together, from the lesson on radio waves. Carlos was not the only top student in the class—he was tied, in fact, with the closest thing he had to a rival in the whole school: the scrawny, bespectacled Reza.

Reza was the son of the former Royal Astronomer of Agrabah, who had consulted with Jafar to make sure the stars aligned on more than one nefarious occasion, which was how his family had found their way to the Isle of the Lost with everyone else.

Weird Science was the class where Carlos always worked the hardest. The presence of Reza, who was every bit as competitive in science lab as he was, only made Carlos work that much harder.

And as annoying as everyone found Reza to be—he always had to use the very biggest words for everything, whether they were used correctly and whether he was inserting a few extra syllables where they might or might not belong—he was still smart.

Very smart. Which meant Carlos enjoyed besting him. Just the other week they had been working on a special elixir, and Reza had been annoyed that Carlos had figured out the secret ingredient first.

Yeah, Reza was almost as smart as he was irritating. Even now he was raising his hand, waving it wildly back and forth.

Their professor, the powerful sorcerer Yen Sid, ignored him. Yen Sid had been sent to the Isle of the Lost from Auradon by King Beast to teach the villain kids how to live without magic and learn the magic of science instead. Carlos remarked once that it must have been a huge sacrifice for him to give up Auradon, but the crotchety old wizard shrugged and said that he didn't mind and that he had a responsibility to teach all children, good or bad.

Yen Sid resumed their lesson by quoting his favorite phrase, "Any sufficiently advanced technology is indistinguishable from magic." The secretive magician smiled from his lectern, his bald head glowing under the light, and his large, gray beard covering half his chest. He had traded in his sorcerer's robes for a chemist's white coat, now that there was no market in magic, and . . . well, no magic to speak of.

Reza raised his hand again. Once again, Yen Sid ignored him, and Carlos smiled to himself.

"Just because there is no magic on the Isle of the Lost does not mean we cannot make our own," Yen Sid said. "In fact, we can create everything we need for a spell right in this classroom. The answer to our situation is right in front of us. From fireworks to explosions, everything can be made from . . . *science*."

"Except, science is boring," said one of the Gastons.

"And also, what's that smell?" said the other Gaston, slapping his brother on the head. "Because—you know—beans are the magical fruit."

"Shut up," Carlos hissed. He wanted to listen.

Reza's hand shot up again. *Me, me, me.*

"I'm talking about the *magic of science*," Yen Sid said, ignoring both Gastons and Reza.

"Excuse me. Excuse me, Professor?" Reza couldn't contain himself any longer. He was practically squeaking in his seat. Carlos snorted.

The professor sighed. "What is it, Reza?"

Reza stood up. "Irregardless, the irrelevancy of my classmates' simplistical commentation bears no meaningfulness to this experiment, in point of fact."

"Thank you, Reza." Yen Sid understood, as Carlos did, that Reza had just said the Gastons were stupid. Which was news to no one at all.

Reza cleared his throat.

"If science is in fact magic, i.e., per se, could one then correspondingly and accordingly posit the postulate that magic is thus, ergo, to wit, also science, quid pro quo, quod erat demonstrandum, Q.E.D.?"

Yen Sid rolled his eyes. Muffled snorts and snickers came from the rest of the class.

"Yes, Reza. Science could be described, in fact, as magic. From certain perspectives. But you don't have to take my word for it. Why don't you start today's experiment and find out for yourself—"

Reza's hand shot up again. The whole class started to laugh.

Yen Sid looked at him sternly. "—like your classmate Carlos here, who, instead of wasting time with more talk, is halfway done with the assignment?" He raised an eyebrow at Reza.

Reza's face turned red. The class laughed harder.

Today's lesson focused on engineering. Carlos's heart warmed as he bent over his desk and applied himself to the task of learning how to make a robotic broom that swept by itself.

It was the solution to his earlier problem. With this invention, he would be able to clean Hell Hall in a jiffy. He even had a name for it: the Broomba.

The Gastons grumbled, but Carlos couldn't even hear them. Not when he was working. He tightened a screw on the motor of his broom.

This was the *real* magic.

• • •

By the end of first period, it wasn't just Carlos who was happy to be back in school. Evie was glad she had decided to show up as well. For one thing, she didn't see any sign of Mal; and for another thing, it was empowering to realize that while her mother might never think she was pretty enough, she was certainly pretty enough for her Selfies Seminar, which only a few students from Selfies 101 were allowed to take. As it turned out, she could have taught the class herself.

"These are amazing!" Mother Gothel gushed as she looked over Evie's homework. The class had been ordered to produce a series of self-portraits, and Evie had spent the hours before Carlos's party hard at work on her portfolio, taking pictures of herself. Beauty required effort, didn't it? Wasn't that what her mother always said?

And, since her mother had made her so aware of every angle and every trick of light and cosmetics, Evie had the best photographs. (Truthfully, this class was nothing; by the time Evie could hold a hairbrush, she had known how to make herself seem ten times more beautiful than she really was.)

It's all smoke and mirrors, she thought, wincing at the word *mirror*. That's how you get to be the fairest of them all.

She tried to ignore the other girls in the class, the step-granddaughters especially, who looked daggers at her.

"It's as if you spend *every second* staring at your own reflection!" Mother Gothel marveled. "Now, that is a feat of self-centeredness!"

Evie smiled. "Why, thank you. I do try."

"Your mother must be so proud," Mother Gothel said, handing back the photos.

Evie only nodded.

After bombing on his Evil World History exam, Jay ducked to hide from an evil step-granddaughter, who waved to him coquettishly, making him late for his Enrichment class. He slipped into the shadows behind a statue in the stairwell.

Crap.

It wasn't as if he hadn't enjoyed dancing with her last night; he liked dancing with her fine, and stealing girls' hearts was practically a hobby. But it wasn't as fun as stealing other things, since hearts came with too many strings attached. And it certainly didn't pay as well.

Besides, Jay liked his freedom.

"Jayyyyyy," her voice sing-songed down the hall. "Oh, Jayyyyy I think you might have something of my grandmother's that I need back. I'm very, very angry at you, you bad boy," she said, not sounding angry at all.

But Jay wouldn't come out of his hiding place behind the statue of Evil Dragon Maleficent. The stone monstrosity, commissioned by Maleficent herself, took up more than half the landing between the school's second and third basement levels, and had become one of Jay's most reliable hiding spots. Soon his predatory dance date gave up the search.

"Phew, that was close." He slid out of hiding and fell into step with Carlos, who frowned at him without looking up from his book as he walked.

"Closer than all the other times?".

"Yeah . . . no. Not really." Jay sighed.

Carlos turned the page, and the two boys headed into Enrichment without saying another word.

Enrichment was literally about enriching oneself by taking from others. The class studied lock-picking techniques, shoplifting secrets—which meant it was Jay's favorite class for the obvious reason—being a thief and all—and today's guest lecturer was none other than the school's creepy headmaster himself, Dr. Facilier.

"There are many kinds of thieves," Dr. Facilier said in his silky whisper. "One can shoplift at the bazaar, or burglarize a home, or steal a rickshaw. But these are, of course, petty exercises. Mere child's play."

Jay wanted to argue. After all, he had Dr. Facilier's bolo tie in his pocket, didn't he? *What are you calling child's play, old man?*

"But a true villain has larger ambitions—to steal an identity, a fortune—someone's entire life! Can someone give me an example of such villainy? Such great enrichment?" The good doctor surveyed the room. "Yes, Carlos?"

"My mother wanted to steal one hundred and one puppies!" Carlos said, almost in a yelp. "That was large."

"Yes, and that was an extravagantly evil dream." Dr.

Facilier smiled, and everyone in the room shuddered at the sight. "Anyone else? Examples?"

"My mother stole Rapunzel's magic to keep herself young?" Ginny Gothel offered. "Rapunzel had really . . . large . . . hair?"

"You have a point there. A very good example surely, of enriching oneself through the abuse of others," Dr. Facilier nodded. He walked over to the blackboard. "Now, I understand that the advanced students among you have your project for Evil Schemes due."

A few heads nodded, including Jay's and Carlos's.

"My own evil scheme was the height of enrichment. Does anyone know it?"

The room was silent. Dr. Facilier looked insulted. He muttered something about "kids these days" and resumed his lecture.

"For my evil scheme, I had turned Prince Naveen into a frog, and voodoo'd his valet to look like him. My plan was for his valet to marry Charlotte La Bouff, and once he did, I would kill her father and take his fortune. If I had succeeded, I would have stolen a man's identity and another man's fortune. A stroke of enrichment!"

The class clapped. A beaming Dr. Facilier bowed, stiffly and quickly.

"Except you failed," Carlos pointed out, when the room was silent again.

"Yes," Dr. Facilier brooded, his face falling. "That's true.

I failed. Disastrously, unfortunately, and decidedly. I was a complete and utter failure. I won neither the princess nor the fortune. Hence, the founding of Dragon Hall, where we must learn from our failures and teach the next generation of villains to do what we were not able to do."

Harriet Hook raised her hand. "What's that?"

"Prepare! Research! Be more evil! Work faster! Think bigger!" Dr. Facilier urged. "So that when the time comes, when the dome falls—and magic is returned to us—and it will be, my children, it will be; evil like us cannot be contained—you will be ready."

Jay scribbled on his notepad. *Be more evil. Think bigger. The Big Score.*

Once again, his thoughts went back to the Dragon's Eye. It was Maleficent's scepter, and the quest for its recovery was Mal's mission. It wasn't his quest, and it wasn't his problem.

But what if it was?

What if it should be?

Mal had asked him to help, and he had blown her off. But what if he told her that he *would* help her? And what if, when they did find it, he stole it right from under her nose? He would be stealing a fortune and her identity as Maleficent's heir all in one swoop, just like Dr. Facilier.

And what if, by chance, it still worked?

His father would finally have his Big Score. Jay would have his Evil Scheme. Between the two of them, they'd find a way off the Isle of Lost, Leftover, and Forgotten.

They didn't belong there anymore, did they?

Jay smiled. He would enrich himself, all right. All the way to becoming the Master of Darkness.

By lunchtime, the rest of the school was still talking about last night's epic howler at Hell Hall, but Mal had no interest. The party was the past; she'd moved on.

She had bigger things to worry about now. All she could think about was how her mother wanted the Dragon's Eye back. And how Maleficent wouldn't see her as anything other than her father's daughter—in other words, a pathetic, soft human—until Mal could prove her wrong.

Mal kept reliving last night's conversation over and over, so that she missed her first few classes and sleepwalked through the rest. She arrived for her one-on-one afterschool seminar with Lady Tremaine still feeling anxious and out of sorts.

"Hi, Professor Tremaine, you wanted to see me about my year-long evil scheme?" she asked, knocking on the open door to the faculty tombs.

Lady Tremaine looked up from her desk with a thin smile. "Yes, come in and shut the door, please." A full thermos of curdled wine sat on the desk in front of her, which didn't bode well. Lady Tremaine only drank sour wine when she was in a sour mood.

Mal knew she was in trouble, but she did as told and sat across from her teacher. "So what's up?

Lady Tremaine snorted. "'What's up' is this . . . sad excuse for a year-long evil scheme. A grudge against one girl? Party tricks? Pranks? This is beneath you, Mal. I expected more from you. You're my best student." She reached for her wine and sipped it, making an appropriately disgusted face.

You expected more? You and everyone else on this island, Mal thought sullenly. *Get in line.*

"What's wrong with my evil scheme?" she asked.

"It's just not evil enough," sniffed Lady Tremaine.

Mal sighed.

Lady Tremaine glared. "I need you to really put your dark heart and foul soul into it. Come up with a truly wicked scheme. One that will bring you to the depths of depravity and heights of wicked greatness of which I know you're capable."

Mal kicked the desk and frowned. She'd thought her evil scheme was pretty wicked. "Like what? And how do you know what wicked greatness I'm capable of, anyway?"

"You are Mal, daughter of Maleficent! Who doesn't know that?" Lady Tremaine shook her head.

You'd be surprised, Mal thought.

Lady Tremaine continued to sip her wine. "I'm sure you'll come up with something, dear. You are your mother's daughter, after all. I expect something truly horrid and legendary for your evil scheme. Something that will go down in *history*," Lady Tremaine said, returning Mal's paper to her. "I'll give you a minute to brainstorm, if that helps."

Mal looked down at the proposal she'd originally written. At first, she bristled at the criticism. She didn't want to hear it.

What was wrong with this? It was evil, pure evil. And it was *bad*, wasn't it? Taking down a princess—that wasn't exactly a nice thing to do. She was going to make Evie pay, wasn't she?

And a vendetta, that was a time-honored evil scheme, wasn't it?

Classic villainy? What was wrong with that?

Mal wanted to crumple the paper in her hand. She didn't have time for this. She had other things on her mind . . . her mother and the Dragon's Eye, for one, that stupid cursed scepter . . .

Hey, wait a minute. . . .

What did my mother say about the Dragon's Eye?

Whoever touches the scepter will be cursed to fall asleep for a thousand years.

Maleficent had only cursed Aurora's kingdom to fall asleep for a *hundred* years after Sleeping Beauty had pricked her finger on a spinning wheel. This curse put the victim to sleep for a *thousand*.

That was like, ten *times* more evil, unless her math was off. Anyway, *much* more evil. *Plus or minus a few zeroes.*

Maybe she should embark on this quest, after all.

And if somehow, along the way, she made it happen that *Evie* was the one who would touch the Dragon's Eye . . .

Well, that would be the nastiest, wickedest plan the Isle would ever witness! A two-for-one! No, a triple play—

She'd take out the princess and win her own mother's respect—as well as the school's evil scheme competition—all at once.

Lady Tremaine was right. All these little petty tricks she had planned to play on Evie were nothing compared to *this*. If Mal sent Evie to sleep for a thousand years—well, what could be nastier than that?

Or, more to the point, *who?*

"I've got it!" Mal said, jumping up from her chair and giving the startled Lady Tremaine a big hug, despite her better judgment (and Lady Tremaine's breath). "Something *so* evil, no one has seen it before—or ever will again!"

"Wonderful, child! It makes me so happy to see you so wicked," sniffed Lady Tremaine, bringing a hankie to her eye. "It brings me hope for our future. Except for, you know. That *hug.*"

Mal smiled triumphantly. Even a sappy hug couldn't get to her now. She couldn't wait to get started. Evil waited for no one.

Her mind started turning.

She couldn't very well embark on an evil quest alone. If she were going to look for a needle in a haystack, or the Dragon's Eye on the island, she would need minions, her own henchmen to command, just like her mother had. She would have to put together a strike team—plus, it would be easier to get Evie to come with her if she were part of a group.

But where would she get minions of her own? Of course, there were always Maleficent's henchmen's kids. Except those boar-like guys stank too much; and as for the goblins and jackals—well, who would run the Slop Shop? Also, as she'd noted before, she didn't speak Goblin. Besides, her mother kept harping about how useless they'd been during the whole Curse-Sleeping-Beauty mission.

Pass.

Mal would have to find her own team. Her own crew of right-hand-men and one yes-woman in particular.

Where to start?

She'd need someone who knew the island back and forth, upside down and sideways.

Someone who could be counted on if they met any trouble, being a whole lot of trouble himself.

Someone who knew how to get his hands on what he wanted.

She just had to convince him to join her.

Maybe she could promise him some kind of reward, or something.

It was already dark when she left school and went straight to Jafar's Junk Shop.

chapter

15

Thick as Thieves

Mal tossed pebbles at the junk shop's window so that they clattered on the sill. "Jay! Are you there?" she shout-whispered. "Jay! Come out! I want to talk to you!" She hurled a few more stones again.

"Who's making that infernal noise? Doesn't anyone know how to ring a doorbell these days?" Jafar demanded as he pushed the window open and stuck his head out. He was about to unleash a string of curses when he saw who was standing outside. "Oh, my dear Mal," he said, his voice still as silky as when he had been advising the Sultan. "How may I be of service?"

Mal was about to apologize when she remembered dark

fairies are *never* sorry. "I'm looking for Jay," she said, trying to sound as commanding as her mother.

"Why, yes, of course," Jafar said. "I will let him know. Please, come inside." There was a pause, and then Jafar bellowed in a booming voice, "JAY! MAL WANTS YOU!"

"THERE IN A SEC!" Jay yelled back.

"What's the deal with villains and birds?" asked Mal, entering the junk shop and finding Iago on Jafar's shoulder. She thought of how Maleficent showered Diablo with so much affection.

"Excuse me?" Jafar asked, while Iago narrowed his beady eyes at Mal.

"Nothing."

Jay appeared. "Oh, hey, Mal, funny you're here, I was just about to head over your way. We should talk more about that—"

"That homework assignment," Mal said, shooting dagger looks at him. Nobody else could know about the Dragon's Eye.

"Right, yeah. Homework. Thanks, Dad, I'll take it from here," Jay said, indicating pointedly for his dad to leave.

Jafar pulled his robe around him and huffed, Iago squawking and flying behind him.

"Is there somewhere we can talk?" Mal asked when she and Jay were finally alone.

Jay motioned to the junk shop. "What's wrong with here?"

Mal looked around the messy shop, noticing a few things that were hers in the pile and taking them back without comment. She supposed it was as good a place as any—and seriously, what was she hiding, anyway? It wasn't as if anyone else would steal Maleficent's Dragon's Eye. Who would be dumb enough to do that . . . ?

She squinted at Jay, who was inspecting a beaker that he'd pulled from his pocket. His dark eyes shone with mischief.

"Where'd you get that?" she asked. "What is it?"

"I dunno. Reza had it in his bag. He was all protective about it, so I took it," Jay explained with a sly smile.

Mal made an impatient gesture. She couldn't wait to get started and couldn't afford to get distracted. "Listen, I know you don't think we can, but we need to figure out how to find that Dragon's Eye. I mean, it does command all of the forces of darkness when it works. And, who knows? Magic might return to the island one day."

Jay raised his eyebrows. "Yeah—I was just about to say the same thing."

"Really?" she asked, shocked that he had taken so little convincing. She began to get a tad suspicious.

Jay blew on his nails. "Yeah. I mean, come on, if it's really here, we need to get our hands on it. But are you sure your mother's right? I mean, she is a little crazy in the horn-head."

Mal rolled her eyes. "You can't deny Diablo's back. He was frozen in stone, but he's alive now. He's already eaten almost everything in our cupboards."

"Whoa."

"I know, right?"

"Iago's the same. I think he eats more than me and Dad combined."

They shared a chuckle.

"Okay, great—I was hoping to start searching as soon as possible," Mal said, willing to overlook the possibility that Jay was only agreeing to help for his own selfish motives. She could handle him.

Jay was about to say something when he turned around, his reflexes swift and suspicious. "What's that noise?" he asked, just as the door to the back room crashed down and Jafar tumbled through, Iago sitting on his stomach.

"I told you that you were too fat to lean on that door!" Iago scolded.

Jafar made a valiant attempt to take back his dignity, and pulled himself up to stand and brush the dust and detritus from his hair. "Oh, we were just about to ask if the two of you wanted dinner, weren't we, Iago? But we couldn't help but overhear . . . forgive me if we are wrong, but did you say that Maleficent's Dragon's Eye scepter is lost somewhere on this island?" Jafar asked, his dark eyes gleaming.

Mal narrowed her eyes at Jay, mentally berating him for

not having found a suitable place for them to talk privately. But it was clear that it was too late, and Jafar already knew everything.

Jafar looked solemnly at the two teenagers in front of him. "Follow me, it's time we had a real conversation."

He led them to his private sitting room in the back of the shop, a cozy den full of jewel-toned curtains and Oriental rugs, tufted satin pillows and brass lamps and sconces that gave it a mournful, exotic, desert air. Jafar took a seat on one of the long, low couches and motioned for them to make themselves comfortable on the ottomans. "When I was released from my genie bottle and brought here to this cursed island, while I was whizzing through the air, I saw what looked at first like just an ordinary forest but upon closer observation was actually a black castle covered in thorns."

"Another castle?" Mal asked. "Covered in thorns, you say? But that would mean . . . that's . . ."

Her mother's true castle. The Bargain Castle was a rental. It wasn't their true home. *The Forbidden Fortress.* Wasn't that what her mother's real home was called? Mal had never paid enough attention, but it certainly sounded familiar. And where else could it be but the Isle of the Lost?

Jafar pulled on his raggedy beard. "Yes. But I'm afraid I can't be sure of exactly where it is, though. This island is far larger than you think, and you could look forever and

never find it, especially if it is hidden in the forbidden zone."
Nowhere, as it was called by the citizens of the Isle.

"Never!" repeated Iago with a ruffle of his feathers.

"That's what I said." Jay nodded.

"I had completely forgotten about seeing the fortress
until now, when you mentioned Diablo's return and his tes-
timony that he saw the Dragon's Eye himself," said Jafar.
"And if the fortress is on the island, perhaps it's not all that's
hidden in the mist."

"But why would it be here?" Jay asked, leaning forward
on his knees and looking at his father intently.

"These things were too dangerous to keep in Auradon.
And with magic made impossible by the dome, they are
harmless now. But if we were to take back what is rightfully
ours, perhaps we might have a chance against that invisible
barrier one day."

"Diablo swears the Dragon's Eye has sparked back to
life. Which means that maybe the shield is not as impenetrable as we thought," said Mal. "But we're still stuck with
not knowing exactly where it is. There's not exactly a map
to Nowhere."

"We can try the Athenaeum of Evil," said Jay promptly.

"The Anthe-what of Evil?"

"The Library of Forbidden Secrets in Dragon Hall—
you know, that locked door that no one's supposed to go
into. The one with the big spider guarding it."

Mal shook her head. "You really think that's anything?

I always thought it was just a way to keep the first-years out of Dr. Facilier's office."

"Well, we have to start somewhere. And I remember Dr. F mentioning in Enrichment that the library contains information about the history of the island."

"Since when do you pay attention in class?" Mal asked disgustedly.

"Listen, you want my help, or not?"

Jay had a point. It was a start, and she'd learned more about the island in one evening at the junk shop than she had in sixteen years. "All right."

"We'll go tomorrow, bright and early," Jay said cheerfully. "Meet at the bazaar for supplies first, as soon as the market opens."

Mal made a face. She hated getting up early. "What's wrong with tonight?"

"The orchestra's playing a concert tonight, there will be too many people around. Tomorrow's Saturday: no one will be there. Easier."

Mal sighed. "Fine. By the way, thanks for your help, Jafar."

"My pleasure," Jafar said with a crooked smile. "Good night."

When Mal had gone, Jay felt his father slither up to him and dig his fingers into his sleeve. "What's up?" he asked, even though he already knew.

"The Dragon's Eye," Jafar cooed.

"I know, I know." Jay nodded. It would be the biggest score of the year.

"I would hate to think you're betraying your friend," Jafar said with a sorrowful look on his face.

"Don't worry, Dad. None of us have any friends," Jay scoffed. "Least of all, Mal."

As they'd agreed, the next morning Jay met Mal at the crowded marketplace so they could "pick up" (read *swipe*) supplies for their journey to find the fortress. Jay hung back and snatched a bunch of fruit from a couple of tents while Mal stopped at a fortune-teller's stand and traded a stolen pair of only *slightly* chipped earrings for a tattered pack of tarot cards.

"What are those for?" Jay asked.

"No one's allowed into the library right? Where all those documents are locked up and sealed . . ."

"And the only person who has the key is Dr. F, and he loves tarot cards."

"Glad to see you're awake," Mal replied.

"So, how sure are you about this whole thing? I mean, a little sure? A lot sure? Just-want-something-to-do sure?" asked Jay, juggling a few bruised peaches.

"I don't know. But I have to at least *try* to find the fortress, especially if the Dragon's Eye is there. Also, don't you think it's weird that we've never left the village? I mean, this island's pretty small, and we've never even *tried* to look around."

"What's there to look at? You said it yourself—we're probably headed for Nowhere."

"But if somehow there's a map of the island in the library, we'll know exactly *where* in Nowhere we should be heading to find the fortress. There's something out there, beyond the village. I know it."

"But say we do get a hold of the Dragon's Eye and it can't *do* anything?" Jay asked.

"Diablo swears that it sparked to life!"

"But how? There's no magic on the Isle. Nada."

"Well, maybe there's a hole in the dome, or something," said Mal.

"A hole?" scoffed Jay.

"I told you, I don't know; all I know is that the raven swears he saw it spark, and my mother wants me to fetch it, like I'm an errand girl. If you're too chicken to come with me, then go back and steal some more crap for your junk shop," Mal said, annoyed.

"I'm not chicken!"

"Yeah—more like a parrot," said Mal.

Jay sighed. She had him there. "Fine," he grumbled. "Maybe you're right: maybe there *is* a hole."

chapter

Lifelong Frenemies

Mal's and Jay's squabbling voices carried throughout the marketplace, and Evie couldn't help but overhear. She was at the bazaar for her first-ever shopping trip. Since nothing had befallen Evie for having left the castle and gone to school, Evil Queen was more convinced than ever that Maleficent had forgotten about their banishment, or at least didn't care that they had returned. Evil Queen was so excited to be back in the village, she was running from storefront to storefront, saying hello to everyone and filling her cart with all sorts of age-defying elixirs and new beauty regimens.

Evie squinted at their faces. Mal was scowling and Jay

looked annoyed, as per usual. Was she imagining it, or did she hear them say something about a hole in the magical barrier? The memory of that burst of light that had shot out of Carlos's invention the night of the party came to her quickly.

"Are you guys talking about a hole in the dome?" she asked, coming up to the two of them.

Mal looked up suspiciously, but when she saw Evie her voice turned thick as honey. "Why, Evie! You're just the person I've been looking for," she said.

"She is?" Jay asked, confused.

"Yes, she is," Mal said definitively. "Now, what were you saying about the dome?"

Evie wondered if she should tell them what she knew. She knew she couldn't trust Mal, and she had an inkling that Jay was behind her missing poison-heart necklace. She hadn't seen it since the party and suspected he'd lifted it when he'd taken her cloak that evening.

"Nothing," she said.

"Tell us," urged Jay, crossing his arms.

"Why should I?" Evie sniffed. Mal had trapped her in a closet! And Jay wasn't any better, really—the little thief.

"Because," Jay said. Then he was stumped. "Um. Because if you don't, Mal will curse you?" he added, even though he didn't sound convinced himself.

"If you haven't noticed, there's no magic on this island," Evie said huffily.

"Not yet," said Mal. "But there may be one day." She took Evie's arm in hers and whispered, "Look, I know we didn't start off on the right foot, but I think we should let bygones be bygones. It's a small island, and we shouldn't be enemies."

"Really?"

"Totally," said Mal with her sweetest smile.

Evie knew Mal wasn't being sincere, but she was intrigued enough to play along with it.

She was about to tell her what she knew about the dome when Evil Queen burst out of Bits and Bobs, wearing a jet-black velour sweat suit with QUEEN embroidered across her derriere. "Evie! I got some new eye shadow for you! Oh!" she said, when she saw Evie wasn't alone. "If it isn't Mal!" she added nervously. "How are you, dear? How's your mother? Is she here? Is she still mad at me?"

"Uh . . ." Mal blinked.

Evie wished her mother would stop talking, but of course that was a fruitless wish. Her mother continued to babble on nervously. "Tell your mother to come around and see me sometime. I'd be happy to give her a makeover! I've seen her photos in the paper. She's looking a bit green lately. She needs a stronger foundation," Evil Queen said.

"I'll uh, let her know," Mal said.

"You do that, sweetheart! And if I may say so, your purple hair is fabulous! It really brings out your cheekbones!" Evil Queen gushed.

"Thank you? I guess?" said Mal, who looked distinctly uncomfortable.

Jay laughed. "Take the compliment, Mal. Sorry, Evil Queen, Mal isn't used to compliments. You know Maleficent has no interest in beauty unless it can be used to glamour someone into doing her will."

"Right. Let's go, Evie," said her mother.

"Oh, can Evie hang out with us?" asked Mal with a syrupy smile. "We were just about to grab a few unhealthy snacks from the Slop Shop."

Evie was torn. On the one hand, she knew she should stay away from Mal if she wanted to be safe, but on the other, she never got to hang out with kids her age.

Evil Queen nodded. "Sure! I'll see you at home, sweetie." As she left, she mouthed, "Reapply your lip gloss!".

When her mother had disappeared into the crowd, Evie picked up the conversation where they had left off. "You guys want to know about the hole in the dome, or not?"

Mal and Jay exchanged glances. "Of course we do," they chorused.

Evie shrugged. "Well, something happened the night of the party that may have to do with the dome."

"Is that right?" asked Mal with a raised eyebrow.

"You need to talk to Carlos," said Evie. "He knows what happened." She shivered from the memory, at the bright light that had emanated from that little machine. For a second there, she had worried that they had broken the universe somehow. She still remembered the vibrant, sharp feeling of electricity in the air. It had felt like . . . magic.

"Carlos? Why? What does he have to do with anything?" Mal demanded as they passed a tent selling colorful scarves, and Jay practiced his parkour by running across the walls and rooftops.

"Because he was the one that did it," said Evie.

"Did what?"

"Punched a hole in the dome."

Jay barked a laugh and dropped down next to them. "Yeah, right—as if that little guy can punch anything. Come on, Mal. We've got work to do." He began to turn away.

Evie stared at Mal. Mal stared at Evie.

"I'm not lying," she said to Mal.

"I didn't think you were," said Mal, her green eyes flashing. Evie met them with her calm blue ones. Finally Mal said, "Okay."

"You actually believe her?" Jay gawked, sounding right then like Iago.

"I think we need to check it all out," said Mal.

"But we're headed to Dragon Hall," said Jay.

"No, we'll head toward Hell Hall first. I want to talk to Carlos," Mal decided. "And you're coming with us, Evie."

Evie didn't argue with that. Something big was going down. Something had started, the night that Carlos had turned on that machine. And against her better judgment, Evie wanted to see how it would end.

So, onward to Hell Hall they went; but now the twosome was three.

chapter

Do You Believe in Magic?

One more day of freedom before his mother came home. Carlos surveyed his domain. Considering that it had been the headquarters of a rather epic party earlier in the week, it didn't look too bad. The Broomba had worked wonders. Then again, the place always was a bit of a wreck, so who would notice?

The iron knight who towered over the staircase was as solid as ever, the draperies just as heavy and dusty, the faded wallpaper and the holes in the walls lending just that ruined touch that other decorators on the island tried to copy, to no avail.

Carlos was enjoying the rare, relative peace in his house when it was shattered by the sound of the front door knocker pounding so hard, he was sure its booming echo could be heard across the entire island.

He opened the door, then slammed it shut when he saw who was on his doorstep. "Go away, Mal—haven't you done enough?" he yelled from inside the house.

"Open up! It's important!" Jay demanded.

"No!"

"Carlos!" That was Evie's voice. "Something happened with that machine of yours the other night. Something big!"

Wait—what? Evie had told them about his invention? But she had promised! He cracked open the door the tiniest bit so that only his left eye was showing. "You told them what happened?" he said accusingly. "I trusted you!"

Evie pleaded, "Come on, open up! I brought you a pillow!"

Carlos opened the door grudgingly. "Fine. You guys can come in. But don't even think of locking anyone in the closet this time, Mal!" He turned to Evie. "Is it made of goose down?" he asked excitedly. He hadn't really believed she would bring him one.

"Yup, the vultures who brought it said the goblin who found it swore it's from one of the Auradon castles," Evie said, handing him a pillow in a blue silk pillowcase with a royal insignia.

He accepted the pillow and led them into the living room, pushed some deflated black balloons off the couch, and glowered at them. "Well, what did my machine do?" he asked.

Mal raised an eyebrow, and he immediately regretted his tone of voice. "I mean, care to enlighten me?" he asked politely.

"Evie?" prompted Mal.

Evie took a deep breath. "Okay, so the night of the party, Carlos switched on this machine he's invented—it's a box that looks for some kind of signal that lets you watch other TV shows—right, Carlos?"

Carlos nodded. "And music, and lots of other things, through radio waves."

"So when he turned it on that night, it let out this huge blast of light!" she said breathlessly. "And it burned a hole right through the tree-house roof! We saw it go right through the dome!"

Carlos nodded.

"And the TV suddenly came alive with all these colors! And there were a bunch of new shows! Not just the usual Dungeon Deals and King Beast's Fireside Chats!"

"But how does that prove it broke through the dome?" asked Mal, who looked skeptical, and Carlos couldn't blame her. He hardly believed it himself.

"Because we've never seen those shows before! Which

means the signal didn't come from the relay station on the Isle of the Lost. Which means it had to have come from a forbidden network on Auradon . . ." said Evie.

"Which means . . ." Carlos prodded.

"The blast broke through the dome. For a second," Evie finished triumphantly.

Mal turned to Carlos. "You really think that your machine did that?"

"It might've," he admitted.

"Do you think there's a possibility it let magic in, and not just radio waves?"

"*Magic* in? I don't know. Why? Do you know something we don't?" There had to be a reason Mal was here. She had to have some kind of angle on this. Mal never paid any attention to anyone unless she wanted something. What did she want?

He could see her weighing her options. Would she tell them? She didn't know him every well except to tease him, and from what he'd observed so far, Mal wasn't fond of Evie in the least. Jay might be in on it—he had to be, otherwise *he* wouldn't be here.

"Fine. I'll tell you guys," Mal said finally. "Jay already knows. But this has to stay between us. And Evie, no hidden backsies."

Evie put up her hands in protest.

"Okay, so the night of the party, my mother's raven, Diablo—who'd been turned into stone by the three so-called 'good' fairies twenty years ago, came back to life. And Diablo swears he saw the Dragon's Eye, my mother's missing scepter, spark to life as well."

Carlos stared at her, and no one spoke for a long moment.

"But that would mean . . ." Carlos said, his eyes blinking rapidly as if he couldn't believe what he was hearing.

"Magic! That magic had been able to penetrate the dome for a second!" Jay said excitedly. He had been silent until now, looking around Hell Hall most likely to see if he had missed pocketing anything good from the other night.

Carlos himself was still trying to process what Mal had told them. It was one thing to get to watch new television shows, but it was quite another to hear that *magic* had penetrated the invisible barrier, and that Maleficent's missing scepter—the most powerful dark weapon in the universe— had been brought back to life.

"Yes," said Mal. "Diablo swears it's true. And so now my mother has tasked me with getting the Dragon's Eye back. Just in case it happens again, the magic returning. So that *this* time, she'll be ready."

Jay coughed. "And so, um, we should get on the road, Mal, before it gets too late," he said. "You know I hate to miss a meal."

Carlos could sympathize with that, especially since meals came so rarely.

"Wait a minute. Before we go, I want to see this box of his," Mal said, motioning to Carlos.

Carlos was about to argue but decided it was wiser to let Mal have her way. "All right," he said. "Let me go get it." He ran through the safe way into his mother's closet and returned with the machine.

He handed it to Mal, who inspected it closely. She shook it, put it up to her ear, and shrugged. It looked just like a regular box to her, nothing special, and certainly not powerful enough to break through the dome.

"Can you make it work again?" she asked.

"I haven't tried."

"Try."

He hesitated for a moment, then fiddled with a few knobs and looked fearfully up at the ceiling. "Okay. Here we go." He pressed the switch.

Nothing happened.

He tried again.

Again, nothing.

He shook his head. "Sorry. Maybe it was just a one-time deal."

Mal crossed her arms, looking stymied. Carlos knew that look—it meant she was about explode. What if Mal thought they were just pulling her leg? Letting her think they had made a discovery, when all along they were just making fun of her? He had to think of something. . . .

"Wanna see the hole in the ceiling?" he offered. If Mal wanted proof, he could give her proof.

Mal thought about it for a minute. "Sure, why not."

Carlos took them to his tree house, and the four of them inspected the ceiling. It was definitely there, a perfectly round, tiny black hole.

"Rad," pronounced Jay, bumping fists with Carlos.

Carlos grinned proudly. He was still hugging his new pillow. He was looking forward to trying it out soon. Would he actually sleep through the night for once without tossing and turning?

Mal peered up at the ceiling. "I don't know how much I believe your little invention actually blasted a hole in the invisible dome, but Jay's right, we should get going."

Carlos sighed, unsure of whether to be relieved or distressed. Mal was about to leave the room when the black box on his desk suddenly began to beep.

Beep.

Beep.

Mal turned around and stared at it. "Why's it doing that?" she asked.

Carlos ran over to check. "I don't know, but it's been beeping on and off since it blew a hole in the roof and the dome."

"Maybe it's looking for a signal?" said Evie excitedly. "Maybe it senses something."

"Like what?" he asked, looking down at this invention with something like awe. He never thought it would really work. But if Diablo was right, then this thing of his might have actually broken the magical barrier. And now Evie was hinting at something more? He'd only hoped to get a glimpse of the outside world, not bring magic back into the island.

"Yeah, what do you mean, Evie?" asked Mal.

"Like maybe now it senses the Dragon's Eye! You said it's never done this before. Maybe it's because that's never happened before. It's never had anything to talk to," Evie said, rather astutely.

"You think it could be communicating with the Dragon's Eye?" asked Mal.

"Like a compass. Or a homing beacon," said Jay. His eyes gleamed as he studied the machine hungrily, and Carlos put a protective hand on his invention. Jay was most likely already calculating how much he could get for something like it at the shop.

"Could be," said Evie.

"She might actually have a point," said Carlos.

"A homing beacon," echoed Mal.

"I was just guessing," said Evie. "I don't know anything about anything." Carlos wanted to tell her that she was selling herself short, when he realized that he always did the same thing.

"No, you don't" said Mal sharply. "But you're still coming with us."

Evie jumped back. "With you? Where? I agreed to come to Carlos's, but . . ." She shook her head and tugged her cloak tightly around her shoulders. "I'm not going anywhere."

"No way, you have to help us find the Eye," said Mal.

"You're a natural at this. You're so good at it. I need help, and you want to help me, don't you? Don't you want to be my friend? I want to be yours, Evie."

"Oh I—I don't know. . . ."

"Shush! It's settled. And I'll take this, thank you very much," Mal said, reaching for the box.

"No way!" Carlos said, as Mal tried to pull it from him.

Mal tugged it to her side. "Let go, Carlos!" she growled.

He yanked it back. She was not taking it. He'd made it himself!

Mal glared. "I mean it! Let go, or you'll be sorry!"

Carlos shook his head, trembling all over.

"Fine. You win. Keep the box, Carlos, but you have to come with us if you do!" Mal ordered.

"Come again? Go with you—where?" No way. He wasn't going anywhere. Especially anywhere dangerous.

Mal told him about the forbidden fortress hidden on the island and where it might be and how they had to find it.

"Nope I'm not going to Nowhere! I'm staying right here," Carlos said, crossing his arms.

"You'll do what I say, you little . . ." threatened Mal.

Carlos opened his mouth to argue, but thought better of it. In the end, it was *Maleficent* who wanted to reclaim her scepter, not just Mal; and if word ever got back to the Mistress of Darkness that he had opposed or hindered the search in any way, he might as well *start* calling himself Slop, because that's what he would be.

"Okay fine, I'll go. But only if Evie goes too," he said.

"Evie?" asked Mal. "You're coming, aren't you, lovely?"

Evie sighed. "Fine," she said. "Fine. I guess I'll come. Beats looking in the mirror all day for flaws."

"So we're good, then?" asked Jay. "Four of us looking for the Dragon's Eye?"

"I guess so. And I guess I want to know what this thing really did," said Carlos. "If it really *did* burn a hole in the dome and let magic into the island."

As if in answer, the machine beeped.

Beep!

Mal nodded. "All right, then, let's go. We've got a library to break into and a map to find."

"Not *just* yet," Carlos said, raising a hand. "We can't go anywhere until my chores are done. And it's laundry day."

chapter

Once Upon a Dream

Her mother was a famous beauty in a land of famous beauties, and so it was only to be expected that Princess Audrey, daughter of Aurora, was gifted with the same lilting voice, lovely thick hair, swan-like neck, and deep, dark eyes that could drown a prince in their warm embrace.

Like a kitten scenting catnip—or perhaps like an isle of banished former villains sensing magic—a young prince could hardly be expected to resist such sparkly, dimpled charms. In point of fact, Princess Audrey, like her mother before her, was exactly the sort of princess who gave princesses their rather princessy reputation—right down to her very last perfect curl and the last crystal stitched into her silken gown.

And so it was to Princess Audrey that Prince Ben went the next day, to lick his wounds and seek some comfort after the disastrous meeting of the King's Council—like the discouraged, catnip-seeking kitten he was.

"It's such a mess," he told her as they walked around the garden of the "Cottage," as Aurora and Phillip's grand castle was nicknamed after King Hubert had declared that the forty-room palace was a mere starter home for the royal newlyweds. "Starter home?" Aurora had said. "What are you possibly imagining that we'll start? A shelter for homeless giants?" The king had not been pleased to hear it, but Aurora was a simple girl and had lived as Briar Rose for eighteen years of her life in an actual cottage in the woods, so she found the castle more than spacious enough for her family. (And at least one or two stray passing giants.)

"So what happens now?" Audrey asked, looking perfectly charming with a flower in her hair. Naturally, it happened to match the silken lining of her dusty-rose bodice. "Surely even a prince can't be expected to do everything right the very first time he tries?"

Easy for you to say, Ben thought.

A dove alighted on Audrey's shoulder, cooing sweetly. Audrey lifted one pale-pink nail, and the dove nuzzled her gentle fingertip. Ben found himself looking around for the royal portraitist.

Ben sighed.

Somehow, even the sight of his beautiful girlfriend wasn't enough to lift the prince's somber mood. "Dad says I have to hold another meeting to fix it. He's disappointed, of course, and he's had to send conciliatory gift baskets of his favorite cream cakes to everyone who was there, so he's not in the best mood. You know how much he likes his cream cakes."

"Frosted or unfrosted?" Audrey asked. "And with currants or chocolates?"

"All kinds," Ben said, sighing again. "More than a dozen each. Mom thinks it's the only way to make peace, although Dad was kind of annoyed to give away so many of his favorite treats."

"They are rather good." Audrey smiled. "And everyone does love cake."

Ben wished Audrey could be more understanding, but her life had been charmed from the beginning as the pampered princess of two doting parents—especially Aurora, who been separated from her own mother and forced to spend her formative years in a fairy foster home, under the threat of a deadly curse. "*My* daughter will never know anything but love and beauty and peace and joy," Aurora had declared. And she had meant it. So it wasn't hard to see now why Audrey couldn't understand how Ben could ever disappoint his parents. *She* never had.

And she never will, he thought.

Like almost everything in Auradon, Audrey was perfectly sweet, perfectly gentle, and if Ben were honest, sometimes perfectly boring. There were other colors, aside from pink and pale turquoise. There were other animals, who liked to do things other than coo and cuddle. There were perhaps also other topics than gowns and gardens and balls and carriages—no matter how good the custom paint job on the latest chariots was.

Weren't there?

"I don't even know what those sidekicks are so upset about," Audrey said. "They're so adorable, and everyone loves them. Why would they bother with things like wages and hours and"—she paused to shudder—"credit?" She stroked the dove. "Those aren't lovely things at all."

He looked at her. "I don't know, exactly. I'd never thought about it before, but I can't stop thinking about it now. I'd never imagined that anyone in Auradon didn't live exactly like we do, in our castles, with our servants. And our silk sheets and breakfast trays and rose gardens."

"I love rose gardens," said Audrey with a smile. "And I love the ones with topiaries shaped like adorable creatures." She giggled in delight at the thought, and the dove on her shoulder chirped back agreeably.

"They said I was rude," he lamented. "And I was."

"The elephants are my favorite. With those cute little trunks."

"But I didn't have a choice—they weren't listening to

me. They also said I lost my temper." He hung his head, ashamed of the scene he had caused.

"But also the hippos. Such lovely teeth. It's such a talent, really, to prune a bush into the shape of a hippo. Don't you think?"

"Yes, but about the meeting . . ."

Audrey laughed again, and it was a tinkle of fairy bells chiming in the wind. Ben realized then that she hadn't heard a word he was saying.

Maybe it's better this way. She doesn't understand what I'm going through, and I don't think she ever will.

Audrey must have seen the frown on his face, because she paused to take Ben's hand in her tiny, perfectly manicured fingers. "Don't worry about it, Ben—everything will work out. It always does. You're a prince, and I'm a princess. This is the land of Happy Endings, remember? You deserve nothing less than everything your heart desires. You were born to it, Ben. We all were."

Ben stopped in his tracks. He had never thought about it like that. It was implied, certainly, in everything they did and everything that was done for them. But to hear the words themselves, from such beautifully shaped, perfectly pink lips . . .

Why us? *How did we luck into this life? How is that fair? To be born into a life without a choice in the matter, without the freedom to be anyone else?*

She laughed. "Don't stop now, silly. I have something to

show you. Something perfectly perfect, just like today." He allowed himself to be pulled—like any good prince in the hands of a maiden princess—but his mind was still far away.

Is this all there is?

Is this even what I want for my life?

They had circled the garden, and now Audrey led him into a secluded patch of wildflowers. A beautiful picnic was laid out on the grass amid the blossoms, in a woodland vale filled with all manner of happy forest animals nuzzling, chirping, and hopping all about. "Isn't it amazing? I had half the groundsmen and three cooks working on it all morning." She leaned in to nuzzle Ben's cheek. "Just for us."

She pulled him down to the embroidered silken blanket. Her initials, intertwined with those of her royal parents, were stitched into the fabric beneath them. The gold silken thread sparkled like sunshine in the grass.

Ben smoothed a loose curl away from the blush of her rosy cheek. "It's lovely. And I thank you for it. But—"

"I know," she sighed. "I didn't bring any cream cakes. It was all I could think about when you mentioned them. I do apologize. But we can sample a good seventeen sorts of other pastries." She held up one shaped like a swan, with chocolate wings. "This one is sweet, don't you think?"

She all but cooed at the pastry. Ben pulled away.

He shook his head. "But don't you ever wonder if there's more to life than this?"

"What could be more than this?" asked Audrey with an

uncharacteristic frown. She put down the swan. "What else is there?"

"I don't know, but wouldn't you like to find out? Explore a little. Get out on our own and see the world? At least, see our own kingdom?"

She sucked chocolate off her finger, and even that was distractingly cute. Ben wondered if she knew it. He suspected that she did.

Then she sighed. "You're not talking about that awful island, are you?"

He shrugged. "Maybe. Don't you ever think about it? How weird it would be to live trapped in one place? Under a dome?"

It was, in fact, the first time Ben could ever remember seeing his princess's princessy feathers ruffled. She wasn't even pouting now. She was practically almost nearly slightly irritated.

"Perhaps, darling, *they* should have considered that before undertaking a life of evil and villainy—which could only lead to an eternity of punishment."

Now Ben was intrigued. He had never seen her like this, and wondered for a moment if he didn't prefer it. At the very least, they were finally having a real conversation.

"You have to admit, an eternity is a rather long time." He shook his head. "They're captives, Audrey. At least here in Auradon, we can travel anywhere and everywhere we please. They can't."

Audrey smiled brightly. "Yes, which reminds me. I told Aziz and Lonnie we would be visiting them today. Carriage picks us up in an hour." She leaned forward, touching his chin with her fingertip. "Time for a new topic. Almost a whole new world, you could say."

But Ben had a stubborn streak in him that wouldn't give it up. "Don't try to change the subject, Audrey. Come on. Don't you wonder about them at all?"

"The villains?"

"Yeah."

Audrey sat back, shaking her head. "No. Good riddance. Mother says one of them tried to put her to sleep for a hundred years! After she'd already spent her entire childhood in foster care and protective custody! My own mother! And then that same horrible woman turned into a dragon who tried to kill Papa." She shivered. Audrey must have had heard the story more times than she cared to say, Ben understood, but she'd never mentioned any of it to him before today.

He didn't blame Audrey for not wanting to talk about it, and he softened his voice now, taking her hand.

"Her name is Maleficent," said Ben, who had studied his fairy-tale history. His mother had read the old tales to him, before he could even read himself. "She was the Mistress of Darkness, the most evil fairy who has ever lived."

Audrey's frown deepened. "Don't say her name here," she whispered. It was practically a hiss, she was so upset.

"She might hear you—and curse you! She takes away every-one and everything my family loves."

Now it was Ben's turn to smile. "No way—that dome will hold them forever." He leaned forward. "And *who* exactly does your family love?"

Audrey smiled in return. One blink, and the storm in her eyes was gone.

"My family loves all who are good and kind and deserv-ing of such love, Your Highness." She held up her delicate hand, and he kissed it obligingly.

I shouldn't give her such a hard time, Ben thought. Not after everything her family has been through.

"Dance with me, sweet prince," she urged.

Ben stood up and bowed. "Happy to please my lady." Dancing in the forest was her favorite thing to do, he knew.

Ben held her in his arms. She was beautiful. Perfect. A princess, who was in love with him. And he was in love with her . . . wasn't he?

Audrey sang softly, *I know you, I walked with you, Once upon a dream . . .*

It was their song, but this time, it caught him off guard.

With a start, Ben realized he didn't know her. Not really. He didn't know her soul, her dreams, and she didn't know his. They didn't really know each other.

And worse, he had never dreamt about her. Not once.

For Audrey, that song might be about him. But for Ben, that song wasn't about her.

No.

Not Audrey.

He had dreamt about another girl.

One with purple hair and green eyes glittering in the dark, a sly smile of mischief on her lips.

Who was she? Where was she? Would he ever meet her?

And would he ever get her out of his head?

Ben closed his eyes and tried to focus on the melody and the girl right in front of him, but the memory of the girl from his dream was too hard to forget.

chapter

19

One Hundred and One
Ways to Find a Map

For the next several hours, Mal, Jay, and Evie helped Carlos with the painstaking task of finishing his mother's laundry. Or, to be more specific, Jay and Evie helped Carlos, while Mal "supervised."

For a woman who lived on a semideserted island full of ex-villains, Cruella sure had an elaborate wardrobe, Mal thought. There were fringed scarves and silky black gloves, fishnet stockings and slinky black dresses, chubby wraps and whisper-knit cardigans, bulky coats and frilly corsets. Cruella De Vil might be exiled, but that didn't mean her clothes were going to be anything less than stunning.

Mal looked around at Evie, who was humming as she folded black-and-white towels. The blue-haired princess had been relatively easy to sway, which boded well for when they actually found the scepter. Mal would make sure Evie would be the first one to touch it, absorbing the curse and falling asleep for a thousand years. It was the evil scheme to end all evil schemes, and Mal was looking forward to sweet revenge, as well as picking up straight E's for the semester.

Meanwhile, Jay was up to his elbows in suds washing a number of black-and-white sweatshirts.

"Isn't this a lot of work?" she asked, feeling exhausted just from watching everyone.

Carlos nodded, his mouth full of safety pins.

"And you do it all?" she asked Carlos. Her mother might ignore her and resent her and scold her, but at least she wasn't Maleficent's virtual slave.

Carlos nodded again. He pulled the safety pins out of his mouth and explained that he was pinning a bustier on a hanger just the way Cruella's old favorite drycleaner in London had. "Yes. But you get used to it, I guess. Don't worry, we're almost all done."

"Thank goblins," said Mal, putting her feet up on a nearby ottoman.

But just as they were putting the finishing touches on the last batch of black-and-white clothing and linens, they heard the roar of a car engine. It screeched to a stop in front of Hell Hall.

Carlos began to shake. "It's her . . . Mother . . . she's back . . . she wasn't supposed to be back till tomorrow. The Spa must have dried up."

Mal wasn't sure why Carlos was so jumpy. No one was as scary as *her* mother after all—what on earth could he be so freaked out about?

A car door slammed, and a heavy accent raspy from too much smoke and yelling rang through the air. "Carlos! Carlos! My baby!" Cruella cried, her throaty voice ringing through the house.

Mal looked at Carlos. *My baby?* That didn't sound too bad, now, did it?

"My baby needs a bath!"

"She knows you're dirty from out there?" Evie asked, confused.

Carlos turned red again. "She doesn't mean *me*," he whispered hoarsely. "She means her *car*. She's telling me to give it a wash."

Evie turned away from the window with a horrified look on her face. "But it's so filthy! It'll take hours!" The red car was splattered with dirt from driving around town, crusted black and disgusting.

"No way are we cleaning that," muttered Jay, who couldn't be looking forward to washing one more thing.

The four of them crept out of the laundry area and into the main room.

Cruella stopped short at the sight of three strange

scraggly teenagers in her house. She still wore her hair in a frizzy black-and-white do. Her long, fur coat trailed on the floor behind her, and she was sucking on a slender black cigarette holder.

Mal gave her a disapproving glance, and Cruella shrugged. "It's vapor. Just vapor, darling."

Mal waved the vapor away.

"Now, enough about my baby, how is my one true love?" Cruella drawled, puffing on her long vapor wand.

The three teenagers turned to Carlos questioningly, but even he looked astounded to hear himself described in such affectionate terms. "Your one true love?" he almost stammered.

"Why, yes, my one true love. My furs!" Cruella laughed. "You've been taking good care of them haven't you, darling?"

"Of course," Carlos said, reddening again.

Mal knew he was kicking himself. But what did it matter if his mother loved him or not? They'd been taught that love was for the weak, for the silly, for the *good*. Love was not for the likes of them. They were villains. The bad guys. The only thing they loved was a wicked plan.

"Who are these clowns?" Cruella demanded, waving her arms toward the group.

"They're my . . ." Carlos stammered.

Mal knew he couldn't say *friends*, because they weren't friends, not really. She had bullied him into going with her

DE LA CRUZ

on a quest, Evie pitied him, and Jay was there only so he could attempt to steal the chandelier.

Either Cruella didn't notice or didn't care. "Where're Jace and Harry?" she asked.

Carlos shrugged.

"Hi, Mrs. De Vil, I'm—" Evie said, offering her hand.

"I know who you are," Cruella said dismissively.

Mal thought it was interesting that everyone knew who Evie was, even though she'd been kept in a castle for a decade.

"Hey," said Mal.

"Oh, hello, Mal—tell your mother I send my love, darling," Cruella said, gesturing with her vapor cigarette and then turning to glare at Jay. "And you, tell your father he ripped me off with that lamp he sold me—the thing doesn't work."

"Yes, ma'am." Jay saluted.

"Well, what are you all standing here for? Didn't you hear me? My baby's dirty, darlings! It's absolutely wretched! I can't live another minute until you give my baby a bath! Now, scram!"

Evie thought they would be stuck at Cruella's forever, but at long last the car was clean, and the foursome arrived at Dragon Hall in search of a map that would hopefully show them where the Forbidden Fortress was hidden on the island. Carlos's compass would help, but if Jafar was right about the island being much bigger than they thought, they would need to be pointed in the right direction first.

Evie still wasn't sure why she had agreed to go with the group. She knew Mal was being false, but part of her was interested in the adventure. After being cooped up in a castle for ten years, she was curious to see the rest of the island.

The school was dead as a ghost town that Saturday afternoon; only a goblin crew had arrived to clean the halls and mow the grass around the tombstones. The four villain kids walked in and descended into the gloom of campus. The hallways were lined with overgrown ivy that seemed to be multiplying by the second, snaking around old portraits of evil villains nobody could name anymore. Evie could've sworn their eyes followed her as she trotted past.

They found Dr. Facilier at his desk, staring into an empty crystal ball.

"Ahh, if it isn't my least-favorite student," he said when he saw Mal.

"Relax, Dr. F, I'm not here to fill your top hat with crickets again."

"What a relief," he said coldly. "How can I help you?"

"We need to get into the forbidden library," Mal said. "The Athenaeum of Secrets."

"Ah, but there's a reason it's called the forbidden library—because students are expressly forbidden to enter," he said sternly.

Evie thought Mal would give up, but instead Mal hopped up on Dr. Facilier's desk, cool as Lucifer. "Yeah, about that," she said, plopping down a pack of tarot cards. "Entrance fee?"

Dr. F picked a few up and held them under the dim reading light beside him. "The Major Arcana. Impressive." He pocketed the tarot set and studied the four students in front of him. "What exactly are you looking for in the library?"

"A map of the island," said Mal. "And make it quick, will you? I haven't got all day."

The giant spider guarding the door moved away as docile as a cat when Dr. Facilier tickled its belly. The door to the Library of Forbidden Secrets opened with a rusty squeak, and Dr. F escorted the four of them through.

Tall, teetering bookshelves housed tattered, waterlogged leather-bound books, covered with twenty years' worth of dust, as well as beakers and vials filled with strange-looking liquids and potions. As Dr. Facilier scurried down the dingy corridors before them, moving through the rows of bookshelves and muttering under his breath, they were only able to make out the faint outline of his glowing candle, casting shadows against the library walls.

"You know he's got bat poop for brains, right? This could all be for nothing," Jay whispered.

Mal shot him a look.

"Just saying," said Jay.

"It's worth a try," Evie said from behind them, stopping briefly to untangle herself from a cobweb. "Otherwise, we'll just be wandering around in the dark, like we are now."

"Yeah, it couldn't hurt," agreed Carlos. He was holding his machine protectively under his jacket.

"Aha! Here we are," Dr. Facilier announced, stopping in front of a row of cases. He pulled out a yellowing rolled-up piece of parchment from one of the dusty shelves. He smoothed out the paper and placed it on a lopsided work-table while the four of them gathered around.

"Um, there's nothing there," Evie pointed out, her voice small. It was true, the map was blank.

"Well, it was written in invisible ink, of course," Dr. Facilier said as if *everybody* knew this. "How's a secret supposed to stay a secret, otherwise?"

Without warning, and to the shock of everyone around, Mal grabbed him by the collar and pushed him up against one of the bookcases, which caused several of the vials to fall and shatter to the floor. "Why, you little rat, have you forgotten who my mother is and how she can have you and everyone on this filthy island . . ."

"Mal!" Evie said in a shocked tone. "Stop it!" She put a hand on Dr. Facilier's trembling arm. "Let me handle this."

Mal turned to her. "Let you *what*?"

"Handle this. Easier to catch flies with honey than vinegar," she said. "Go on, let go, gently, gently."

Mal slowly let go of Dr. Facilier, whose knees would have given out if Evie hadn't caught him. "Now, Dr. F, there has to be a way to make the ink visible, doesn't there?"

Dr. Facilier mopped his sweaty brow with a raggedy silk handkerchief. "Yes, there is."

"Good," said Evie. "Now, tell us how."

The headmaster pointed shakily to the vials that had shattered on the ground. "The antidote was kept there. But now it's gone."

Evie glanced at Mal, who looked stricken. Mal put her head in her hands and groaned.

"Uh, Mal?" Carlos asked softly, tapping her shoulder.

"Go away, Spotty," she snapped.

"Listen. I know how to make the elixir. To see the ink."

They all turned to him, including Dr. Facilier. "You can do magic?" Mal asked. "But how?"

"No, no, it's not magic, it's just a little chemistry—you know, Weird Science," Carlos said. "Come on. Evie, bring the map."

They left Dr. Facilier back in his office giving himself a tarot reading, and followed Carlos to the Chem Lab, where they watched him pull various bottles, beakers, and powders off the shelves.

"You're sure this isn't magic?" asked Jay skeptically.

"I'm sure. It's science. Like what humans have to do." Carlos mixed a few drops of liquid here, a dash of powder here . . . but then he frowned. "Wait a minute, I can't find the binder."

"The what?"

"Reza—he must have stolen it from the lab last week! He hates me. Ugh." Carlos's face crumpled. "I'm sorry, Mal. I don't think I can do it, after all. Not without the thing that puts it all together and sparks the chemical reaction."

"Reza stole a vial from the lab?" Jay asked.

"He must have," said Carlos. "It's not here."

"This vial, perhaps?" Jay grinned, holding up a small stoppered test tube filled with sparkly liquid that he had shown Mal earlier.

"Where'd you get that?!"

"From Reza's backpack. Takes one to know one," said Jay.

Carlos poured a few droplets into his beaker and mixed it all together. A puff a smoke blew out. "Voilà," he said. "Antidote to invisible ink." He poured the mixture over the map.

And just like magic, the Isle of the Lost began to form before their eyes, including the hidden and forbidden zones. The Forbidden Fortress appeared, a menacing-looking castle of spiky walls and twisty towers, located on the edge of the island. Right in the middle of Nowhere.

chapter

20

Goblin Wharf

al thought Jay's having the secret vial on hand was a pretty decent stroke of luck, which made her think that maybe they were on to something here. Maybe it was her destiny to find Maleficent's Dragon's Eye. "Do you have the compass?" she asked Carlos.

Carlos nodded. The box beeped, as if to agree.

According to the map they would have to walk way past the village right to the edge of the shore, and from there the path would take them to the fortress.

They set off, Carlos in front with Jay, Evie just behind, and Mal holding up the rear. She watched them walk in front of her. She knew Jay would steal the Dragon's Eye for himself at the first opportunity, that Evie was trying to get on her good side and curry favor, and that Carlos had only joined them to fulfill his curiosity.

But it didn't matter. Somehow, they all had a common goal. To find the Dragon's Eye. Better yet, she wasn't going into Nowhere alone.

Mal had her gang of thieves.

Her very own minions.

And that was progress indeed.

Her evil scheme—the big nasty one—was working.

The path away from the village and toward the shore was smooth at first, but soon became rocky. Mal began to flag. Her feet hurt in her boots, but she soldiered on grimly, now leading the way and following the directions on the map. Behind her she could hear Evie's light steps, Jay's stomping ones, and Carlos's tentative ones.

"Heigh ho, heigh ho, it's off to work we go," Carlos sang under his breath.

Evie shuddered. "Don't."

"What do you have against dwar— Oh, right," he said. "Sorry."

"It's okay."

"So that was your mom, huh?" said Evie.

"Yup, the one and only Cruella De Vil," Carlos said, bypassing some poison ivy and pointing it out to the rest of the group to avoid. "One-way ticket to crazy town, right?"

"She's not so bad," said Evie, who ducked below a low-hanging branch of a creepy oak tree. "At least she doesn't do this thing that my mom does, where she pretends to be a Magic Mirror telling me I'm far from the fairest of the land."

Carlos stopped in his tracks, and he and Jay looked at her, shocked. Even Mal turned around to stare at her.

"Really? But you're gorgeous," Jay said. "I mean, you're not my type, sweetheart, but you've got to *know* you're good-looking."

"Do you really think so?" she asked.

"Nah, you're mom's right—you're ugly," Jay teased.

"That sucks that she does that," said Carlos quietly.

"Whatever," Evie said nonchalantly. "It's not like I care."

"You really mean that?" asked Carlos.

"I mean, it's not like your mom is any different, right?" Evie pointed out. They were the children of the most evil villains in the world. What did they expect: love, joy, sympathy?

"I guess not."

"And your dad, Jay? Doesn't he only care about the shop?"

Jay brooded on that. "Yeah, of course. But what else is he supposed to care about?" he asked honestly.

Mal listened to their conversation, finding it oddly soothing to have other people around, for once. She'd never really liked companionship before; but then again, Maleficent had always insisted that they lived apart from the pack—superior, alone, and bent on revenge.

Lonely, Mal thought. I was lonely. And so were they.

Evie, with her beauty-obsessed mother; Carlos, with his screeching harpy of a parent; Jay, the happy-go-lucky thief with a quick wit and dashing smile, who could steal anything in the world except his father's heart.

The gray fog surrounding the edge of the shore loomed closer. Soon they would have to walk through the mist and enter Nowhere. When they did, would they also become *nobody*? Mal wondered. She cracked her knuckles. Her knees began to ache.

They trudged on in silence for a while, when a sharp whistle cut through the air. It was from Jay, who had been scouting ahead. Evie took a step and crunched twigs loudly underfoot, while Carlos looked up fearfully.

Mal whistled back.

Jay jogged to where the three of them were huddled together.

"What is it?" Mal hissed.

"I saw something—in the shadow. Hide!" he whispered fiercely, disappearing behind a rock.

Carlos yelped and tried to climb a tree, the bark scratching his knees. Evie screamed softly and dove behind some blackberry bushes.

But Mal froze in place. She couldn't move, for some

reason. At first it was because she felt annoyed to think that any daughter of Maleficent would have to hide from *anything*. But as the shadow loomed larger and approached, she worried she had made the wrong decision.

The shadow had a pair of large horns and a spiky tail. Was it a dragon? But her mother was the only dragon in these parts, and had lost the ability to transform into one, once the magic-shielding dome had been put in place.

Then there was a moan, a terrible wailing unlike anything they had ever heard.

It was a hellhound, for sure. A creature of myth and legend, a creature of tooth and fang, blood and fur.

Then the creature emitted what could only be called an adorable purr.

"Beelzebub!" Carlos cried from the tree.

The monster emerged from the shadows, and a little black cat with a wicked grin appeared on the path. The shadow had distorted its ears to look like horns and its tail to appear as if it had spikes. But it was just a little kitty.

"You know this foul beast?" asked Mal contemptuously, to hide her embarrassment at having been scared. Her heart was still beating loudly in her chest.

"It's just my cat," Carlos said. "I got her when I was little." He added sheepishly, "She's one of Lucifer's litter. She's my evil sidekick."

"Oh, cool. I got one too. You know, at my birthday party," said Evie. "Mine is Othello, a baby parrot—well, not such a baby anymore. Othello's got quite the mouth on him too. Not sure where he learned all those words."

"Cool—you got one of Iago's babies? I got two electric eels—Lagan and Derelict. You know, from Flotsam and Jetsam. They're *huge* now. Monsters," said Jay. "They hardly fit in their aquarium anymore."

Carlos let the cat rub his cheek. "Go on, Bee. Go back home, stop following us. I'll be back soon—don't worry."

"What's your evil sidekick?" Evie asked, turning to Mal.

Mal colored. She remembered exactly when they had each received their sidekicks—at that fabulous party long ago, to which she had not been invited. "I don't have one," she said shortly.

"Oh!" said Evie, and turned away, looking embarrassed.

Don't worry, thought Mal. *You'll pay soon enough.*

Finally they stood face-to-face with the gray fog that circled the island and marked the edge of Nowhere. The mist was so thick, it was impossible to see what lay beyond it. It would have entailed a walk of faith to see what was on the other side. And all their lives, the four had been told to keep away from the fog, to stay back from the edge of the gray.

"Who goes first?" asked Jay.

"Not me," said Evie.

"Nor me," said Carlos.

"Duh," sniffed Mal. "As if either of you would."

"Mal?" asked Jay. "After you?"

Mal bit her lip. It was, after all, her quest. "Yeah. I'll go, cowards." She squared her shoulders and tensed. She stepped into the fog. It was like walking through a cold rain, and she shivered. She reminded herself that there was no magic on the island, and that nothing could hurt her; but even so, the gray darkness was impenetrable, and for a moment she felt like screaming.

Then she was on the other side.

Still whole.

Not disintegrated.

Not *nothing*.

She exhaled. "It's fine," she called. "Get over here!"

"If she says so," muttered Jay. Evie followed, then Carlos.

Finally the four of them were on the other side of the fog, standing at the edge of Nowhere.

"Whoa," said Carlos.

They all looked down. They were standing literally at the water's edge. One more step, and they would have fallen off the rocky piece of land that was the Isle of the Lost and into the deep sea below, to become an alligator's dinner.

"Holy Lucifer, what the heck are we supposed to do now?" Mal asked.

"I don't know, but this thing won't shut up," Carlos said. It was true. The compass in his box was beeping wildly now, and the closer Carlos stepped toward the strip of rocky, foggy beach, the faster it beeped. "It's over there. It has to be," he said, pointing to the sea.

"Well, I forgot my swimsuit and I don't really enjoy being eaten by reptiles, so it's all on you guys," Jay said, backing away from the water.

"It can't be *in* the water," Mal said, yanking out the map from her pocket. She gasped. "Guys. Come here." They all gathered around Mal. "Look! There's more!" More ink had appeared, and this time, they saw that the fortress wasn't technically on the Isle of the Lost at all but was located on its own island, or rather its own piece of floating rock, which just so happened to be named the Isle of the Doomed.

"Well, that's cheery," Carlos said.

"And just how are we supposed to get over there?" Evie asked.

Mal studied the map and pointed to a spot labeled GOBLIN WHARF.

"We'll hitch a ride from one of our friendly neighborhood goblins to row us over, of course," Mal said, pushing past them and starting up the muddy beach toward the docks where the goblins unloaded the Auradon barges.

"There's no such thing as a friendly goblin," Carlos sighed, but like the rest of them, he followed behind Mal.

They arrived quickly at the busy port. Mostly because the alligators had taken to snapping at them from the shallow water by the beach, and they'd sprinted, screaming, toward the dock.

The wharf was bustling with activity. Goblins pushed their way past the foursome, emptying cargo from the big Auradon ships that were allowed in and out of the magic dome. They placed the rotting and rotten goods onto the splintering wooden boardwalk and jumped on and off each other's makeshift rafts and boats. They hooted and hollered in their Goblin tongue, tossing bags of scraps and leftovers—clothing, food, cosmetics, electronics, everything the people on Auradon didn't want anymore or had no use for, onto teetering rickshaws to sell at the market.

"We'll need to pay for passage," Mal said. "They're not going to take us over there for free."

The four of them emptied their pockets to pool enough of a sum of trinkets and food to pay their way across to the Isle of the Doomed. It took some haggling—Jay did most of the talking as he spoke a bit of Goblin from having worked at the shop—but they finally secured a spot on a scrap boat. That is, a boat that collected anything and everything that fell off the Auradon Dumpsters. It was a scavenger of scavengers, the lowest of the bottom feeders.

As it turned out, a goblin's boat was not constructed to hold four teenage villains. The floating wooden box creaked and groaned as Mal and the others boarded.

"If I die," Jay said darkly, "you still can't have any of my stuff."

"We'll be fine," Evie said. But she seemed to say it more for her own benefit than anyone else's.

The goblin snickered and started the ancient, rusty motor, and off they went into the thick fog.

It was odd to see the Isle of the Lost from the water. It almost looked . . . pretty, Mal thought. The forest was lush and green around the edges of the island, and the rocky beach jutted out dramatically into a rolling blanket of navy-blue water. In the distance, she could see Bargain Castle. From far away, it seemed to be gleaming in the fading sunlight.

"Funny how different things look from far away, huh?" Evie said, following Mal's gaze back toward Isle of the Lost.

"Yeah, sure, whatever," Mal said, turning her back on Evie. That same ache was settling in her gut again, and she didn't like it. She didn't like it one bit.

Mal could only be sure they'd arrived at the Isle of the Doomed because the engine had stopped. They still couldn't see five feet in front of them. Mal scrambled blindly out of the boat and onto the rocky beach, followed quickly by the rest of the team. The goblin quickly sped off.

The fog lifted slightly as they made their way through the brush. Soon they were standing in front of a gate covered with a painful-looking bristly forest of thorns. And beyond the gate, high on a craggy mountaintop, stood a large black castle, a ruined, forbidding wreck silhouetted against the night sky.

The thorns around the gate grew thick and twisted, so sharp, they would stab or scrape anyone who dared come near. Worse, the thorns were covered with deadly poisonous spiders; and the whole place had a toxic and sinister air.

They stood, paralyzed, unable and unwilling to figure out what to do next, while the black box in Carlos's hands kept beeping incessantly. If it was indeed communicating with the Dragon's Eye, it was clear that the scepter was somewhere behind the thorny gates.

Mal scrunched up her face, frustrated.

It was Jay who broke the silence.

He handed Mal and Evie each a silver dagger, and Carlos some bug spray. He himself hauled a red-handled machete.

"You carry an ax in your pocket?" asked Carlos.

"Who doesn't?" Jay said with a smile. "When you steal enough things from all over the place, I find that you always arrive prepared."

Mal had to admit that Jay's loot came in handy right then.

Jay hacked a path with his machete, and the others followed close behind. Mal slashed at a branch of thorns with her silver dagger, and the branch withered and shrank from her knife. Evie did the same on the other side, and Carlos sprayed a hairy tarantula with his spray, so that it fell off a branch, dead.

It would be hard work, but they were used to it by now. Deeper they went into the dark forest, making their way to the castle above.

chapter

21

Tale as Old as Time

Just be yourself, there are other ways to show strength than your father's kind. Ben's mother's words rang in Ben's ears as he sat down to meet with Grumpy, who had been elected to represent the dwarfs and sidekicks in their petitions.

Great. Wonderful. Just perfect. A one-on-one with Grumpy.

Ben shook his head. He suspected *anyone* else would have been a better person to negotiate with than the crabby old dwarf.

Last time they'd met, the infamous dwarf had been insulted by a sugar cookie.

These talks were doomed.

Ben wished that people would stop telling him to be *himself.* It sounded like such simple advice—and maybe it would have been, if he had had any idea who *himself* was.

But who *was* he?

Prince Ben, son of King Beast, heir to the throne of the great kingdom of Auradon?

He was certainly nothing like his father, who knew how to enforce his rule without forcing it on his subjects. Ben cringed to recall how he had stood on the table and yelled.

That wasn't who he was.

He was Prince Ben, son of King Beast *and* Queen Belle, heir to the throne of the great kingdom of Auradon.

And if, like his father, he was meant to inherit the throne—then it would be on his own terms, as his mother's son and not just as his father's heir.

Because, like his mother, Ben was quiet and gentle and loved nothing better than to disappear into a great, thick book. His childhood hadn't been about hunting or sword-fighting or besting someone else on the field.

It had been spent in a library.

He shared his mother's love of reading, and he always had. Ben's fondest memories were of sitting next to Queen Belle at the hearth of her magnificent library's enormous fireplace, reading by her side. He'd be digging into a pile of books dragged from the lower shelves, while hers were always taken from the very highest. It was paradise.

Once, when his father had discovered they had spent

the entire day hiding in the library and scolded them for skipping out on a royal luncheon banquet "for the sake of a story," his mother had mounted a passionate defense.

"But these aren't just stories," she'd said. "They're whole kingdoms. They're worlds. They're perspectives and opinions you can't offer, from lives you haven't lived. They're more valuable than any gold coin, and more important than any state luncheon. I should hope you, as king, would know that!"

King Beast's eyes had twinkled, and he had lifted Queen Belle into his powerful arms with one easy motion. "And, as you're my queen, I should hope you would know how much I love you for that!" Then he'd gathered up his young son, and the three of them had made a late lunch of cream cakes in the garden.

Of course.

Ben smiled. He hadn't thought about that day in a long time.

He found himself thinking of it still as Lumiere ushered the older dwarf into the conference room.

Grumpy nodded to him and took a seat across from the prince, his short legs swinging like a child's. "What's this all about, young man?" He coughed. "I'm not in the mood for any of your tantrums." He eyed the table uneasily, as if the boy was about to leap upon it, even now. The plate of sugar cookies and the goblet of cider in front of him, he left untouched.

"Thank you for meeting me today," said Ben. "I thought this might be easier if it was just the two of us talking. Since everything got a bit—loud—before."

"Hem," said Grumpy. "We'll see about that. You don't plan to hop on the table again or shout like an animal, do you?"

Ben flushed. "I apologize for my behavior the other day. I was . . . a fool."

"You— What?" Grumpy was caught off guard.

Ben shrugged. "I admit it. I didn't know what I was doing, and I made a mess of everything. And I certainly don't blame you for not wanting to take me seriously now."

Grumpy looked at him grumpily, if a little pleasantly surprised. "Go on."

Ben smiled. It was a start, and he'd take it.

"You see, I called you in because I read all one thousand and one pages of your complaint."

"Really? All one thousand?" asked Grumpy, sounding impressed in spite of himself.

"And one." Ben smiled again. He was a fast reader, and a concerned listener, and if he was truly going to be *himself*, he was going to need to use both talents in his favor to settle this complaint once and for all.

"From what I could gather, it appears what you and your colleagues are demanding is to be heard, and to have a voice in your future. Something more than just a seat at the Council."

"It's not that much to ask is it?" asked Grumpy keenly.

"No, it's not," Ben acknowledged. "And I think we can come to a simple agreement."

"What do you propose?"

Ben shuffled the papers. He thought about it, and about how to say it. How had his mother put it? *Perspectives and opinions I can't offer, from lives I haven't lived.*

Ben smiled. "I propose listening to the people who know best."

Grumpy raised an eyebrow.

Ben consulted his notes. "Let's start with the mermaids. They should charge a silver coin for every undersea tour. And I'll talk to Ariel about giving Flounder's collecting for Ariel a break."

Grumpy nodded. "Sounds reasonable. Okay."

"I've also set up a college fund for the Dalmatians—all one hundred and one of them will be eligible for financial aid through the Puppy Grant." Ben pushed a black-and-white-spotted folder that contained all the pertinent forms across the table.

Grumpy accepted it. "Pongo will appreciate that," said Grumpy. "But what about us miners?"

"Half of everything you mine must still remain the property of the kingdom," said Ben. He knew his father would settle for no less.

"Half? What about the rest of the diamonds? Where does that go?" asked Grumpy, sounding alarmed.

"The other half will go to a 401D Fund. A retirement fund for dwarfs, to take care of your families and your children. Tell Bashful not to worry."

"Sounds fair enough." Grumpy nodded, in spite of himself. "What about the restriction of magic? Just between you and me, those three fairies make a lot of noise."

"The three good fairies will have to take their complaint up with the Fairy Godmother. I can't do anything about it myself, I'm afraid. But I'll get them a meeting with her. That much I can do."

"And Genie's request for unlimited travel within the kingdom?" Grumpy frowned. At this point, he looked like he was struggling to find things to still be grumpy about.

"Approved, so long as he clears his itinerary with the palace beforehand." That was a difficult concession to make, as his father did not want the "blue-skinned-maniac popping up everywhere without notice," but he had been able to convince King Beast that as long as the subjects were warned about Genie's arrival, all would be well.

Grumpy folded his arms. "What about the woodland creatures? They're working their paws and hooves to the bone."

"I've had a team install dishwashers, washer-dryers, and vacuum cleaners in every household. It's time we realized we're living in the twenty-first century, don't you think? Forest woodlands included?"

"Meh," said Grumpy. "I don't care much for modernity,

but I think our furry friends will appreciate it. It's hard to do dishes by hand, without, you know, hands."

Ben tried not to laugh.

"As for Mary and the mice, from now on, they will be well compensated with the finest cheese in the kingdom, from the king's own larders." Ben let the last paper drop.

"Fair enough." Grumpy nodded.

"So we have a deal?"

Grumpy put out his hand. "Deal."

Ben shook it. He was more relieved than he let on. (At least, he hoped he wasn't letting it on. At this point he was sweating so much, he couldn't be entirely certain.)

"You know what, young man?" huffed Grumpy with a frown.

Ben steeled himself for a grouchy comment, but none came.

"You're going to make a good king," the dwarf said with a smile. "Give your father my best, and send your mother my love."

"I will," said Ben, pleased by how well the meeting had turned out. He pushed his own chair back from the ancient table. His work was done, at least for today. *But if this is what being king is all about, then maybe it isn't as hard as I thought.*

The dwarf picked up his stocking cap and hopped down from his seat, turning toward the council-room door.

Then he paused.

"You know, son, sometimes you remind me of her." Queen Belle was much beloved in the kingdom.

Ben smiled. "You know, I really hope I do."

Grumpy shrugged, pushing open the door. "Not nearly so pretty, though. I'll tell you that much. And your mother, she would have made sure we had a cream cake or two. And at least a few currants in the cookies."

Ben laughed as the door slammed shut.

chapter
22

Gargoyle Bridge

*E*very moment of this adventure had already proven to be a little more adventurous than Carlos had anticipated.

This revelation might have been a problem for the average man of science who didn't like to run the tombs and who kept to the labs as much as possible. Sure, Carlos had felt a little seasick on the journey over to the Isle of the Doomed, but he'd been able to hold it down, hadn't he?

If he looked at it like that, he'd already proven himself to be a better adventurer than anyone could have reasonably expected.

That's what Carlos told himself, anyway.

Then he told himself that he'd done better than anyone else in Weird Science would have. He actually laughed out loud at the thought of his classroom nemesis in this current situation, which had prompted Jay to shove him and ask if he didn't think he was taking the whole mad scientist thing a little too literally.

"I'm not crazy," Carlos reassured his fellow adventurers. Still, willing himself not to yak into the churning sea itself had required more than his share of exhausting determination, and by the time the four of them were back on land and all the way clear of the thorn forest—no worse for wear save for a few scratches and itchy elbows—Carlos was more than glad to find a real path leading up to the dark castle on the hill above them.

Plain old dirt and rock had never looked so good.

Until it began to rain, and the dirt became mud, and the rock became slippery.

At least it wasn't the sea, Carlos consoled himself. And the odds of a person actually drowning in mud and rocks were incredibly slim.

Besides, his invention was now beeping at regular intervals, its sensor light flashing more brightly and more quickly with every step that drew them closer to the fortress. "The Dragon's Eye is definitely up there," Carlos said excitedly, feeling a scientist's enthusiasm at a working experiment. "If this thing is right, I'm picking up on some kind of massive surge in electrical energy. If there is a hole in the dome, it's leaking magic here somehow, different from the Isle of the Lost."

"Maybe the hole is right above this place," said Evie.

"Yeah, I can feel it too." Mal nodded, still moving forward along the path. "Do you guys?" She stopped and looked at them, shielding her eyes from the rain with one hand.

Carlos looked at her in surprise. "Feel what? This?" He held up his box, and it beeped in her face. Mal jumped back, startled, and Jay laughed.

"Whoops," Carlos said. "See what I mean? The energy is surging."

Mal looked embarrassed. "I don't know for sure. Maybe I'm imagining it, but it almost feels like there's some kind of magnet pulling me up the path."

"That is so creepy," Evie said, stopping to wipe sweat off her forehead with the edge of her cape. "Like, it's your destiny, literally, calling."

"Well," said Carlos, "no, not really. If it were *literally* calling, it would be, you know, *calling* her."

Jay laughed.

Evie glared at him. "Okay, fine. Literally pulling like a magnet, only not really, because it's, you know, destiny. Are you happy now?"

"Literally?" Carlos raised an eyebrow.

Jay laughed again, which made Carlos feel good, though he couldn't exactly explain why, not even to himself.

"Don't you guys feel it?" Mal sounded nervous. Nobody said anything, and she sighed, turning back to the muddy path.

They'd only made it up past the next curving switchback in the path when Mal stumbled and fell, sending a slide of rock down the trail behind her.

"Who-ahh," Mal yelped, her arms flailing. The dark stones were so slick with rain that she couldn't right herself, only slipping on the rocks again.

Evie caught Mal before she tumbled headfirst down the stony path. Both girls flew backward into Jay, who almost toppled Carlos behind him.

"I got you," said Evie, helping Mal to regain her balance.

"Yeah, and I got you," Jay said.

"Which is great for everyone but me," Carlos said, barely keeping one arm around his device as the other held Jay off him. "The human doorstop."

"I am definitely in the wrong shoes for this," Evie said, wincing at the sight of her own feet.

"We need flippers, not shoes. The rain has turned this whole trail into a mud river. Maybe we should all hold hands," Jay suggested. "We'll work better if we're all together."

"Did you really just say that?" Mal shook her head, sounding disgusted. "Why don't we just sing songs to cheer each other up and then weave flowers out of the mud and move to Auradon, while we're at it?"

"Come on, Mal." Carlos tried not to smile. He knew

that Mal, of all of them, had the hardest time with anything more beneficent than Maleficent.

"Do you have a better idea?" Jay looked embarrassed.

"If you wanted to hold my hand, you know, you could have just asked," teased Evie, as she offered it to Jay, waggling her fingers.

"Well, now," Jay winked. "You don't say."

Evie laughed. "Don't worry, Jay, you're cute—but thieves aren't my style."

"I wasn't worried," said Jay smoothly, grasping her hand in his firm grip. "I just don't feel like taking a mud bath today."

"From a physics perspective, it does make sense. If you want to talk about Newton's second and third laws," Carlos added, trying to sound reassuring. "You know, momentum and force, and all that."

"What he said." Jay nodded, holding out his hand to Mal.

Carlos watched him, wondering if Jay and Evie were flirting, and if that was why Mal seemed mad. No. Mal and Jay bickered like siblings. And Jay and Evie were just trying to cover up the fact that they were scared. Jay had told him earlier that he thought Evie was cute, all right, but he thought of her like he did Mal, which meant he didn't think of her at all. Carlos thought that if the girls were had been their sisters, Mal would have been their annoying, grumpy sister while Evie would have been the manipulative, pretty one. And if Jay had been his brother, he'd be the kind who was either laughing at you or punching you when he wasn't busy stealing your stuff.

The longer he thought about it, the more Carlos decided it wasn't so bad to be an only child, after all.

"Come on, Mal. Just take it. Even Newton agrees," Jay said, wiggling his fingers at Mal, while still grasping Evie's hand tightly in his other hand.

Mal gave up with a sigh, grabbing it after only a slight hesitation. Mal then held her hand out to Carlos, who grabbed it as if it were a lifesaver, seeing as he knew his physics better than any of them.

Somewhat awkwardly, and little by little, the four of them pulled and pushed and helped each other slosh their way up the muddy path, sweaty palms and muddy ankles and cold feet and all.

Before long the pathway curved once again, and now the thick rain cloud surrounding it seemed to part on either side of the four adventurers, revealing a sudden and dramatic vista—what appeared to be a long and slender stone bridge, half-shrouded in mist, that jutted out above a chasm in the rock directly in front of them.

"It's beautiful," Evie said, shivering. "In a really terrifying way."

"It's just a bridge," Carlos said, holding up his box. "But we definitely have to cross it. Look—" The light was flashing so brightly and so quickly now that he covered the sensor with one hand.

"Duh," Jay said.

"It's not just a bridge," Mal said, in a low voice, staring at the gray shape in front of her. "It's *her* bridge. Maleficent's bridge. And it's pulling me. I have to cross it. It wants me to get to the other side."

"It's not the bridge I'm worried about," Carlos said, looking into the distance. "Look!"

Beyond the bridge and mist, a black castle rose from a pillar of stone. The bridge was the only way to reach the castle, as sheer cliffs surrounded the black fortress on all other sides.

But the castle itself was so forbidding, it didn't exactly look like a place that wanted to be reached.

"That's it," Mal breathed. "That has to be the Forbidden Fortress." The darkest place on their dark isle—Maleficent's old lair, and ancestral home.

"Sweet," Jay said. "That's one sick shack."

Evie studied it from behind him, still shivering. "And I thought our castle was drafty."

"I can't believe that we actually found it." Carlos stared from his box to the castle. "And I can't believe it was so close to the island all along."

Mal's eyes were dark, and her expression was impossible to read. She looked almost stunned, Carlos thought. "I guess that explains the rain. The Forbidden Fortress hides itself in a shroud of fog and mist. It's like a moat, I guess."

Carlos examined the air around him. "Of course it is. A defensive mechanism, built into the atmosphere itself."

"I'm sure my mother designed it to keep everyone she didn't want out."

She didn't say the rest, so Jay said it for her. "Which meant, you know, *everyone*."

Carlos found it hard to look away from the black tower on the hill. No wonder the citizens of the Isle of the Lost were told to keep away. Here was concrete proof of villainy, of the power of darkness and infamy.

Maleficent's darkness.

It wasn't just any evil. What loomed in front of them was the most powerful and most storied darkness in the kingdom.

Carlos suddenly felt it—the magnetic pull Mal had tried to describe. He could feel it thrumming in the air, in the very stones beneath his feet. Even if magic was no longer a factor, there was power here, and history.

"Feel that?" Carlos held his vibrating hand up into the air.

"I can too," Evie said, picking up a rock from the mud. It rattled in her fingers as she held it. "Destiny," she announced dramatically.

Jay pointed at the lightning that crackled in air above the black turrets. "Me too. I guess it's time."

Mal didn't say a word. She only stared.

"Hold on, now. We're not in any rush," Carlos said. "We need to do this right, or—" He didn't finish the sentence. He just shrugged.

Then he caught Mal's gaze and knew she felt the same way.

"Look," Jay said, yanking back an armful of overgrown vines that covered the stony steps leading up to the main ramp of the bridge. He tossed them to the side.

"What are those horrible, ugly creatures?" Evie made a face. "No, thanks. I'll stay on this side of those things."

Because now that the vines were gone, they could see that the entire bridge appeared to be guarded by ancient stony gargoyles. The winged gryphons glared down at them from where they perched, flanking the bridge on either side.

"Lovely," Jay said.

Carlos stared. It wasn't only Mal who could see her mother's hand in every stone around them. The carved creatures sneered in exactly the same way Maleficent did, their teeth pointed, their mouths cruel.

Mal looked at them, frozen.

Then Carlos realized it was because she was paralyzed by fear. "Mal?"

She didn't answer.

She can't do this alone, Carlos thought. None of us can.

It's no different from pulling each other through the mud. It's just physics, if you think about it. It's science.

But then Carlos tried not to think about it, because his

heart was pounding so loudly, he thought the others would hear it. He began to recite the periodic table of the elements in his head to calm himself down. Atomic numbers and electrons were always somewhat comforting in times of stress, he'd found.

And the more numbers he recited, the easier it was to put one foot in front of the other.

Which is exactly what he did.

Carlos stepped up on to the first stone paver that led to the sloping bridge. Just as he did, the stone gargoyles began to flap their wings in front of them.

"Whoa!" Jay said.

"No," Evie said. "Just, no."

"How is this possible?" asked Jay. "There's no magic on the island."

"The hole in the dome," said Carlos. "It must have sparked the castle to life or something, like a chemical reaction." It made sense—not only had Diablo been unfrozen, but the whole fortress as well.

Carlos moved his way up the next step, and then the next, until he was standing level with the main ramp of the bridge itself. Mal and Evie and Jay now followed behind him.

The creatures growled as they came to life around them, the bridge rumbling beneath their feet. The gryphons' horrible eyes glowed green, illuminating the fog around them, until they were practically shining a spotlight on the four intruders. The gargoyles uncurled their hunched backs, now almost doubling themselves in height.

Evie was right, Carlos thought. They were really ugly things, with snaggly teeth and forked tongues. He couldn't look away from the hideous faces hovering over him. "This must be residue, left over from the magical years," he said. "Whatever did this was probably part of the same power that sparked Diablo to life."

"The same power?" Mal looked spellbound. "You mean, my mother's?"

"Or the same electromagnetic wave." Carlos thought about his last Weird Science class. "I'm not sure how to tell the difference anymore."

Jay swallowed as a gargoyle leaned down, looking as if it could spring at Carlos at any moment. "Right now, I'm pretty sure the difference doesn't matter."

"Who goes there?" boomed the gargoyle to the right of Carlos.

"You cannot pass," said the one on his left.

"Yeah? Says who?" Carlos took a step back, as did the rest of the group following behind him. They looked at each other nervously, unsure of what to do next. They hadn't known about the gargoyles, hadn't expected a fight. This was going to be more difficult than they expected, maybe even impossible.

But it didn't matter. Even Carlos knew there was no turning back now.

"You ugly things need to move!" said Mal, shouting from behind him. She glared at the gryphons. "Or I'm going to make you!"

The gargoyles growled and grimaced, flapping their stone wings as a threat.

"Any ideas?" Carlos looked over his shoulder nervously. "We don't have weapons or magic. What would we fight with? Besides, how do we fight something made of stone?"

"There has to be a way," Mal said. "We have to pass!" she shouted again. "Let us through!"

"Yeah, I'm not sure that's working." Evie sighed.

The gargoyles glared at the children with glowing eyes, their fangs bared, their stony wings beating the wind. "You cannot pass," they said again in unison—and just as the creatures spoke, the thick gray clouds surrounding the long stone ramp dissipated, revealing a gap in the bridge, a forty-foot gulf with nothing below but air.

The bridge was broken, virtually impassable.

"Great," Jay said. "So it's over. Fine. Whatever. Can we go now?"

The others just stared.

Carlos had to admit Jay was probably right.

There was no apparent way to reach the castle. They had come all this way only to fail. Even if they could pass the gargoyles, there was no way to cross the bridge since *there was no bridge*. It was hopeless. Their journey was ended before it had truly begun.

Carlos stepped back and noticed something carved in the stones at the foot of the bridge. He sat down to read it.

"What is it?" Mal asked, kneeling next to him.

He brushed away the dirt and moss to reveal a sentence carved in the stones: *Ye who trespass the bridge must earn the right of way.*

"Great. So what are those, like, directions?" Mal looked at the others. "What does that mean? How do we earn the right of way?"

Evie shook her head as she glanced back up at the gargoyles and the broken bridge. "I don't know, Mal. We don't seem to have earned anything."

"And technically, we are trespassers," Jay said.

Evie frowned. "I think we should go. Maybe the bridge was destroyed—maybe it's been like this for years. Maybe no one gets in and out now."

"No. Those words have to mean something. But is it a riddle, or a warning?" Mal asked. She looked at the gap in the bridge and pushed her way past the others, toward the edge. She was determined to figure it out.

"What are you doing?" Carlos yelled. "Mal, wait! You're not thinking straight."

But she couldn't wait, and she didn't stop.

He took a step back, Jay and Evie flanking him. "Go after her," Carlos said. "Pull her from the break in the stone before she falls. This is crazy."

Jay nodded and followed her.

"It's so sad," Evie said. "To have come this far."

"I know. But half a bridge might as well be no bridge at all," Carlos muttered. He put down his machine and turned it off so that he wouldn't have to listen to its beeping. The noise of the sensor—more proof of how close they'd come to finding the source of the power—only made things that much worse.

The moment Carlos killed the machine, the light in the gargoyles' eyes faded. The eerie green glow receded back into their black stone sockets.

"Wait—did you just—"

Carlos looked incredulous. "Turn off the monsters? I think so." He called out to Mal, who was now standing with Jay, just a few feet from the break in the stone ramp. "They're like big doorbells, Mal. When we try to cross, they turn on. When we go to leave, they turn off."

"So they're another defense mechanism?" Evie looked unconvinced.

"Maybe." Carlos studied the bridge. "Anything's possible. At least, that's what I'm starting to think."

Mal came running back. "So maybe it's just a test. Look," she said, approaching the gargoyles, their eyes once more glowing. "Ask me your questions!" she called up to the guardians of the bridge. "Let us earn the right of way."

But the gargoyles didn't answer her.

"Maybe you're not turning it on right," Evie said.

"Maybe this is just a waste of time." Jay sighed.

"No, it's not," Mal said, giving them a beseeching look. "This is my mother's castle. We've found it, and there has to be a way in. Look at the inscription on the stone—it has to be some kind of test."

Jay spoke up. "Carlos said they're like a doorbell. But what if they're not? What if they're like the alarm system in a house? All we would have to know to disable them is the code." He shrugged. "I mean, that's what I would do, if I was trying to break in."

Of any of us, he would know, Carlos thought.

"So what's the code?" Mal turned back to the gargoyles, her eyes blazing. "Tell me, you idiots!"

She drew herself up to her full height and spoke in a voice that Carlos knew well. It was how Cruella spoke to him, and how Maleficent spoke to her minions from the balcony. He was impressed. He'd never seen Mal so like her mother as now.

Mal did not ask the gargoyles, she commanded them.

"This is my mother's castle, and you are her servants. You will do as I bid. ASK YOUR RIDDLE AND LET US PASS!" she ordered, looking as if she were home—truly home—for the first time.

Because, as they could all now see, she was.

A moment went by.

The mists swirled, in the background, ravens cawed, and green light pulsed in the distant windows of the castle.

"Carlossssssss," hissed the gargoyles, in disturbingly creepy unison. "Approaaaach usssssss."

Hearing his name, Carlos took a step forward with an awestruck look on his face. "Why me?"

"Maybe because you touched the step first? So the alarm is set on Carlos mode?" Jay scratched his head. "Better you than me, man."

"Time for the pass code." Mal nodded. "You got this, Carlos."

Then the gargoyles began to hiss again. "Carlossssssss. First quessssssstion . . ."

Carlos took a breath. It was just like school, he thought. He liked school. He liked answering questions that had answers, right? So wasn't this just another question? That needed just another answer?

> "Ink spot in the snow
> Or red, rough, and soft
> Black and wet, warm and fast
> Loved and lost— What am I?"

No sooner had the gargoyles stopped speaking than rumbling began beneath their feet. "Carlos!" Evie cried, stumbling as she tried to stand in place.

"What?" Carlos ran his hand through his hair anxiously. His mind was reeling.

Ink is black. Snow is white. What's red and rough? A steak?
Who loves a steak? We haven't had those in a while, anyway.
And what does any of this have to do with me?

"Answer the question!" Mal said. The light was once more fading from the gargoyles' eyes.

"It's—" said Carlos, stalling. He was stuck.

Black. White. Spots. Red. Loved. Lost.

"The puppies. My mother's puppies, the Dalmatians. All one hundred and one of them. All loved and all lost, by her." He looked up at the stone faces. "Though I think the love part is debatable."

Silence.

"Do I need to say the names? Because I swear I can tell them to you, every last one of them." He took a breath. "Pongo. Perdita. Patch. Lucky. Roly Poly. Freckles. Pepper . . ." When he had finished speaking, the mist once more congealed around the bridge. Carlos let out a sigh.

It hadn't worked.

"Wait!" Mal said, pointing to the spot where the mists had congealed. "It's doing something." The gray mist parted, revealing a new section of the bridge, a piece that had not existed a moment ago.

The gargoyles cleared a path, and the four of them ran out onto it, hurrying to the newly formed edge, waiting for the next question.

"NEXT RIDDLE!" Mal demanded, just as a ferocious

wind blew at them. Carlos was beginning to get the feeling the bridge had more than a few ways of getting rid of unwanted visitors. He swallowed.

They needed to hurry.

Or rather, he did.

"Carlossssssss. Next quesssssssstion."

He nodded.

"Like a rose in a blizzard
It blooms like a cut
A red smear
Her kiss is death,"

the gargoyles hissed in their eerie unison, turning to face them, claws raised. Their muscles flexed and their tails whipped, their forked tongues raking their fangs. It looked as if they might pounce at any moment.

Once again, the bridge began to shift beneath their feet.

"'Her kiss is death,'" echoed Carlos. "It has to be about my mother. Is that the answer? Cruella De Vil?"

The bridge began to shake even harder.

Wrong answer.

"But it *is* about your mother!" said Evie, suddenly. "A rose in a blizzard, it blooms like a cut . . . her kiss . . . it's about what color lipstick she wears! Cruella's signature red!"

Carlos was dumbfounded. "It is?"

"A red smear—see? It means it's something she puts on. Oh, I know what it is!" Evie said. "The answer is Cherries in the Snow! That has to be it; it's been everywhere this season. I mean—judging from what's been thrown away on the Dumpster barges."

Mal rolled her eyes. "I can't believe you know that."

The wind whipped up again, and the four of them locked hands, holding on to one another for support. They pressed their shoulders together, bracing themselves against the gale.

Evie cursed. "It's not Cherries in the Snow? I could swear that was it. Red with a pinkish undertone. No, wait—wait—it didn't have a pink undertone, it was darker. *Redder.* A 'true red'—what did the magazines call it? Frost and Flame? No—Fire and Ice! That's it! Cruella's pout is made of Fire and Ice!"

The gargoyles paused, their eyes glowing. They stood in place as the mist once more congealed around the bridge, then thinned to reveal another new section.

Carlos relaxed. Jay whooped—and even Mal clapped Evie on the back as they advanced across the bridge.

One more answered question, and the way would be clear.

"Ask your last riddle!" Mal charged them.

The gargoyles looked crafty.

"Carlosssssss. Last quesssssstion."

He nodded.

Mal looked at him encouragingly.

Here it goes, one last time.

> *"Dark is her heart*
> *Black like the sky above*
> *Tell us, young travelers—*
> *What is her one true love?"*

The creatures hissed in unison, and as soon as they finished speaking, they walked toward the four, teeth shining, claws raised, wings flapping. The gargoyles would tear them to shreds if Carlos answered incorrectly—the four of them saw that now.

Carlos had to get it right, not just to cross the bridge but to keep them all alive. "'Dark is her heart'—they must mean Maleficent, right?" He turned to Mal. "But it could mean any of our mothers."

"My mother has no true love. My mother loves nothing and nobody! Not even me!" said Mal, with a slight pang that Carlos knew all too well.

"Don't look at me. I don't even *have* a mother," Jay said.

"Beauty!" Evie called out. "That's mine. I know . . . it's a little cliché."

But the gargoyles were not interested in anything anyone had to say. Coming closer, parting the mists, their tails swishing: "WHAT IS HER ONE TRUE LOVE?" they demanded, looking from Evie to Carlos to Mal to Jay.

"My *father*?" Mal ventured.

Carlos shook his head. If Maleficent was anything like Cruella, she hated Mal's father with a vengeance. Cruella had forbidden any questions about his own, no matter how curious Carlos was, how much he wanted to know. As far as Cruella was concerned, Carlos was hers alone. Maleficent had to be the same.

The gargoyles were nearly upon them. They were taller than Carlos had realized, maybe eight or nine feet. They were enormous, and their weight made the bridge groan beneath their every step.

Carlos didn't think even the periodic tables could help him now.

"WHAT IS HER ONE TRUE LOVE?" the gargoyles asked again, extending their massive wings. When they flapped, the mists swirled about them.

"The Dragon's Eye?" Mal guessed. "That's all my mom cares about."

"Being the Fairest One of All!" Evie shouted. "Her, or me. In that order!"

Jay just shrugged. "I can't help. I'm pretty sure the answer isn't Jafar, Prince of Pajamas."

At first it looked as if the gargoyles were shaking their heads, but Carlos realized it was because the bridge was rumbling so much. Everything was quaking, and the gargoyles were nearly upon them. His teeth began to clatter. Evie lost her balance and slipped, almost falling over the side, but Carlos caught her in time. Jay held on to a crumbling post and held out his hand so that Carlos could hold on to him, forming a link to Evie.

"Hurry! Somebody'd better come up with something," Jay grunted. "I can't hold on much longer."

Evie screamed as she dangled off the bridge, Carlos clinging to one of her blue gloves, which she was slipping out of, one finger at a time.

"THINK, MAL! What does Maleficent love?" Carlos yelled. "She has to love SOMETHING!"

"WHAT IS HER ONE TRUE LOVE? ANSWER THE RIDDLE OR FALL INTO DARKNESS," the gargoyles intoned.

"Diablo?" Mal screamed. "Is it Diablo?"

In answer, the bridge buckled under her feet, and Mal slid down, only by luck managing to hold on to Jay, who was anchoring everyone. The entire castle was shaking. Stones flew down from its ramparts, and the towers threatened to crumble on top of them.

The bridge began to sway dangerously.

"Wait!" screamed Jay. "You guys! They're not talking about Maleficent! They're still talking about Cruella! Quick—Carlos—what is her one true love?"

Carlos couldn't think. He was too scared. He couldn't even put a sentence together. And he was even more frightened by what the answer *would* be.

Maybe that was why he hadn't guessed right, this time.

I can't bear to say it out loud.

Jay's voice echoed. "CARLOS! WHAT IS YOUR MOTHER'S ONE TRUE LOVE?"

He had to say it.

He'd almost always known.

Sometimes, like this afternoon, he would think she meant him, but he really knew better.

Because she *never* meant him.

Not once. Not ever.

Carlos opened his eyes. He had to say it, and he had to say it now.

"HER FURS! FUR IS HER ONE TRUE LOVE!" he yelled. She said it all the time. She had said it that afternoon in front of everyone.

"All my mother cares about is her stupid fur coat closet and everything in it. But you guys already know that."

It was the truth, and like any truth, it was powerful.

In the blink of an eye, the four of them were standing on the other side of the gargoyle bridge, and everything was set to rights once more. There was no more swaying or rumbling, no one was falling over the side, and the gargoyles had all turned back to stone.

Although Carlos would swear that one of the stone gargoyles had winked at him.

They were safe, for now.

"Nice work," said Mal, breathing heavily. "Okay, now—where to?"

Carlos shakily looked at the beeping box in his hands. "This way."

he Forbidden Fortress lived up to its name. Once the four adventurers had found their way in through its massive oaken doors, it was almost impossible to tell the darkness of the shadow world outside the castle from the shadow world within. Either way, it was intimidatingly dark, and the farther Jay and Carlos and Evie and Mal crept inside, the more their nervous whispers echoed through the ghostly, abandoned chambers.

Jay wished he'd worn something warmer than his leather vest. Mal's lips were turning blue, Carlos's breath appeared in white clouds as he spoke, and Evie's fingers felt like icicles when Jay grabbed them. (Once. Or twice. And strictly for warmth.) It was colder than Dragon Hall inside, and there was no chance of anything getting any warmer; there were no logs on the fireplace grates, no thermostats to switch on.

"That's modern castle living." Evie sighed. "Trade in one big, cold prison for another." Mal nodded in agreement. Privately, Jay thought that Jafar's junk shop seemed downright cozy in comparison, but he kept that to himself.

Inside every corridor, a dense fog floated just above the black marble floor. "That has to be magic. The fog doesn't just *do* that," Mal said.

Carlos nodded. "The refracted energy seems stronger here. I think we're closer to the source than we've ever been."

As he spoke, an icy wind blew past them, whistling in through the shattered stained-glass windows high above them. Each step they took reverberated against the walls.

Even Jay the master thief was too intimidated to try and take anything, and kept his hands to himself for once.

Of course once they did find the scepter, he'd have to man up. Jay knew that, and he'd made his peace with it—no matter how well they'd all gotten along on the way there.

Villains don't have friends, and neither do their children. Not when you get right down to it.

None of them had come there out of loyalty to Mal, or friendship. Jay knew what he had to do, and he'd do it.

Until then, his hands stayed in his pockets. If this haunted place was selling it, he didn't want it.

"What's that?" Jay asked, pointing. Green lights flashed through half-shattered panes of glass, but he couldn't figure out the source.

"It's what we've been tracking all along," Carlos answered. "That same electromagnetic energy: it's going crazy." He shook his head at the flashing lights on his box. "This fortress was definitely exposed to something that's left a kind of residue charge—"

"You mean, an enchantment?"

He shrugged. "That, too."

"And so, even after all these years, this place is somehow still glowing with its own light?" Evie looked amazed.

"Cool," Jay said.

Mal shrugged it off. "In other words, we're getting closer to the Dragon's Eye."

"Yep," said Jay. Like the rest of the group, he knew what everyone else in the Isle and the kingdom knew—that the evil green light meant only one terrifying person.

Even if it probably reminded Mal of home.

Corridors led to more corridors, until they passed through dark hallways full of framed paintings shrouded in cobwebs and dust. "It's a portrait gallery," Evie said, straining to see the walls through the shadows. "Every castle has one."

"Mal, stop it—" Jay shouted, looking behind him and jumping away.

Mal reached out and tapped his shoulder. She was

standing right in front of him. "Hello? I'm not back there. I'm over here."

"Crap. I thought that picture was you." He pointed.

"That's not me. That's my mother," Mal said with a sigh.

"Whoa, you really do look like her, you know," Jay said.

"You two could be twins," Evie agreed.

"That, my friends, is called genetics," Carlos said with a smile.

"Gee, thanks—I look like my mother? Just what every girl wants to hear," Mal replied. Still, Jay knew different. What Mal wanted, more than anything, *was* to be just like her mother.

Exactly like her.

Every bit as bad, and every bit as powerful.

That was what it would take for someone like Maleficent to even notice her—and Jay could tell that this portrait gallery was only making Mal want it that much more desperately.

"Now, what?" Mal asked, as if she were trying to change the subject.

Jay looked around. Before them were four corridors leading to four different parts of the fortress.

A foul draft issued from each of the paths, and Jay could have sworn he heard a distant moan; but he knew it was only the wind, winding its way through the curving passages. He yanked a matchbook from his pocket and lit a match, muttering a quick "eenie-meanie-miney-mo."

"How scientific," Carlos said, rolling his eyes.

"You got your way, I got mine. That one," Jay said, pointing to the corridor directly in front of them. Just as he did, the wind blew out from that same passage, and the foul stench of something rotted or dead came along with it.

The wind snuffed the burning match out.

Evie held her nose, and Mal did the same.

"Are you sure about this?" Mal asked.

"Duh, of course not. That's why I played eenie-meanie-miney-mo! One corridor is as good as the next," Jay said, entering the corridor and not waiting for the rest to follow. It was the first rule of breaking into an unknown castle: you never let it get to you. You always act like you know what you are doing.

Jay had a feeling this fortress was playing with them, offering them choices when really all roads probably led to the same place. It was time to take matters back into his own hands.

"No, wait—you don't know where you're going. Carlos, check your box-compass-thing," said Mal.

Carlos brought the box up to the intersection. It beeped. "Okay, I guess maybe Jay's right."

"Of course I am."

They followed Jay into the dark corridor.

Carlos held the beeping box in his hands, the sound echoing off the stony walls. It led them to a dank, cold stairway that led further downward, deeper into darkness. The air felt colder and damper and in the eerie silence came a distant rattle, like bones striking rock, or chains rattling in the wind.

"Because that's comforting." Evie sighed.

"The dungeon," said Mal. "Or you might know it as the place where my mother encountered the lovestruck Prince Phillip."

Evie's eyes were wide with awe. It was probably the most famous story in all of Auradon. "Maleficent was going to lock him down here for a hundred years, right? That would have been fun."

Carlos looked around. "She nearly pulled it off, didn't she?"

Mal nodded. "If not for that trio of self-righteous, busy-body, blasted good fairies." She sighed. "End of scene. Enter Isle of the Lost."

"I don't know about you, but I feel like we've been down here a hundred years already. Let's get on with it," Jay said.

He was more alert than he'd been all day, because he knew he was on the job now.

It was time to get to work.

Jay found a dungeon door. Carlos held the box inside, listening for its beep. "This is the one."

He went ahead with the box, while Jay and Mal and Evie helped each other slowly down the steps, bracing themselves against the wall as they went. There was no rail, and the treads were coated in a black moss. Every step squished in the darkness, and it felt as if they were stepping on something living and wet.

"Suddenly the whole mud river thing doesn't seem so bad," said Evie.

"Seriously," Jay said.

Mal didn't say a word. She couldn't. She was too distracted. Even the moss smelled like her mother.

It only grew thicker as they delved deeper into the dungeon. There were layer upon layer of gauzy cobwebs, a spider's tapestry woven long ago and forgotten. Every step they took pulled apart the threads, clearing a way forward. All of them were quiet, hushed by the lingering menace in the air as their footsteps squished in the gloom.

"Here?" Mal asked, stopping in front of a rotten wooden door hanging partly off its hinges. When she touched it, the frame collapsed, sending the wood clattering against the floor. Even the heavy iron straps that had once bound the door fell against the stones and the wood, making an awful racket.

"Maybe we shouldn't touch anything," said Carlos, scrutinizing the device in his hands.

Mal rolled her eyes. "Too late."

"I think this is it," Carlos said.

Jay hoped he was right, that the box had led them to the Dragon's Eye.

He couldn't imagine what Mal would do to poor Carlos

if it hadn't. And Jay himself needed to get on with the job at hand.

Mal nodded, and Jay pushed aside what was left of the door. As they entered, he couldn't help but notice that the shattered remains of the door and its frame looked like a kind of mouth—a panther's mouth—and they were stepping through its open jaws, into the mouth of the beast.

"Did any of you notice—"

"Shut up," Evie said tensely. They had all seen the same thing, which couldn't be good. That was probably why nobody wanted to talk about it.

The four of them walked inside. The room was impossibly dark. There was not even a hint of light, not a glow from a distant window or a torch. Jay reached out, looking for a wall, something to touch.

"Maybe we should find a flashlight or something in Jay's pockets, before we touch any—" Carlos warned, but it was too late.

Jay struck something with his hand, and the room was suddenly filled with the deafening sounds of metal and stone colliding and grinding and tinkling all around them.

And just as suddenly, they were bathed in the brightest light, a glow that burst from every corner of the room. The golden brilliance filled their eyes—and before they knew what was happening, the room was suddenly filling with sand.

Sand, sand everywhere . . . and they were falling into it, covered in it.

Evie screamed. Mal started to thrash. Carlos lost hold of his box. Only Jay stood perfectly still.

It wasn't a dungeon, it was a *cave*.

A cave filled with sand . . . and, from what Jay could barely make out amid the massive dunes now surrounding him . . . treasure.

He looked around at the king's ransom of jewels that glittered in between the dunes. Mound upon mound of gold coins shimmered in the distance, while hills of gold coins stretched as far as the eye could see. There were crowns and coronets, jeweled scepters and goblets, emeralds the size of his fist, diamonds as brilliant as the stars, thousands of gold doubloons and silver coins. There were larger things too: great obelisks, and coffins, lamps and urns, a pharaoh's head, a winged staff, a chalice, and a sphinx made of gold.

A king's ransom, he thought. *That's what this is.*

Evie pushed the sand away and sat up, wearing a new crown on her head, quite by accident. "What is this? Where are we?"

"I can assure you this is not part of my mother's castle," said Mal wryly, as she spat out some sand and blew her purple bangs out of her eyes. She stood up, brushing sand off her leather jacket. "More residue from the hole in the dome?" she asked.

Carlos nodded. "It has to be. There's no other explanation."

"Wait a minute, where's the scepter?" she asked Carlos, looking around. She sounded nervous. "It has to be here, right? Has anyone seen it?"

Carlos removed a golden bucket that had fallen on his head and picked up his box from where it was balanced on what looked like an ancient golden sarcophagus. He blew sand from the drive and checked the machine again. "It's still working, but I don't know. It's not beeping anymore. It's like it lost the signal, or something."

"Well, find it again!" Mal barked.

"I will, I will. . . . Give me a second, here. You have no idea what sand can do to a motherboard. . . ."

Meanwhile, Jay was stuffing every pocket he had with as much of the marvelous loot as he could carry.

This was the answer to his dreams . . . the stuff he had been longing for . . . heaven on earth . . . the Biggest Score of his life, and his father's!

It was . . . it was . . .

It dawned on him that he knew exactly where they were.

"The Cave of Wonders!" he cried.

"Come again?" asked Mal.

"This is the place—where my father found the lamp."

"I thought Aladdin found the lamp," said Carlos.

"Yes, but *who* sent him there?" asked Jay with a superior smile. "If it wasn't for Jafar, Aladdin would have never found it. Hence it was my father's lamp all along." He looked annoyed. "But nobody ever mentions that part, do they?

And my dad said he thought there might be other things hidden in the mist—he must have suspected this might be here too."

"Fine. Cave of Wonders. More like Basement of Sand," said Mal. "More important, how do we get out of here?"

"You don't," said a deep voice.

"Excuse me?" said Mal.

"I didn't say anything," said Jay, who was now wearing numerous gold chains around his neck and stacking diamond bracelets up his arm.

"Who was that?" asked Evie nervously.

They looked around. Nobody else seemed to be there.

"Fine. It's nothing. Now, let's find that door," said Mal.

"You won't," said the booming voice again. "And you will be trapped here forever if you don't answer me correctly!"

"Great," Jay groaned.

"Is this another riddle? This whole fortress is, like, booby-trapped or something," Evie grumbled.

"Multiple defenses—I told you," Carlos said. "Burglar alarm. Probably for the Dragon's Eye, don't you think?"

"Cave? Should I call you Cave?" asked Mal.

"Mouth of Wonders will do," said the voice.

Evie made a face. "That's a terrible name."

Mal nodded. "Okay, Mouth, what's the question?"

"It is but a simple one."

"Hit us," Mal said.

The booming voice chuckled.

Then it asked in somber tones, "What is the golden rule?"

"The golden rule?" Mal asked, scratching her head. She looked at her team. "Is that some kind of jewelry thing? Jay?"

But Jay was too busy grabbing as much gold as he could get and didn't seem to hear the question.

Carlos began frantically reciting every mathematical rule he could thing of. "Rules of logarithms? Rule of three? Rules expressed in symbols? Order of operations?"

"Is it maybe something about being nice to each other?" asked Evie tentatively. "Do unto others what you want done unto yourself? Some kind of Auradon greeting-card nonsense?"

In answer, the cave began to fill with sand again. The Mouth of Wonders was not happy, that much was clear. Sand appeared from everywhere, filling the room, filling the spaces between the stacks of gold coins, rising like water filling a sinking ship. They would soon suffocate if they did not give the Mouth the correct answer.

"It's the Cave of Wonders, not the Fairy Godmother!" shrieked Carlos. "The Cave doesn't care about being kind! That's not the golden rule!"

The cave continued to fill with sand.

"Come on—this way!" Mal tried to climb the stacks of gold coins—thinking she could avoid the sand by getting closer to the ceiling—but they collapsed beneath her each time she attempted to scale them, and she only ended up buried in more treasure. She tried again, and this time Evie gave her a push from behind, so that she was able to grab on to the tall statue of a sphinx.

She mounted the creature's back and reached to pull Evie up beside her, but the sand was still rising, already engulfing her leg, threating to keep her down.

"I can't make it!" Evie shouted.

"You have to!" Mal yelled back.

But Evie had disappeared under the flood of sand.

Jay couldn't believe it when he watched her go under. "Evie—"

"Come on—" Carlos said, feeling beneath the sand for her. "She has to be down here. Help me find her."

"I can't find her," Jay shouted.

Evie popped back up, spluttering, spitting coins out of her mouth. Mal and Carlos and Jay looked relieved.

"Here—" Now Mal offered Carlos a hand to pull him up, but the sand was already at his chest. "C'mon," she cried, "climb the sphinx!"

"I can't," he said.

"What?"

"My leg is caught."

Evie climbed up on the sphinx and tugged at his arm on one side, and Mal from the other, but no matter what they did, Carlos didn't budge an inch. He was stuck, and the sand was still rising around him. It came from the walls and from the floor, and now Evie noticed that it was coming from the ceiling too.

Mal tugged again at Carlos's arm, but instead of pulling him from the sand, she pulled him out of Evie's grasp. Evie tumbled into the ever-growing mounds of sand, crashing against chalices and crowns.

The sand covered her: first up to her knees, then her shoulders . . .

Carlos reached for her, and they held hands as the sand kept rising.

"At least I have my heels on," Evie said, trying to sound brave. The sand was up to her neck, and Carlos could barely keep his chin above the surface now.

"JAY! WHERE'S JAY?" yelled Mal, looking around, coughing up sand as she frantically held Carlos by the arm. "JAY!"

Jay was flailing in the sand; it was in his hair, in his eyes. He was also covered with gold doubloons. *Gold. So much gold.* He'd never seen so much gold in his life. He had all the gold in the world, it felt like.

He would die buried in gold. . . .

The golden rule . . .

What is the golden rule?

Why, he knew the answer to that.

He could almost hear his father whispering the answer in his ear.

Meanwhile, Carlos and Evie had disappeared beneath

the sand again, and Mal herself was about to go under.

The sand was nearly at the ceiling. Soon there were would be nowhere to escape to—no way to avoid the sand, and no air in the chamber. They were running out of time and out of room.

But Jay knew the answer.

Jay knew he could save them.

"WHOEVER HAS THE MOST GOLD MAKES THE RULES! THAT'S THE GOLDEN RULE!" Jay cried triumphantly, raising a fist in the air.

There was a great booming chuckle, and the sand slowly started to melt into the drains. Soon Jay and Mal and Evie and Carlos were standing right back in the fortress, out of the dungeons altogether.

The Cave of Wonders had disappeared, but then so had all its treasure.

"Fool's gold," said Jay sadly, looking at his empty pockets. "All of it."

chapter

24

Funhouse Mirror

*E*vie thought her heart would never stop pounding.
She could still taste the sand from that cave. So
this was what true evil was like—like sand in the mouth
and gargoyles on attack. If this was what magic did, she was
glad there was a dome.

Also, she had practically lost a heel back in there.

Evie shook her head. This was the second time the
Forbidden Fortress had almost gotten the better of them.
Did Maleficent know she was sending her own daughter
into a trap? And if so, did she care? Probably not: this was
the feared and loathed Mistress of Darkness, after all. Evil
Queen was a fool to think she could compete with someone

like that, and Evie almost felt like a fool for trying to compete with the Mistress of Darkness's daughter.

Now that she thought about it, Evie almost felt sorry for Mal.

Almost.

Carlos's machine was beeping again.

The four crept through the ruined castle. Bats screamed and fluttered over their heads, and the crumbling marble floor beneath them seemed to shift and slide in order to bear their weight.

Evie stumbled. "What *is* it with this place? Is there a fault line that runs under this island?"

"Well," Carlos began.

"Joke. That was a joke." Evie sighed.

There was nothing too funny about their current situation, however. It was a miracle that the surrounding ocean hadn't completely swallowed the castle and the entire mountain by now. Evie could hear the scampering of rats inside the walls, and chills ran up her spine.

Even the rats were looking for safer ground, she thought.

"This way," Carlos said, motioning to a narrow passage in front of him.

They followed, trailing behind Carlos, the machine beeping, the sound growing louder. "Now this way," he said, rounding one turn, then another. Evie was right behind him as they followed, the passage growing narrower. "And now—"

"What's going on?" asked Evie, cutting him off. "Because

I know my sizing, and I didn't just double in diameter in the last two and a half minutes."

Indeed, the passage had narrowed to nearly her shoulders' width. If it got any narrower, she would have to turn sideways. A lump formed in her throat, and her stomach began to roil—she felt as if this were no longer a corridor. It was crack, a fissure, and it felt like it might close on them at any moment.

Mal raised her voice. "Is it just my imagination, or are we wedged inside a mountain like—"

"A piece of string dangling down a pipe? Toothpaste squeezed inside a straw? A hangnail in this cuticle right here?" Jay said, holding out his hand. "Dang, this one really hurts."

"Are you describing the things you've stolen today? Because those are all terrible analogies," Evie said, looking at Jay. "And I'm saying that as someone who was castle-schooled by a woman who thinks the three R's are Rouging, Reddening, and Reapplying."

"Maybe we should go back," Carlos said, giving voice to Evie's fear. "Except—I think I might be stuck." Just then, the walls shook, the castle rattled, and a chip of stone fell to the floor. The shard was big enough to do damage, and it narrowly missed Evie's perfect nose.

She cried out. She wanted to retreat, but she couldn't, the corridor was too narrow. "Maybe it's some kind of trap! Let's go—it doesn't look safe!"

"No," Carlos said. "Look! There's another passage," he added, wedging himself forward until he could pry first one hip and then the other out from the narrow corridor to a just-wider one.

As she and Jay and Mal followed him, Evie was so relieved that she didn't even remember to complain about her nose.

This new passage turned right, then left. The walls were farther apart here, but they were oddly sloped, some tilting inward, others outward. The effect was dizzying, as even the ceiling was sloped in spots, and the corridors kept branching, splitting into two or sometimes three directions.

And always, the rumbling continued beneath them.

"Something doesn't like us," Jay said.

"We're not supposed to be in this place," echoed Evie.

"We need to hurry," Carlos said, trying to sound calm, though he had to be as scared as any of them.

Another stone broke free of the wall, shattering as it hit the floor, nearly crushing Evie's head. She jumped back this time, shuddering. "What *is* this place?"

"We're in some kind of maze," Mal said, thinking aloud. "That's why the corridors keep turning, why passages keep splitting off and narrowing. It's some kind of twisted maze, and we're lost in it."

"No, we're not. We've still got the box," Carlos replied. "It's the only thing that *is* keeping us from getting lost in here." The machine was still beeping, so they just kept following him. Evie only hoped he was right and that he knew where he was going. He must have, though, because the winding corridors soon gave way to more open spaces, and all of them breathed a sigh of relief.

Even when the hallways ran long and straight again, the castle was still rumbling, the walls still tilting; and the ceiling was even lower now where they found themselves.

"It's not random," Carlos said, suddenly. "It's in a rhythm."

"You're right," Jay said. "Look. The rumbling seems to go along with your beeping box. When the box lights up, the walls start to move."

Evie stared. "You mean, he's the one doing it?"

Carlos shook his head. "Actually, I think it's the waves. Imagine how old this castle must be. What if, each time a wave strikes the foundation, a stone falls, or the floors rumble?"

Mal swallowed. "I just hope the castle itself doesn't crumble before we find the scepter."

Evie bent down so her head wouldn't hit the ceiling. All of them except for Carlos had to crouch down now to avoid it.

"It's a room made for mice," said Mal.

"Or dwarfs?" asked Evie.

"Or children?" guessed Jay.

"No," Carlos said, quieting the others, pointing to something in the dark distance. They followed the line of his gaze, seeing at first a pair of green glowing eyes, then another and another.

"Goblins," said Carlos. "This is where the goblins live. That's why the ceilings are so low and the corridors are so strange. This isn't a place for humans," he said, and when he finished, the air filled with a terrible, raucous laughter, the sound of claws tapping and teeth grinding. The box had led them right into the goblins' den.

"Super," Mal said.

"Yeah, good work," Jay snorted.

Evie just glared at Carlos.

And these weren't the friendly, enterprising goblins of the wharf or the rude ones from the Slop Shop. These were horrible creatures that had lived in darkness without their mistress for twenty years. Hungry and horrible.

"What do we do?" Jay asked, cowering behind Carlos, who had flattened himself against the wall of the corridor.

"We run," Evie and Mal cried, one after the other.

They ran toward the only open passageway, the goblin horde shrieking in the darkness, following behind them, their spears beating against the walls.

Jay shouted, "I guess they don't get a lot of visitors."

"Maybe they should stop eating their guests," Carlos said, nearly tripping over what he hoped was not a bone.

"That door!" Evie said, pointing to a heavy wooden door. "Everyone in!"

They hurried through the doorway, and Evie slammed the door after them, throwing the lock and sealing the goblins out.

"That was close," said Mal.

"Too close," Jay echoed. The goblins could still be heard on the far side of the door, cackling and tapping it with their spears.

"Maybe they just like to scare people?" Evie said. "I heard they were mostly harmless."

"Yeah, mostly," said Carlos, sucking his hand where a spear had almost hit it. "Let's not wait around to find out."

When it sounded as if the goblins had gone, Evie cracked open the door. She made sure they were alone before she nodded to Carlos. They continued down the narrow hallways finding nothing but empty chambers until she spied a light shining from a hidden hallway. "Over here!" she called.

She walked toward the light excitedly, thinking it might be the Dragon's Eye glinting in the dark.

And stopped short—because she was standing in front of a mirror.

A dark, stained, cracked mirror, but a mirror nonetheless. Evie screamed.

"A monster!" she said.

"What is it?" Mal asked, following and looking over Evie's shoulder. Then Mal screamed too.

Carlos and Jay bumped up next.

"A beast," Evie yelled. "A hideous beast!"

Evie was still screaming and pointing to her reflection. In the mirror, an old woman with a crooked nose and wearing a black cape pointed right back.

The hag was her.

"What's happened to me?" she asked, her voice, rough and quavery. Worse, when she looked down, she saw that her formerly smooth skin was saggy, wrinkly, and dotted with liver spots. She looked at her hair—white and scraggly. She was an old beggar woman, and not just in the mirror.

She wasn't the only one.

Mal was frowning at her reflection. She had a warty nose, and her head was mostly bald except for a few white strands. "Charming. It's got to be some kind of spell."

Jay shook his head. "But—once again, and let's say it all together now—there's no magic on the island."

"There was a moment—for a single second—when my machine burned a hole in the dome, and I think maybe that was what did it."

"Did what, exactly?" Evie asked, looking spooked.

"Brought Diablo back to life, sparked the Dragon's Eye and the gargoyles and the Cave of Wonders, and probably everything that used to be magical in this fortress," said Carlos. "I mean, maybe. Or not."

"I don't know, I don't think I look THAT bad," said Jay, who grinned at his reflection. He was chubby and pasty, bearded and gray, and looked exactly like his father. He too was wearing a black cloak. "I look like I got my hands on a whole lot of cake in my life, at least."

"Speak for yourself," said Carlos, who was frightened to see that in old age he resembled his mother, feature for feature: knotted neck, high cheekbones, bug-eyed glare. "I think I'd rather face the goblins than this."

"I'm with you." Evie couldn't look at herself for another moment.

She began to panic; her throat was constricting. She *couldn't* look like this! She was beautiful! She was—

"Fairest," agreed the mirror.

"Not the voice!" Evie shouted, before she realized what, exactly, she had heard. Because this time, it wasn't her mother doing her Mirror Voice, as it so often was.

It was an actual Magic Mirror. On an actual wall.

They all turned to the mirror, whose human-esque features had appeared as a ghostly presence in the reflective glass.

"Fairest you are, and fairest you will be again,
If you prove you are wise
and declare all the ingredients needed
for a peddler's disguise,"

said the Magic Mirror.

"It's a word problem!" said Carlos, gleefully. He loved word problems.

"No, it's not. It's a spell," Jay said, looking at him like he was crazy.

"I knew it!" said Mal.

"What's a peddler's disguise?" asked Jay.

"Obviously—it's *this*. It's what's happened to *us*," said Mal. "Evie, do you know what goes into making a peddler's disguise? It sounds like if we can name all the ingredients, we can reverse the spell."

"Not us," Carlos pointed out. "Evie. It says, you know, the Fairest." He looked at Mal, suddenly embarrassed. "Sorry, Mal."

"There's nothing fair about me now," Evie said. "But I have heard of the Peddler's Disguise, though." Her eyes were back on the glass, still riveted by her awful looks in the mirror.

"Of course you have. It's only your mother's most famous disguise! Remember—when she fooled Snow White into taking the apple?" said Mal impatiently.

"Don't pressure me! You're making me panic. It's like, I used to know it, but now I can't think of anything except *her*." Evie pointed at her reflection. "I'm paralyzed."

"I don't know. I think it's kind of cool," Jay said. "You could steal a whole lot of stuff, looking like that."

Carlos nodded. "He does have a point. You might want to give the whole getup a test run."

Evie started to wail.

"Not helping," Mal scolded.

Evie wailed all the more loudly.

"Evie, come on. That's not you. You know that. Don't let my mother's evil fortress get under your skin," Mal said, sounding as passionate on the subject as Evie had ever heard her sound about anything at all.

"This is what my— I mean, Maleficent does. She finds your weaknesses and picks them off, one by one. You think it's an accident that we stumbled across this Magic Mirror, right when we happened to have the Fairest along for the ride?"

"You think it's on purpose?" Evie looked calmer, and even a little intrigued.

"I think it's a test, just like everything else in this place. Like Carlos and the gargoyles, or Jay and the Mouth."

"Okay," Evie said slowly, nodding at Mal. "You really think I can do it?"

"I know you can, you loser. I mean, *Fairest* loser." Mal grinned.

Evie grinned back.

Okay, maybe she could do this. "I have studied that spell a hundred times in my mother's grimoire."

"That's the spirit," Mal said, thumping her on the back.

"I can see the words of the spell as clearly as if it were before me now," Evie said a little more loudly, standing a little straighter.

"There you go. Of course you can. It's a classic."

"A classic," Evie said to herself. "That was what I called it. Remember?"

Could she?

Then she looked her old, ugly self right in the eye.

"'Mummy dust, to make me look old!'" she cried.

Suddenly, her wrinkles disappeared. Carlos whooped with joy, because his had vanished as well. And he'd hated seeing Cruella's frown lines on his face.

Evie smiled. "'To shroud my clothes, black of night!'"

In a flash, they were wearing their own clothes again.

"'To age my voice, an old hag's cackle!'" she said, and even as she said it, her real voice returned, young and melodic once again.

Jay laughed in delight, and it was no longer an old man's gruff chuckle.

"'To whiten my hair, a scream of fright!'" said Evie, watching as her hair went back to the dark, beautiful blue hue. Mal's thick purple locks returned, and the black seeped back into Carlos's white hair.

Evie was almost done now, and her voice gained confidence as she remembered the last words of the incantation. "'A blast of wind to fan my hate, a thunderbolt to mix it well, now reverse this magic spell!'"

All four of them cheered and yelled and jumped around like crazy idiots. Even Evie was grinning now.

She had never been so happy to see herself in the mirror, and now that she was herself again, she found that for once in her life, nobody even cared how she looked. Not even her.

It was like magic.

chapter
25

Dragon's Curse

As she trudged behind the others, Mal thought about what she'd said to Evie—how everything at the Forbidden Fortress had been a test.

Carlos had faced the gargoyles, and Jay, the Cave of Wonders. Evie had endured the Magic Mirror.

What about me?

What's in store for me?

Was danger—in the form of a challenge all her own— waiting for her, just behind the next castle door?

Or would it be even more like my mother to ignore me alto-gether? To leave me alone, and think I wasn't worthy of any kind of test at all?

She closed her eyes. She could almost hear her mother's voice now.

What is there to test, Mal? You aren't like me. You're weak, like your father. You don't even deserve your own name.

Mal opened her eyes.

Either way, nothing changed the place where they were standing.

Maleficent's home. Her lair.

Mal was on her mother's turf now, whether or not she was welcome there. And she knew that whatever happened next was about the two of them, test or not. Quest or not.

Even, Dragon's Eye or not.

Mal couldn't shake the feeling that something or someone was watching her; she'd felt it since she left home that morning, and the presence was even stronger in the fortress. But every time she looked over her shoulder there was nothing. Maybe she was just being paranoid.

Past the mirrored hallway, Mal and the others walked through a corridor hung with purple and gold pennants and great tapestries, depicting all the surrounding kingdoms. It was hard to tell one from the next, though, mostly because the dust was so thick. As they walked, they even made tracks across the dusty stones, as if they were instead trudging through hallways of snow.

But on they went.

The corridors bent and twisted, the floor sometimes

seeming uneven, the walls angling one way or the other, making them all feel as if they were in a dream or a funhouse or someplace that didn't really exist.

A fairy tale come to life.

A castle—only, the way castles looked in nightmares.

Every wall and every stone was rendered in shades of gray and black, a faint green glow sometimes seeping through a wedge here and there.

Mother's home, Mal thought every time she noticed the green light.

The total effect was excruciating for all four of them— even for Mal.

Or, especially for Mal.

The cracked stained glass windows were the only other source of color. The old glass was mostly broken, and sections of the windows lay entirely in ruins, their shards dashed across the floor. Mal and the others had to step carefully to avoid slipping on one of pieces. The long, window-lined corridor gave way to an even taller and wider corridor, and before long, Mal knew they were approaching some place of significance, a great chamber, perhaps even the heart of the castle itself.

Mal walked toward her fate, as Evie had said. Her destiny, if that's what it was.

Mal could feel it, the now familiar pull toward something unknown, something that perhaps belonged only to her.

It was there in front of her, buzzing and vibrating, just as it had been since the first moment she'd stepped inside the Thorn Forest. It pulled at her, beckoned her, even taunted her.

Come, it said.

Hurry.

This way.

Was it her really destiny calling to her, after all?

Or was it just another failure waiting for her in the throne room? More confirmation that she would never be her mother's daughter, no matter how hard she tried?

She stopped at a pair of doors twice the height of a grown man.

"This is it. It's here."

She looked at Carlos, and he nodded, holding up the box. She saw that he had switched it off some time ago. "We didn't need it anymore," he said, looking right at Mal.

Jay nodded to her. Even Evie reached for her hand, squeezing it once before she let it go again.

Mal took a breath. She felt a chill up her spine, and goose bumps all over her arm. "This was Maleficent's throne room. I'm sure of it now. I can feel it." She looked up at them. "Does that sound crazy?"

They shook their heads, no.

She pushed open the doors, taking it all in.

The darkness and the power. The shadow and the light.

Ceilings as high as the sky, and as black as smoke. Windows spanning whole walls, through which Maleficent could manipulate an entire world.

"Oh," said Evie involuntarily.

Carlos looked like he wanted to bolt, but he didn't.

Jay's eyes flickered across the room as if he were casing the joint.

But Mal felt like she was all alone with the ghosts.

One ghost, in particular.

This was where her mother used to rage and command, where she had shot out of the ceiling as a green ball of fire to curse an entire kingdom. This was her seat of Darkness.

They pushed farther inside, Mal at the front. Carlos and Jay and Evie fell like a phalanx of soldiers behind her, almost in formation.

The black stones beneath their feet were shiny and slick, and the entire room was haunted by an aura of deep malevolence. Mal could feel it; they all could.

This had been a sad, angry, and unhappy home. Even now, the pain of that time burned its way through Mal, deep into her bones.

She shivered.

There was an empty place in the middle of the room where her mother's throne used to be. It had sat upon a great dais, flanked by two curving sets of stairs. The room was round and ringed with columns.

A great arc cradled the place where the throne had once sat, guarding an empty spot. The tattered remains of purple tapestries moldered on the walls.

"There's nothing left," Mal said, kneeling on the one dark spot that no longer held a throne. "It's all gone."

"You all right?" asked Jay, who was nervously blowing on his hands to warm them.

She nodded. "It's . . ." she faltered, unable to find the words to describe what she was feeling. She had listened to all her mother's stories, but she didn't think they were *real*.

Not until now.

"Yeah," he said. "I know." He shrugged, and she realized he'd probably felt the same way when they were in the Cave of Wonders. Mal knew Jafar and Iago talked about it all the time, but it was hard to imagine, hard to picture a world beyond what they knew of the Isle.

It had been, anyway.

Now everything was different.

Jay sighed. "It's all real, isn't it?"

"I guess so," Mal nodded. "Every last page of every last story." *Even the curse,* she thought, for the first time in hours.

The curse.

Someone has to touch it.

Evie has to touch it, and sleep for a thousand years.

"So, where is it?" Carlos asked, looking around the cold stone room.

"It has to be here somewhere," said Evie, turning to look behind her.

"Maybe we should split up," Jay said, a glint in his eye.

"Think," Mal said. "My mother was never without it. She held it even as she sat upon her throne." Mal moved back to the spot where the throne no longer stood. "Here."

"So where would it be now?" Carlos frowned.

"It wouldn't be where anyone else could touch it," Evie said. "Try asking my mother if she'll let you touch any of her own Miss Fairest Everything memorabilia."

Mal flinched at the word *touch*.

The curse was waiting for all of them—or at least, one of them—just as the Dragon's Eye was.

"But she'd want to see it, of course. From her throne," Jay said. Mal nodded; they'd all seen Jafar orient himself in his kitchen, directly behind his stack of coins.

"Which would be—" Mal spun slowly around. She could picture her mother sitting here, clutching the staff, feeling powerful and evil and well, like herself as she reigned over the kingdom.

She shook her head.

My mother would have no problem cursing any of the people in this room for ten thousand years, let alone one.

"There. Look!" cried Evie, spotting a tall black staff with a dim green globe at its top against the far wall.

It was, just as they had predicted, exactly in Mal's line of vision from the missing throne, but raised by some sort of magical light a good twelve feet into the air. Far out of the hands of any interlopers—and yes, where it could not be touched.

Of course.

There it was.

It's really here. The most powerful weapon of all Darkness.

Evil lives! indeed.

"It's right here!" Evie was closest to it and reached for it eagerly.

She shot her hand up into the air, extending her fingers. The moment she did, the Dragon's Eye began to shake, as if something about Mal herself was prying it loose from the very light and air that bound it.

Evie smiled. "I've got it—"

Mal saw Evie's hand curl toward it, almost in slow motion. The scepter itself seemed to glow, as if it were beckoning Evie toward it.

Everything around Mal seemed to blur until she could only see Evie's small, delicate fingers and the bewitched Dragon's Eye, just beyond her grasp.

In a split second Mal had to make the decision: could she let Evie touch it and be cursed into a deep, death-like sleep for a thousand years?

Or would she save her?

Stop her?

Do something . . . *good?*

While betraying her own mother's wishes, and giving

up on her own dream of becoming something more than a disappointment?

Was she content to remain only a Mal her entire life?

Never a Maleficent?

She froze, unable to decide.

"No!" cried Mal finally, running toward Evie. "Don't!"

What just happened? What was she doing? Why couldn't she stop herself?

"What?" asked Evie, shocked, just as a familiar voice boomed from the Dragon's Eye.

"WHOEVER AWAKENS THE DRAGON WILL BE CURSED TO SLEEP FOR A THOUSAND YEARS!"

Maleficent's voice was coming from the staff even now, echoing and reverberating around the room.

Her mother really had left an impression behind her. What remained of her power and her energy crackled off the walls of the room, sparked to life by one accidental moment and latent until now, when it had victims to torture.

Evie's fingers brushed the air next to the staff.

While Mal's hand closed upon it, and when it did . . .

She fell to the floor, asleep.

Mal blinked her eyes. She could see herself lying on the floor of the throne room, purple hair spilling out like a stain beneath her head.

Her three companions huddled nervously around her.

So I'm sleeping, then? Or *am I awake? Or maybe I'm dreaming?*

Because Mal knew she was seeing something else as well.

She wasn't in the Forbidden Fortress anymore.

She was in a palace, and there was good King Stefan and his queen and a baby in a cradle.

They were happy. She could see by the light in their faces, and by the way their eyes never left the child.

Almost like a magnet, Mal thought. *I know how that pull feels.*

A huge, gaily-dressed crowd of courtiers and servants and guests assembled in a beautiful throne room around them. There were two good fairies hovering above the cradle, their wands making beautiful sparkles in the air. It was all so sweet, it was sickening.

Mal had never seen anything like it, not up close like this. Not in some kind of insipid storybook.

What is this?

Why am I seeing this?

Then a green ball of fire appeared in the middle of the room, and when it dispersed, Mal saw a familiar face.

Her mother.

Tall, haughty, beautiful, and scorned. Maleficent was angry. Mal could feel the cold heat rising from her very being. She stared at her mother.

Maleficent addressed the crowd gathered around the royal family.

"Ah, I see everyone has been invited. The royalty, nobility, the gentry, and the rabble. I must say, I really felt quite distressed at not receiving an invitation."

What was her mother talking about? Then Mal realized. Maleficent had not been invited to Aurora's christening. Mal had never known this was the reason her mother hated parties and celebrations of all kinds.

But she knew exactly how her mother felt.

The hurt.

The shame.

The anger.

The desire for revenge.

Mal had felt exactly the same thing, hadn't she? When Evil Queen had thrown her party for Evie, all those years ago and kept her out?

Mal watched as her mother cursed the baby Princess Aurora to sleep a hundred years if she pricked her finger even once on a spindle. It was some fine spellcraft, and Mal was proud of her mother's efficiency, her power, her simple rendering. One prick of one finger could bring an entire royal house crashing down. It was a beautiful, terrible destiny. Well-woven. Deeply felt.

Mal was proud of Maleficent. She always had been, and she always would be. Maleficent had raised her daughter alone, and gotten by as best she could. If only because there was no one else to do it.

But her mother was made for Evil; she was good at it.

And in that very moment, and for the very first time, Mal finally understood that it wasn't just pride that she felt. It was pity. Maybe even compassion.

She was sad for her mother—and that was something new.

The crowd saw a monster, a terror, a devil, a witch, cursing a beautiful princess. But Mal saw only a hurt little girl, acting out of spite and anger and insecurity.

She wanted to reach out and tell Maleficent it would be all right. She wasn't sure it was true, but they'd somehow gotten along this far, hadn't they?

It'll be all right, Mother.

She had to tell her.

But she woke up before she could.

Mal blinked her eyes open. She was in the throne room at the Forbidden Fortress. Jay, Carlos, and Evie were standing around her nervously.

When she had fallen asleep she had been holding the Dragon's Eye scepter in her hand. But when she woke up, it was nowhere to be seen.

chapter

The Girl with the Double Dragon Tattoo

"You're awake! But you're supposed to be asleep for a thousand years!" cried Evie. "How?"

Mal rubbed her eyes. It was true—she was awake. She wasn't cursed. Why was that? Then she realized.

Prove that you are my daughter, prove that you are mine, her mother had ordered her. *Prove to me that you are the blood of the dragon. Prove you are worthy of that mark on your skin.*

The mark of the double dragon etched on her forearm. That had to be it. She held it up, showing the others.

"It couldn't hurt me," said Mal. "My true name is

Maleficent. Like my mother, I am part dragon, and so I am immune to the Dragon's curse."

"Lucky you," Jay said, eyeing the impressive tat.

Mal smiled proudly down at the marking she bore.

If she had been her father's daughter, weak, human, she would be asleep by now. For a thousand years. But she wasn't. She was strong, and awake, and had proven to everyone that she was her mother's daughter.

Hadn't she?

And when she brought her mother the Dragon's Eye—

"But wait—where is it?" Mal said, looking around accusingly at the trio. "I had it right in my hand!"

"Good question," said Jay, sounding a little wounded himself.

"It's gone. When you grabbed it, there was a flash of light that blinded us for a second, and when we could see again, it was gone," said Carlos. He shrugged. "Easy come, easy go."

The other three glared at him.

"Easy?" Evie raised an eyebrow, looking as tough as she possibly could.

Mal narrowed her eyes. "Jay, come on, hand it over."

"I swear, I don't have it!" said Jay, emptying his pockets to show her. "I planned to take it. I wanted to take it. I was even going to take it out of your own hand, while you were sacked out."

"And?"

He shrugged. "Just didn't get around to it, I guess."

"None of us have it," said Evie. She folded her arms, looking annoyed. "And by the way, you knew the curse was on that staff and you had all of us come with you anyway? What was up with that?"

Mal kicked a stone with her toe. "Yeah. I didn't really work out the plan very well."

"So why didn't you let me touch it, then? Wasn't that your evil scheme all along?"

Mal shrugged. "What are you talking about? I just didn't want you to. It wasn't yours to touch."

"Be honest. You were going to curse me, weren't you? You were going to let me touch that thing and end up taking the thousand-year nap?" Evie sighed.

Jay looked up. Carlos backed away instinctively. Mal knew neither one of them wanted to get anywhere near this conversation. She knew that because she felt the same way herself.

"I guess that was the plan." Mal shrugged. *You don't have to explain yourself. Not to her.* But she found, strangely enough, that she wanted to.

"Is this still about the—you know?" Evie looked at her. "Come on."

Mal was embarrassed. "I have no idea what you're talking about."

"Sure you don't," Jay muttered. Even Carlos laughed. Mal glared at both of them.

Evie rolled her eyes. "The party. My party. Back when we were little kids."

"Who can remember that far back?" Mal said, sticking out her chin stubbornly.

Evie looked tired. "I begged my mother to invite you, you know. But she refused; she was still too angry at your mother. They've competed for everything for as long as they've known each other."

Mal nodded again. "I know. Because of that stupid election about who would lead this island, right?"

Evie shrugged. "You know what they say. *Magic Mirror on the wall, who's the biggest ego of them all?*"

Mal smiled in spite of the entirely awkward nature of the conversation.

Evie looked her straight in the eye. "Look, my mom messed up. But the party wasn't that great, really. You didn't miss much."

"It wasn't a howler?"

"Not anything like Carlos's at all." Evie smiled.

"That's right. I'm legendary," Carlos said.

Mal glared at him. "As if I didn't have to almost beat you into having that party?"

She looked back at Evie. "Look, I didn't mean to trap you in Cruella's horrible closet." Mal glanced at Carlos, adding, "The one she loves more than her own son."

"Ha-ha," Carlos said, not laughing at all. Well, *sort of* not laughing. Actually, he was kind of laughing. Even Jay was having a hard time keeping a straight face.

Evie giggled as well. "Yes, you did."

"Okay, I did." Mal smiled.

"It's all right." Evie smiled back. "I didn't get caught in any of the traps."

"Cool," said Mal, even as she was embarrassed by her softness.

Carlos sighed.

Jay punched him in the gut with a grin. "Come on. At least your mom doesn't only wear sweat suits and pajamas."

"Let's not talk about it," said Evie and Mal, almost in unison.

"Yeah. Enough with the violins. We got a long walk home," Jay said. "And I'm not all that sure that this place has a back door."

Mal had a hard time keeping her mind on finding the way out of the fortress, though.

She was soft, and she was worried.

She had just saved someone's life, practically. Hadn't she?

What kind of self-respecting second-generation villain did anything of the sort?

What had happened to her grand evil scheme?

Why hadn't she just let Evie be cursed by Maleficent's scepter? Weren't princesses *meant* to sleep for years and years anyway? Didn't that basically come with the job description?

What if my mom is right?

What if Mal really *was* weak like her father—and worse, had a propensity for good somewhere in her black little heart?

Mal shuddered as she walked along behind the others.

No. If anything, being immune to the curse just proved she was definitely *not* her father's daughter. One day she too would be Maleficent.

She *had* to be.

But whether she was Maleficent's daughter or not, she had failed.

She was returning home empty-handed.

Boy, did she not want to be around when her mother found out.

chapter

27

The Descendants

This wasn't the victory lap Mal had imagined when she'd first set off in search of the Forbidden Fortress.

Defeated, the unlikely gang of four began to retrace their steps, just looking for the way out. They had lost everything, as usual. By any reasonable standard—or by her mother's infinitely *less* reasonable standards, Mal thought—they were utter and complete failures, every last one.

Especially her.

The moment they retreated from the throne room, though, Mal couldn't help but feel a shiver of relief at also leaving its darkness behind.

Although, oddly enough, the fortress had a different feel now, like it was dead. Mal couldn't feel the same energy it had before.

"Do you think the hole in the dome's plugged up again?" she asked Carlos. "It feels different in here."

"Maybe," he said. "Or maybe the magic it sparked is spent, now."

Mal looked up at the sky. She had a feeling there wouldn't be any more magic on the island.

Nobody said a word as they found their way back to the hall where the Magic Mirror was now just an ordinary surface—especially not Evie, who avoided so much as a glance at it.

Nobody said a word, either, as they hurried once again over the crumbling marble floor, this time avoiding both the scampering rats and the fluttering bats—going nowhere near any goblin passages or suffocating mazes or dusty tapestry rooms or portrait halls—until they reached the vast, empty cave that had so briefly become the sand-filled Cave of Wonders.

Especially not Jay, who only quickened the pace of his own echoing footsteps until he once again found the rotting wooden door that had brought them there the first time.

And Carlos seemed in a particular hurry to get through twisting passages that led to the black marble–floored, dark-fogged halls of the main fortress. As he pushed his way out the front doors, the gargoyle bridge once again faced them.

Faced *him*.

When the others caught up to Carlos, they stopped and stared over the precipice where he stood. The dizzying depths of the ravine below were, well, dizzying. But he didn't seem in any hurry to step back up to the bridge this time.

"It's fine," Evie said, encouragingly. "We'll just do what we did before."

"Sure. We cross one stupid bridge." Jay nodded. "Not very far at all."

That was true. On the other side of the bridge, they could just make out the winding path leading its way down through the thorn forest, from the direction they'd originally come.

"We're practically home free," Mal agreed, looking sideways at Carlos, who sighed.

"I don't know. Do you think it looks a little more, you know, crumbly? After all those tidal earthquakes we were feeling back there? It doesn't seem like the safest plan." He looked at Mal.

Nobody could disagree.

The problem was still the bridge. It was all in one piece this time, with no missing sections—but they all knew better than to trust anything in the fortress.

And not one of them dared set foot on it, after last time. Not after the riddles. Though they'd made it over easily enough the first time, once they'd answered the riddles, they hadn't thought about having to go out the way they'd come.

"I don't know if I can do it again," Carlos said, taking

in the faces of the once again stone gargoyles. He winced at the thought of their coming to life again.

In Mal's own mind, she hadn't gotten much past imagining the scene where she reclaimed her mother's missing scepter and came home a hero. She had been a little foggy on the actual details beyond that, she supposed; and now that the whole redemption thing was off the table, she really didn't have a backup plan.

But as she looked at Carlos, who stood there shivering, she suspected, at the memory of collapsing bridges and fur coats and a mother's true love that wasn't her son, Mal figured out a way across.

Mal stepped in front of him. "You don't have to do it again." She took another step, and then another. "I mean, you don't get to hog all the cool bridge action," she said, trying to sound convincing. "Now it's my turn."

"What?" Carlos looked confused.

The wind picked up as Mal kept moving forward, but she didn't stop.

Mal pulled her jacket tightly around her and shouted up at the gargoyles. "You don't scare me! I've seen worse. Where do you think I grew up, Auradon?"

The wind howled around her now. She took another step, motioning for the other three to move behind her.

"Are you crazy?" Jay shook his head, sliding behind her.

"Mal, seriously. You don't have to do this," Carlos whispered, ducking behind Jay.

"Definitely crazy," Evie said, from behind Carlos.

"Me, crazy?" Mal raised her voice even higher. "How could I not be? I go to school in a graveyard and eat expired scones for breakfast. My own mother sends me to forbidden places like this, because of some old bird and a lost stick," she scoffed. "There's nothing you can throw at me that's worse than what I've already got going."

As she spoke, Mal kept pressing forward. She had crossed the halfway point of the bridge now, dragging the others right behind her.

The wind roared and whipped against them, as if it would pick them up and toss them off the bridge itself, if she let it. But Mal wouldn't.

"Is that all you've got?" She stuck out her chin, that much more stubborn. "You think a little breeze like that can get to someone like me?"

Lightning cracked overhead, and she started to run— her friends right behind her. By the time they reached the other side, the bridge had begun to rock so hard, it seemed like it would crumble again.

Only, this time it wouldn't be an illusion.

The moment Mal felt the dirt of the far cliff safely beneath her feet, she stumbled over a tree root and collapsed, bringing Carlos and Evie down with her. Jay stood there laughing.

Until he realized that he wasn't the only one laughing.

"Uh, guys?"

Mal looked up. They were surrounded by a crowd of goblins—not unlike the ones who had chased them through the goblin passages of the Forbidden Fortress. Except these particular goblins seemed to be of a friendlier variety.

"Girl," one said.

"Brave," said another.

"Help," said a third.

"I don't get it," Evie said, sitting up. Mal and Carlos scrambled to their feet. Jay took a step back.

Finally, a fourth goblin sighed. "I think what my companions are trying to articulate is that we're incredibly impressed by that show of fortitude. The bravery. The perseverance. It's a bit unusual, in these parts."

"Parts," repeated the goblins.

"It talks," Evie said.

Mal looked from one goblin to another. "Uh, thanks?"

"Not at all," said the goblin. The goblins around him began to grunt animatedly—although Mal thought it might be laughter, too. Carlos looked nervous. Jay just grunted back.

The fourth goblin sighed again, looking back at Mal. "And if you'd like our assistance in any way, we'd be more than happy to help convey you to your destination."

He looked Mal over.

She looked him over, in return. "Our destination?"

He suddenly became flustered. "You do seem far away from home," he said, adding hastily: "Not to presume. It's a conclusion I draw only from the irrefutable fact that neither you or your friends seem, well, remotely goblin-esque."

The goblins grunt-laughed again.

Jay stared. "You're about two feet tall. How would a guy like you get people like us all the way back to town?"

Evie elbowed him.

"Not to be rude," Jay said.

"Rude," chanted the goblins, still grunt-laughing.

"I'm pretty sure that was rude," Carlos muttered.

"Ah, there you have it. Alone, we are but a single goblin, perhaps even, a brute." The goblin smiled. "Together, I'm afraid we are a rather brutal army. Not to mention, we pull an excellent carriage."

"Pull!" The goblins went nuts.

An old iron carriage—like the kind you might have seen Belle and Beast ride away in, except black and burnt and nothing that either the queen or king of Auradon would so much as touch—appeared in front of them.

No less than forty goblins manned either side, fighting for a grip on the carriage itself.

"Why would you do that?" Mal said, as a good seven goblins battled the broken door open. "Why are you being so nice?"

"A good deed. Helping a fellow adventurer. Perhaps there's a chance for us to get off this island yet," said the goblin. "We have been sending messages to our dwarf kin asking King Beast for amnesty. We've been wicked for such a very long time, you know. It does get tiresome after a while. I would kill for a cream cake."

"Currants," said a goblin.

"Chocolate chip," said another.

Mal had to admit, she was starting to feel a little exhausted herself. She knew, because she slept the entire way home, without even being embarrassed that her head was resting on Evie's shoulder.

When Mal returned to the Bargain Castle, she fully expected her mother to scream invectives at her for failing in her quest. She opened the door slowly and stepped inside, as quietly as she could, keeping her eyes on the ground.

It was no use. Maleficent was on her throne. "So, the prodigal daughter returns," she said. Her voice sounded different.

"Mother, I have something to . . ." Mal stopped, looking up.

And stared.

And then stared some more, in about ten different varieties of shock.

Because she found herself staring at the long black staff with the green globe at its top that her mother was holding.

The Dragon's Eye.

"Is that—" She couldn't speak.

Maleficent nodded. "Yes, it is the Dragon's Eye. And

yes, you did fail me. But thankfully, not all my servants are as useless as you."

Mal ignored the word *servant*. "But how?"

Maleficent laughed. "Silly child, what do you know about quests?"

"But we found it in the Forbidden Fortress! I just touched it—an hour ago!" said Mal. "It was in your own throne room. Suspended on the wall. Where you could see it, from where your throne used to sit."

Her mother eyed her. Mal couldn't be certain, but it was possible, for the briefest of all split-seconds, that her mother was the slightest bit impressed.

"I touched it, and that thing knocked me unconscious."

"You touched it? You don't say," said Maleficent. "Well, good job, you. You really are as soft as your father."

Mal bristled. "I don't understand."

"You touched the Dragon's Eye? Instead of tricking one of the others into doing it? Such weakness. I didn't want to believe the news when I heard it." Maleficent banged her staff upon the floor next to her feet. "How many times, Mal? How much more will you shame me?"

She rolled her eyes. "I sent Diablo out after you to retrieve the Eye for me. He must have taken it from you while you were sleeping off the curse." She shook her head. "I knew you wouldn't have it in you to do what needed to be done, and I knew I couldn't take any chances. It appears I was right. Again."

Diablo cawed proudly.

So she'd been right about feeling as if they were being followed. Of course. That was Diablo.

Mal felt like giving up. It never mattered, how hard she tried, or what she did, she would never impress her mother.

Even now, her mother had eyes only for the Dragon's Eye.

"The only thing is, it's broken," said Maleficent with a frown. "Look at the eye, it's dead." For a moment, she sounded like the same angry little girl who had cursed a baby over a party invitation. Mal remembered all too well, and she looked at her mother through new eyes.

"Well, the dome is still up," said Mal, finally. "It keeps the magic out." It was down for a brief moment, but there would be no magic on the island anytime soon.

"Maybe. Or maybe you broke the eye when you touched it," Maleficent accused. "You are such a disappointment."

Meanwhile, at Jafar's Junk Shop, an angry Jafar was berating Jay, who had returned home empty-handed. "So you're saying you did find the Dragon's Eye, did you? So where is it, then?"

"It disappeared!" Jay protested. "One minute we had it, and then we lost it."

"Right. And this had nothing to do with a certain noble deed performed by a certain daughter of evil for a certain other daughter of evil?"

Jay froze. "Excuse me?"

The words *good* and *deed* were chilling, particularly on the Isle, and particularly when coming out of his father's mouth.

"Did you think goblins keep secrets particularly well, boy? The news is all over the island."

"I swear. That's what really happened. I swear on a stack of stolen . . ." Jay blanked. He couldn't think of a single thing to steal at the moment.

But to be honest, for once in his life, he didn't even care.

"You are such a disappointment," Jafar snorted.

Over at Hell Hall, Carlos was getting an earful after Cruella finally discovered her furs in disarray in her closet. "Who has been in here? It looks like a wild animal was trapped with my furs! What imbecile would do such a thing?"

"A wild one?" Carlos winced. He knew it was pointless to even try. Not when the closet looked like this.

His answer was a scream, and it was bloodcurdling. Even in his mother's signature, shrill octave.

"I'm sorry Mother," whimpered Carlos. "It won't happen again! I know how much you love your furs." The words were almost a whisper. He could see the faces of the gargoyles from the bridge, mocking him as he said them.

Then he could see Mal, Evie, and Jay laughing at her with him, and he had to keep from secretly smiling, himself.

Cruella sniffed. "You are such a disappointment!"

• • •

Over at the Castle-Across-the-Way, the Evil Queen was lamenting the state of Evie's hair. "It's like a rat's nest! What happened? You look awful."

"I'm sorry Mother, we ran into . . . well . . . uh . . . let's just say I couldn't find a mirror."

I found one, she thought. *Just not the kind you want to look at.*

Not when you're supposed to be the fairest of them all.

"Just promise me these rumors I'm hearing aren't true," her mother said. "All this talk of a virtuous act." She shuddered. "The goblins are saying such horrid things about the four of you."

"You know that goblins are horrible creatures, Mom." Evie hid her face. She didn't know what to say. To be honest, she didn't even know what she thought. It had been a strange few days.

Not entirely bad, but strange.

The Evil Queen sighed. "You forgot to reapply blush again. Oh dear, sometimes, you're such a disappointment."

Mal sat out on the balcony, hearing the sounds of laughter and mayhem from down below. Then, a shout.

"Mal!" Jay called. "Come down!"

She ran downstairs. "What's up?"

"Oh nothing, just trying to get away from our parents and disappointing them again," said Carlos.

"You too, huh?" asked Mal. She turned to Jay and Evie. "And you?"

The three of them nodded.

"Come on, let's go to the market," said Evie. "I need a new scarf."

"I can get you one," said Jay, waggling his eyebrows. "Oh, and Evie—here you go," he said. "I believe this might be yours."

"My necklace!" said Evie, putting the poison-heart charm around her neck once more, with a smile. "Thanks, Jay."

"I found it."

"In his pocket," said Mal, but even she was grinning.

With a whoop, the four descendants of the world's greatest villains ran through the crowded streets of the Isle of the Lost, causing havoc, stealing and plundering together while the citizens of the island ran the other way. They were truly rotten to the core.

Even Mal started to feel better.

And in fact, as they laughed and sang, Mal wondered if this was what happiness was like.

Because even though the four of them weren't quite friends yet, they were the closest things they had to it.

"You will join
me for dinner. . . .
That's not a
request!"
—Beast, Beauty
and the Beast

epilogue

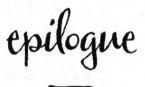

Sunrise Over Auradon

While the band of four villain kids was causing havoc in the streets of the Isle of the Lost, Prince Ben was looking out the window from his high vantage point in Beast Castle, lost in a few thoughts of his own.

It was true that Grumpy the dwarf had told him he'd make a good king, but privately, Ben wondered if he was right.

More to the point, he wondered if becoming a good king was even something he cared about at all.

Did it matter? What he cared about? What he wanted?

Trapped, Ben thought, staring out over the vast expanse of the kingdom. That's what I am.

He looked up at the sky, as if it held the answers. The blue wash was bright and clear as usual, and he could see all the way to the distant horizon, where Auradon itself dissolved into nothing but misty shoreline and azure water.

No.

Not nothing.

Ben thought of his dream of the island.

The Isle of the Lost. That's what everyone called it, even his father.

He considered again what it would be like to live as they did, trapped underneath the magical dome, just as he was in his royal life.

They were prisoners, weren't they? His father tried to pretend that they were not, but even Ben knew otherwise. They were exiled to the island by order of the king.

Just as Ben was able to live in the castle because he was the king's son. And because my father loves me, Ben thought. And because I was born to this.

It was impossible to stop thinking about it.

He flinched.

"Ouch," Ben said, as a needle poked him again in the armpit.

"Sorry, sire; forgive me sire." Lumiere, who was measuring him for his coronation suit, quailed.

"Quite all right," said Ben, who looked kingly, at least

according to Lumiere, in the royal blue velvet suit with yellow piping. It had belonged to King Beast, who had worn it at his own coronation. "It was my fault—I moved."

"Your mind is elsewhere, sire," said Lumiere sagely. "As befitting a future king of Auradon."

"Perhaps," said Ben.

For a future king, he was surprised by how little he knew about the Isle of the Lost. How did the villains fare, beneath the dome? How did they live, eat, take care of themselves? How were their families? What were their hopes and dreams? What did they see when they stared out the windows of their own castle or cottage or cave?

Ben remembered he had heard that a few of them had children. Some would have to be his own age by now, wouldn't they? He wondered how they dealt with living in the shadow of their infamous parents.

I imagine that for them, it's a lot like this, he thought, staring down at his royal beast-head ring, the one just like his father's. Wearing his father's suit, fitted by his father's tailor. Standing at the window of his father's castle.

We're all trapped. I'm as trapped as they are.

The more Ben thought about it, the more he knew it was true. He hadn't chosen to be born a prince and become a king, just as they hadn't chosen who their parents were. They were prisoners for a crime they themselves had not committed.

That was the greater crime, wasn't it?

It's not fair. It's not our fault. We have no say in our own lives. We're living in a fairy tale someone else wrote.

In that moment, Ben suddenly understood why it was that the sidekicks wanted more for their lives: because he found he wanted even more than *that*.

He wanted things to change, throughout Auradon.

Everything, he thought. *For everyone.*

Was that even possible? On the other hand, how could it not be? How could he possibly keep going with the way things were now?

Ben thought about it.

If he was going to be king, he would have to be himself, his mother had said. And he was different from his father. That was clear to everyone, even Lumiere. Ben would rule, but he would rule differently.

He would make different rules and proclamations.

His mind wandered again to the image of the purple-haired girl with the bright green eyes. The girl from his dream.

Who was she?

Would he ever meet her?

Was she one of them? One of the lost souls on that cursed island? He had a feeling that she was.

And just then, he had a flash of inspiration.

One that would change the fates of both Auradon and the Isle of the Lost forever.

Why not?

It's about time.

His mind was made up.

"Sire! Where are you going?" cried Lumiere as Ben suddenly leapt away from the needle and thread, a flurry of straight pins and bespoke chalk and measuring tape flying into the air around him.

"To find my parents! I have something to tell them, and it can't wait!" said Ben. "I've got the most brilliant idea!"

TO FIND OUT WHAT HAPPENS NEXT . . .

premieres on the Disney Channel in 2015

acknowledgments

When I was a little girl growing up in the Philippines, the first movie I ever saw was *Cinderella*, which had been my mother's favorite movie as a child. It was the first movie I ever watched with my daughter, and it also became *her* favorite movie. (*My* favorite is *Sleeping Beauty*.) Disney magic was a huge part of my childhood, and now it is a huge part of my daughter's. It was wonderful to watch the old movies again with her while I was writing this book, as well as share the new Disney Channel movie that inspired it. I still can't believe that I got to play in this universe and with these characters who defined my childhood. It's been a magical journey, and I owe my thanks to the people who helped me on my way. My publishing family—my editor, Emily Meehan, my publisher, Suzanne Murphy, and everyone at Disney Hyperion, especially Seale Ballenger, Mary Ann Zissimos, Simon Tasker, Elena Blanco, Kim Knueppel, Sarah Sullivan, Jackie DeLeo, Frank Bumbalo, Jessica

Harriton, Dina Sherman, Elke Villa, Andrew Sansone, and Holly Nagel, who have seen me through countless books and launches, thanks for keeping the faith! Marci Senders, who put together a wickedly awesome design, and Monica Mayper, who made sure every villainous dangling participle fell into place. Disney Consumer Products grand poobahs Andrew Sugerman and Raj Murari throw the best parties. Jeanne Mosure is my hero. Big thanks to Rebecca Frazer and Jennifer Magee-Cook from Team Descendants, and all the lovely folks at the Disney Channel, especially Jennifer Rogers Doyle, Leigh Tran, Naketha Mattocks, and Gary Marsh. It was a thrill to meet director Kenny Ortega, production designer Mark Hofeling and the stars of the movie, Dove Cameron, Booboo Stewart, Cameron Boyce, Sofia Carson, and the inimitable Kristin Chenoweth. Screenwriters Sara Parriott and Josann McGibbon's script was hilarious and inspiring. My agent, Richard Abate, is the man. Melissa Kahn is awesome. Thanks and love to the DLC and Johnston families, especially my nephews Nicholas and Joseph Green and Sebastian de la Cruz. I get by with a little help from my friends, especially dear Margie Stohl. My husband, Mike Johnston, is a creative genius, and he and our daughter, Mattie Johnston, make everything worthwhile.

I hope you enjoyed the book and that it created a whole new set of Disney memories. You won't want to miss the movie. Thank you for reading!

xoxo

Mel